Suddenly Sorceress

ERICA LUCKE DEAN

Suddenly Sorceress
A Red Adept Publishing Book

Red Adept Publishing, LLC
104 Bugenfield Court
Garner, NC 27529
http://RedAdeptPublishing.com/

ISBN-13: 978-1-940215-21-1
ISBN-10: 1-940215-21-8
Library of Congress Control Number: 2013957092

First Print Edition: December 2013

Cover and Formatting: Streetlight Graphics

To my kids,
For never letting me forget the world is full of magic.

Prologue

"YOU'RE TOO SEXY, MY ASS!" I tried to tune out the Right Said Fred ringtone as I fished my fiancé's cell phone from the pocket of his discarded Dockers. I glared at the flashing caller ID. "You just don't give up, do you?"

That was lucky number thirteen. Thirteen missed calls in the span of an hour. Thirteen calls he was unable to answer.

Because of me.

After pressing *ignore* one more time, I shoved the phone back into the pocket where it belonged, hoping it would muffle the sound somewhat. I didn't know why I didn't just turn off the damn thing. I'd endured his ridiculous ringtone more times than anyone should have to, obviously determined to punish myself. Between the maddening song and the horrible smell, I certainly felt punished. Even if it wasn't nearly enough.

Way down deep in my bones, I knew my life had been forever changed. Even if I could somehow fix things—put them back to normal—*nothing* would be the same again. Not ever.

Swallowing against the crystal ball-sized lump in my throat, I dropped Matt's pants where I'd found them, along with his shirt, his boxers, and his shoes, and I collapsed onto the rumpled blankets on the bed.

That sort of thing didn't happen in the real world. Only small children or crazy people believed in... no, I refused to even think the word, let alone say it. *It's impossible.* But I'd seen it with my own eyes, and *whatever* it was, it definitely *wasn't* normal.

My scruffy housecat made another frantic orbit around my feet as the phone sounded again, the self-centered lyrics looping, making me cringe. Apparently, he'd also grown weary of the tune.

If only I could say the choice of ringtone was ironic, a product of his wry sense of humor. But he didn't have much of a sense of humor. Matthew Green was *exactly* that arrogant. Despite every despicable thing he'd done to me, every insult, lie, and betrayal that had led us there, I truly wished Matt could answer his stupid phone himself. Unfortunately, wishing didn't seem to be on my side that morning.

Stifling a groan, I pulled myself from the warmth of the bed to dig the phone out of Matt's pocket again. *Geez, persistent much?* With a deep, cleansing breath, I mashed down the button to accept the call.

"Matt! Where are you?" Matt's receptionist, Ginger, snapped before I had a chance to say hello. "Friday's your busiest day. Do you have any idea what time it is? You've already missed two appointments."

Even without caller ID, I would have recognized her breathy Betty Boop voice. She sounded as though she'd been sucking helium all morning. I didn't know her well, but I suspected she was banging my fiancé.

"We'll be lucky if there's enough time for a quickie before the next patient arrives," she continued in a whisper.

Yep... definitely banging him.

"And another thing." Her sweet baby voice morphed into a feral growl. "Candy's been standing outside your office all morning. I thought you said you were done with her? I'm not kidding, Matt, if I find out you're still screwing her, I'm going to cut off your balls."

Apparently, I was engaged to a pathological cheater. Of course, I hadn't known that when I agreed to marry him. There were a lot of things I didn't know about Matt. Then again, there was a lot I didn't know about *me*.

"Well? Aren't you going to say anything?"

"Uh... hi, Ginger." I cleared my throat and resisted the urge to "*say anything*." "This is Ivie. Matt can't come to the phone. I... uh... don't think he's going to be able to... uh... make it into work today." I managed to stammer through the basics without my voice cracking.

"Oh, hi, Ivie." Her voice changed again; she sounded as if she'd been sucking lemons. She didn't even have the decency to be embarrassed. "What's wrong with Matt? He hasn't missed a day in... Actually, I don't think he's ever called in sick."

My eyes darted to the closed bathroom door, and I shuddered. "He's really not feeling like himself today." Understatement of the century.

"Is he sick?"

"Um... I definitely don't think anyone wants what he has." I tiptoed around the answer. I wasn't good at coy, but I gave it my best shot.

"Oh... Well, in that case, maybe it's best if he stays home." I could almost see her coiling a lock of her thick red hair around her finger as she spoke. "Just tell him I hope he feels better, and not to worry. I'll reschedule his appointments for him. Do you think he'll be well enough to come in Monday?"

I tamped down a flicker of panic. "I really hope so." *But I seriously doubt it.*

After listening to Ginger rant for a minute about missed appointments and the difficult task of rescheduling, I ended the call, staring at the bathroom door as if I expected a silent command to open it. I closed my eyes and tried to imagine the door swinging wide and my fiancé sauntering out. I popped open one eye. The door hadn't moved—not even a crack.

For far too long, I'd avoided that room. With three tentative steps, I closed the distance between myself and the master bathroom, covering my mouth and nose with one hand as I cracked the door. I'd almost gotten used to the foul odor in the bedroom. It was bad but not unbearable. The stench in the bathroom was overwhelming. The fumes poured out, bringing tears to my eyes. The small space reeked worse than when I'd locked him in there last night. It smelled as if someone had cooked up a potion of burning tires and rotten eggs in a boiling vat of sour ammonia, and even that comparison wasn't quite bad enough.

Blinking back the sting of tears, I scanned the room. I didn't see him anywhere, just a puddle that looked suspiciously like urine in one corner and in the other, a makeshift bed fashioned out of—were those my good bath towels?

No Matt.

A quick rush of adrenaline kick-started my heart. *What's happened to him now? This is bad. Very, very bad.* As if things weren't bad enough already. What sort of person was I? What I'd done was unspeakable, so horrible even *I* didn't know what I'd done.

Just as I was about to have a full-blown panic attack, he slunk out from behind the hamper. I should have been relieved he was still alive, but I wasn't sure if his current state was much better. He stared up at me—his beady little black eyes blinking in the harsh fluorescent light—so much smaller than he used to be and covered in a thick pelt of black and white fur. My fiancé.

The skunk.

One

MAYBE I SHOULD HAVE STARTED from the beginning—when everything first spun out of control— the day of the annual farm field trip.

Thursday was the kind of day that inspires mass suicides... or improper Valium use at the very least. The sort of day that could only happen once in a person's lifetime. I certainly hoped so anyway.

In theory, the outing should have been loads of fun—visiting the cows, touring the milking facilities, feeding the chickens and pigs, even a hayride through the pumpkin patch. But I hated it. Hate wasn't nearly strong enough a word. Loathe. Detest. Abhor. Despise. I practically broke out in hives on the first day of October in bitter anticipation of what was to come.

Even before that—the moment the permission slips were printed with the date. October twenty-fourth.

Doomsday.

Bright and early that morning, Helena Ferrell, our lead teacher, corralled the miniature debutantes and future billionaires onto the bright yellow deathtrap doubling as our transportation. "Okay, everybody into the bus." She winked at me and snagged a little boy by his jacket as he was about to take my feet out from under me. "Come on, no need to push."

"Thanks," I mouthed. Then, with as genuine a smile as I could muster, I stepped out of the way of the rush. My only wish was to head in the other direction, away from what lay in store for me at the end of that bus ride. In hindsight, I should have stayed in bed. "Hey, Helena, I'm not feeling well." I sidled up to her petite frame and pressed my palm to my forehead. "I think I have a fever. I should probably go home."

"Suck it up, Ivie. You don't have a fever. You're probably just having hot flashes brought on by anxiety." Helena grinned, twisting her chestnut hair into a ponytail. "We're going to a farm, not the gas chamber. I thought you *liked* animals."

"Of course I like animals. But after last year..." I was reluctant to jinx myself by even thinking about last year.

"Don't be ridiculous." Ever the optimist, Helena patted my shoulder as if I were a child, despite our barely existent age difference. "Last year was your first time. You're a second year teacher now. Older and wiser, right? Besides, *nobody* could have such bad luck two years in a row. You know what they say, lightning doesn't strike twice in the same place."

With an exaggerated sigh, I nodded. Like it or not, the field trip was part of my job. A job I loved every other day of the year. I flashed her a forced smile and moved to the back of the bus to oversee the rowdiest of the bunch. I wished I taught something safe—like auto shop. Power tools had nothing on kindergarteners. Especially at my ultra-snobby school. The parents drove Hummers and BMWs, and the kids had trust funds and iPhones.

No joke. Three of my kindergarteners had iPhones. I didn't even have an iPhone, and I was marrying a doctor. Okay, a *chiropractor*. But that was close enough for my mother. She would have been just as excited if I were marrying Dr. Seuss. (Oh, the places I'd go!) As long as he had Dr. in front of his name, she was happy.

Once the kids were all present and accounted for, the bus groaned out of the school parking lot. Destination: the Maxwell Dairy Farm. I adored my students—for the most part —but armed with nothing more than my meager charm and a cell phone with 911 on speed dial, I was naïvely determined to make it through my second farm field trip unscathed.

The idea exhausted me, and the wheels on the bus nearly lulled me to sleep. The ride was shorter than I remembered, but I supposed time moved more quickly as I marched ever closer to my doom. We pulled into the long drive leading to the barn and I tensed from my hair to my toes.

"We're here." Helena winked at me as she bellowed over the excited chatter. "Everyone stay in your seats until the bus stops."

My lips twitched as I tried to return her smile, and she laughed at my pitiful attempt.

"Ivie, if I didn't know better, I'd think you were terrified." Helena pulled out her clipboard with the day's agenda. "What's to be afraid of? They're just cows, right?"

"Right." I nodded, staring at the black and white bovines grazing and potentially plotting my demise.

Didn't she understand my relationship with cows was strictly dietary? I glanced at my leather riding boots. Cows came in handy in many ways. Even for city girl, Ivie Marie McKie. The name had a nice ring to it, especially with my father's Scottish brogue—the one I didn't have.

Of course, it would be Green soon. Ivie Green. It sounded like a paint color. Or a lawn service. *Green...* just like the grass in the nearby pasture. After a quick scan of my surroundings, I climbed out of the bus and realized I'd left my life, and my favorite clothes, in the hands of fate.

"Miss Key." Robby Patterson, one of the boys in my class, butchered my name as he tugged on the hem of my blouse.

I looked down at the top of his blond head. "What is it, Robby?"

He pointed to my boots. "You stepped in poop."

Helena was wrong. Lightning most definitely strikes twice in the same place.

"Those are riding boots, aren't they?" Helena smirked. "They're meant for this environment."

"They're Ralph Laurens," I said, wiping my feet on a clump of clean hay.

"Maybe you shouldn't have worn someone else's boots on farm day." She winked, scooting past me to corral her class.

The whispers and giggles of the group of moms-slash-chaperones behind me caught my attention.

"Should he be wearing that shirt with kids around?"

"I doubt the kids would understand anyway."

"Still, highly inappropriate."

I spun to catch them gesturing toward the barn, then whirled again just in time to see the back of a tall, nicely built man in a dark-blue T-shirt and a pair of well-worn jeans.

"What's wrong with his shirt?" *Other than the fact that it clings to his body in a most distracting way?* I asked the short chubby mom with the Grumpy Cat sweatshirt.

"Wait for it." She grinned.

As he turned, I elbowed Helena. "Check that out." I pointed with my chin.

"Veterinarians do it doggy style," she mouthed and burst out laughing. He lifted his face in our direction.

"Oh, my God. He heard us." I whipped around as if that would make me invisible. *If I can't see him, he can't see me, right?*

Helena shifted her attention back to the hot guy and nudged me. "He's checking out your butt."

I made another dizzying spin to face him again.

I heard one of the moms whisper, "What butt?" as he tipped his baseball cap at me, his lips curving into a cocky smile.

Helena asked, "Do you think we can get him to take off the Ray-Bans and the hat? I'd like to see if his face is as amazing as the rest of the package."

I couldn't have agreed more. If the face matched the rest of him, he would be the most perfect specimen of man I'd ever laid eyes on. I peeked around Helena to get another look. "I wonder who he is."

"Oh, that's the vet. He's here on a call. Something to do with the goats," a cheerful female voice said from behind me. "I'm sure he wouldn't mind talking to the kids while he's here. I could go ask if you like."

"That would be great," Helena answered before I could stop her. The last thing I needed was to come face to face with the guy after shamelessly gawking at him. "Come on, kids. We're going to go meet the veterinarian." Helena rounded up the group and herded them toward the barn and the hot doc.

I hung back to watch for stragglers. Or to hide behind a group of five-year-olds. Either way.

Engaged women are *not* supposed to flirt, I reminded myself. Especially when one is an engaged kindergarten teacher on a field trip with students. But flirt I did, staring at him from across the pasture like a—like a goat in heat. If I hadn't been so busy smiling in his direction, feeding off his sideways glances, I might have paid closer attention to where I was walking. I might have seen the path I was on... or what was directly in front of me. Things might have ended up okay. But I was never that lucky.

"I was wrong, you know." Helena bit back a smile, checking each student's name off her clipboard as we boarded the bus two hours later. "Your luck really is that bad."

I glared at her, scrubbing a wet paper towel through my hair. "I told you that this morning." Thankfully, the handsome vet had disappeared during the Goat Incident.

But not before witnessing the entire mortifying scene. It would take hypnosis to purge *that* from my memory. I could never face him again. Not that it mattered. I had no business worrying about another man when I had a fiancé at home. A perfectly respectable chiropractor with a bizarre fascination with *Zoolander.* "Whose brilliant idea was it to plan a field trip during mating season?"

"I suppose it could have been worse. At least you still have all your fingers and toes." Giggles punctuated her words.

Of course, I had more to lose than toes. My pride, for one.

Also amongst the day's casualties—coming in slightly behind Robby Patterson's two front teeth, which were probably going to fall out soon anyway—the field trip took out my favorite pair of brown leather boots. They were also my *only* pair of brown leather boots, and they had been a ridiculous extravagance even on sale. I also lost a pair of Rag & Bone jeans—the Golden Snitch of Goodwill finds—and my favorite white button-down shirt. It wasn't a designer label, and it wasn't expensive, but I absolutely loved that shirt. That shirt had managed to survive multiple run-ins with spaghetti sauce, at least one pomegranate martini, and cat vomit, all without as much as a shadow of a stain.

The bloodstains—thankfully, not mine that time—would have probably come clean. And the L-shaped tear in the sleeve could have been stitched. But to my deepest regret, no amount of scrubbing could *ever* eradicate the abject humiliation. My brain might need a thorough bleaching for good measure.

Helena opened her mouth to say something else, but I gave her my best bitch-face, scrunching up my features until I imagined I resembled a constipated pug. "Not another word about the goat."

"Chin up, Ivie." Helena snickered. "At least you got lucky."

"Not funny, Ferrell." I wadded up the dirty paper towel and lobbed it at her. Even at close range, I missed.

She coughed around a laugh. "Oh, trust me. It's funny." Helena stood to address the children. "Come on, kids, let's sing. *Old MacDonald had a farm, E-I-E-I-O, and on his farm he had a goat...*"

The kids continued singing, but Helena and the other teachers, and most of the chaperones, dissolved into a fit of giggles at my expense. Mrs. Patterson glared at me as if I'd purposely seduced a goat in front of her precious child.

"I'm never going to live this down, am I?"

"Never." Helena gave my shoulders a quick squeeze, wrinkling her nose. "Wow, you really do stink."

I felt cursed. But I didn't believe in curses. Well, I didn't then. After the excruciating ride back to the school with a busload of five- and six-year-olds, I headed home to pour myself a glass of wine, take a hot bath, and relax. That was the plan anyway. Before I could even step inside the house, I got a text message from my best friend.

Chloe: How was your Ygirsday?

I glanced at the message as I fumbled for my keys. The auto-correct on her phone always messed up Thursday. Chloe never bothered to fix it.

Me: Sucked!

Chloe: How was the farm? You're texting, must still have all your fingers.

Me: Don't even ask.

Chloe: Wedding shopping tomorrow am. Pick you up at 8?

Me: Can't.

My phone rang. Chloe didn't even give me a chance to say hello before starting in on me. "Ivie Marie McKie, you haven't even shopped for your dress yet. What sort of bride are you?"

"The sort that has to work for a living?"

"Screw work. I may not be a fan of the groom, but you can't expect me to allow my BFF to show up for her own wedding looking less than amazing. Seriously, I'm not taking no for an answer. Besides, there's a huge sale at Coach tomorrow."

A sale at Coach. *Figures.* "Forget it! I'm not going." I wanted to laugh, but I didn't want to encourage her. The seconds ticked by while I waited for her to say something before I realized she'd hung up on me. Chloe considered ignoring a sale at Coach a mortal sin.

When I'd first met the trust fund baby, Chloe had an infinite credit line on her American Express card, and she knew how to use it. I called her a serial swiper our freshman year of college, and I was only half joking. She spent more on shoes and purses than I paid for my car.

About a year ago—right around the same time the ink dried on our college diplomas—Chloe was forced to get a real job. Her father had cut her off. He said independence was for her own good, and it worked. Sort of. She got a job as a promotions director for a radio station, where she pulled in considerably more than my annual salary, plus bonuses. She didn't have to worry about a house or a car because her father had already bought her both before pulling the plug on the money. Of course, she'd had to make horrible sacrifices due to her poverty. She couldn't afford to buy Gucci, Coach, or Ralph Lauren until they went on sale. Even then, she still dropped a month's worth of groceries at a clip. No matter how hard I tried to avoid the impromptu excursions, she always seemed to find a way to drag me along, kicking and screaming the whole way.

Once safely inside my house, I shed my ruined clothes, shoved my boots into a black garbage bag, and threw them into the back of my bedroom closet, prepared to let them stay there indefinitely. Unlike my spoiled blouse and jeans, I wasn't quite ready to chuck them into the trash...

yet. They'd set me back enough money to buy a cheap car. I wasn't about to just throw them away.

After a long hot shower, where I scoured away traces of goat semen and saliva, I changed into a pair of red flannel pajama pants, a ratty blue sweatshirt, and my fuzzy bunny slippers. While bunnies were also notoriously horny, I didn't mind them humping my feet.

Thursday—like almost every other night—was a Swanson frozen dinner night, so I tossed a Salisbury steak with corn and mashed potatoes into the microwave and ate standing up in the kitchen. After pouring myself a glass of cheap chardonnay, I lit a fire and snuggled into my favorite leather chair to read *Pride and Prejudice* for the umpteenth time. Several chapters and a bottle of wine later—Mr. Darcy had just botched his proposal to poor Elizabeth—I realized *my* soon-to-be husband was still missing in action.

I'd like to say I was worried. Or that I missed him. We were supposed to be getting married, so I should have been at least a *little* concerned, right? Instead, my mind drifted back to the farm... and the goat... and the hot veterinarian. I barely gave a second thought to what may or may not have happened to the grown man who obviously didn't think enough about me to call. Even *before* my crush on the sexy animal doctor, I had had that twinge of doubt as to why we were still together.

When I hadn't heard from Matt by ten and I'd gotten his voice mail yet again, I called the gym to ask if anyone had seen him. Sometime after eleven, I called the local hospitals. All of them. He may not have been the most attentive man, but he never stayed out so late without at least checking in.

I should have known better. That little voice inside my head should have spoken up. But as far as internal voices went, mine was as quiet as a church mouse. By the time his key hit the lock at ten minutes before midnight, I was officially furious.

Two

THE FRONT DOOR SLAMMED, AND I stopped pacing around our bedroom, prepared to let him come up with a dozen excuses—none of which would be sufficient for making me worry half the night away. I expected to listen to his pathetic apology. I wasn't ready for him to stomp up the stairs and confront me.

The first thing I noticed about him was the state of his white dress shirt: untucked, half the buttons undone, and the rest misaligned. "Ivie, I need my grandmother's engagement ring."

No, "Hello." No, "We need to talk." Just, "I need my grandmother's engagement ring." I tucked my left hand into the sleeve of my sweatshirt, instinctively protecting my precious, and jutted my chin out in defiance like a child. "Why do you need my ring?"

"Not *your* ring. My *grandmother's* ring. You don't need to know why; you only need to know I need it back."

My eyes traveled up to his twisted smile and the red wine mustache circling his mouth like the Kool-Aid smiles my kindergarteners wore. "Are you drunk?" My body thrummed with an undercurrent of raw fury.

His barking laugh caught me off guard, and I flinched. "I had a glass of wine, but no, I'm not drunk. I've just finally come to my senses."

"What are you talking about?" His senses? A contradiction in terms if I'd ever heard one. I stepped toward him then stopped. I had no idea what I wanted to do or, more importantly, what I should do.

"I've met someone else." He leaned against the bedroom doorframe. "I'm in love with Candy. She's just..." He actually sighed like a freaking teenage girl.

A choking sound came from my throat, and his eyes flashed with irritation.

"I know what you're thinking. It's not just the sex." He sneered. "But believe me, the sex is amazing. We're flying to Vegas to get married tomorrow afternoon. Now give me my grandmother's ring." He held out his hand as if he thought I'd pull it off my finger and hand it over without another word.

My mouth fell open. I'd met Candy. I didn't know what to say. My fiancé was leaving me—for the aerobics instructor? "You're breaking up with me?" I struggled to spit out the words. "For *Candy*?"

He nodded, moving away from the doorway. "I'll be gone until Tuesday. That should give you plenty of time to pack. I need you out by Monday night."

I followed him into our bathroom. Visions of me living out of the trunk of my powder-blue Beetle flitted through my brain. "You want *me* to move *out*?"

Matt rolled his eyes as he shoved his shaving things into an overnight bag. "I thought I made that obvious. My *wife* will be moving in with me."

Unable to think straight, I gaped at him. I knew we weren't *happy*, but we weren't *unhappy* either. The words *comfortable*, *content*, and *settled* popped like soap bubbles in my head.

He stared at the big black cat weaving around my feet. "And don't forget to take that damn mangy cat with you."

I scooped up the mass of black fur I'd taken in a few months earlier, hugging him. Looked as though we were both about to be strays. "You're supposed to be marrying *me*! You can't ask for the ring back and marry someone else just like *that*." My voice sounded frantic.

Matt smiled. "Actually, I can marry anyone I want. I know I should say I'm sorry, but I'm not. You and I aren't married. We aren't *getting* married. Truth be told, I've come to realize there's nothing at all exciting about you, and Candy has made me see I'm far too young to settle for someone so... *boring*. This is *my* house. You have no claim to it. Seriously, if you're still here when I get back from my honeymoon, I'll have you arrested for trespassing."

Nothing exciting about *me?* Matthew Green was, very literally, the least exciting man I knew—his whirlwind Las Vegas elopement notwithstanding. He organized his sock drawer by color. He slept with a mouth guard to protect his capped teeth. For crap sake, the man wore tighty-whities!

I put the color in his black and white TV show. *I* added the soundtrack to his silent film. For the first time since we'd met, I realized I was living a farce. Our entire relationship was meaningless. How did I end up with such a colossal stinker? That's when my anger billowed up like a white sheet on a windy day, blinding me.

The cat darted out of my grasp, and my hands balled into tight fists, snapping open before clenching again. My blood ran like hot oil through my veins, and I had a strange taste in my mouth—metallic but almost sugary. I remembered thinking, *how dare he?* Horrible images zigzagged through my mind as I thought them so loudly I may as well have been screaming. A string of unspoken obscenities bubbled up to my lips. And then... *nothing*.

As Friday morning dawned, Matt was still missing, and I was still coming to grips with the fact that Thursday wasn't a dream.

Retracing my steps, I dredged up as much detail as I could remember from the great big blank that was last night. After Matt came home, he'd asked for his ring back. There was a flash of light, then a delicious warmth coursed through me. His clothes lay in a lump where he'd been standing. In his place sat a little black skunk.

I gnawed on my already jagged thumbnail until it throbbed in sync with my heartbeat, chipping my favorite polish in the process. I thought there had to be some logical explanation, but after several hours of soul-searching, I could come up with only one possible conclusion.

I'm a witch.

Especially when I realized the skunk responded to "Matthew." I mean, what were the odds they would have the same name?

After my immediate horror, and all the varying levels of disbelief that came along with it, dissipated, I settled into what could only be shock. I tried to be rational. What was done was done. He was a skunk. And since no matter how hard I tried, I couldn't seem to wish the whole thing away, I decided to recreate my steps—the ones I could remember.

With my eyes squeezed shut, I concentrated and struggled to envision Matt as he used to be—as he should have been. I waited for the surge of heat to return. *Nothing.* I couldn't summon his human image, as if he'd been obliterated from my memories. Wiped clean. Well, not quite clean. I saw bits and pieces—random flashes.

I pictured the exact shade of blue in his colored contact lenses and the precise way his highlighted hair swept back away from his square face. Rationally, I knew what he looked like, but I couldn't bring his face into view. Not even a flicker.

Digging through my dresser drawers, I searched for a photograph of Matt. I couldn't find one. There were pictures of me—lots of them—with my arm draped around nothing and kissing air. Not a single photo included Matt, as though he'd been erased from every one.

Poof. Like magic.

I should have spent the entire night trying to find a way to reverse whatever spell had transformed Matt, but I didn't. The shock and anger had completely worn me out.

The rollercoaster of emotions made me hungry too—in many disturbing ways—so I'd trekked down to the kitchen at one o'clock in the morning for the pint of Chunky Monkey in the freezer. It was Matt's favorite flavor, but he couldn't eat it *now.* I had no idea what skunks ate. After devouring the ice cream and an entire bag of Double Stuf Oreos—more calories than I normally ate in two days—I crawled into the guest room bed with my laptop. I planned to do a Google search for magical incantations—and what to feed skunks—but instead, I drifted off, fuzzy slippers along for the ride.

I didn't mean to fall asleep. I mean, how *could* anyone sleep after turning their fiancé into vermin?

Like a baby actually. Probably the best night's rest I'd ever had. Other than numerous erotic dreams starring a criminally sexy—but conspicuously faceless—veterinarian, I was dead to the world. I woke up from my reoccurring sex dreams feeling refreshed and alive, cleansed of all negative feelings. Then my conscience hit me. *So much for my good mood.* I mean, who had decadent dreams after turning her fiancé into a woodland creature? *I do, that's who.* The first thing I did when I got out of bed was call in sick for the third time that week.

I hadn't been sick the other two days either. I supposed the first day loosely qualified. My mother had to have a root canal and begged me to go with her. How could I say no? I was her only child, and since my poor father blew himself up in a freak accident, a science experiment gone wrong, more than twelve years ago, I was all she had left.

Basically, she played the guilt card.

The other day I'd spent shopping with Chloe. Prada had had an unprecedented sale, and Chloe refused to go alone. I could have said no, but honestly, surrender was easier. Since our first day as college roommates, she had decided I would be her exclusive shopping partner. We were practically inseparable—until I moved in with Matt. Since then I'd still talked to her on the phone at least once a day.

The chorus of "Girls Just Wanna Have Fun" blared from my phone.

"Hey, Chl—"

"I know you said no, but you absolutely *have* to go with me to Coach," Chloe blurted. "Do you remember the bag I dreamt about? The hobo with gold flecks in shimmering, soft, buttery leather, with the silk lining and thick leather strap?"

Chloe's newest quest was to locate the perfect fall bag. She knew exactly what she wanted and had described it to me so many times I could pick it out of a lineup. She spoke about the purse with a divine reverence. She didn't care how much it cost; finding it was her life's mission. Of course, the elusive purse didn't exist. She had literally dreamed it, calling me the next morning to tell me she'd fallen in love. In all the years I'd known Chloe Jamison, she had never professed to love a man, but she'd fallen for many a leather handbag. According to Chloe, something about the shape of the perfect hobo and the sumptuous feel of leather against her skin made life worth living.

After two weeks of exhausting every avenue, she had yet to find anything even remotely resembling her dream bag. Had that discouraged her? Not a chance. The challenge, and knowing that bag was out there and needed her, drove her to search harder. She was determined to drag me along for the ride.

How could I ever *forget that bag?* "Yes, of course, I remember, but—"

"Well, I saw an ad showcasing a purse almost exactly like it. Even on sale it's ridiculously expensive, but who needs groceries, right?" She laughed. "I'll just have to arrange a few dinner dates for the next week or two."

Chloe had enough boyfriends to keep herself in dinner dates for a month. It came with being model beautiful. Men fell for her big blue eyes, perfect body, and luxurious, long vanilla-blond hair. *Natural* blond hair. Hating her should have been easy, but I didn't know anyone who hated Chloe. Her personality was infectious. In a non-STD way.

"I'm coming to pick you up, and don't even try to say no. The simple fact that you answered tells me you didn't go to work today, so you have absolutely no excuse."

I glanced down at the clothes I'd slept in. And although I couldn't see my hair, I was sure we were talking wild nest. "I can't. It's just... it's not a good day for me."

"Ohhh nooo," she said. "I am *not* letting you weasel out of going. I'm pulling into your driveway now. Hey, is that Dr. Doolittle's car?" She emphasized Doolittle as if it were two words—*Do Little*. "You know what, never mind, it doesn't matter. You've got thirty seconds to change out of your flannel pajamas and get your butt out the door, or I'm coming in."

I had absolutely no way to stop her. And *I* was supposed to be the witch. Chloe had her own way of weaving a spell to overtake free will. I hoped my appearance would distract her from her mission long enough so I could, in fact, weasel out of going. The call had barely disconnected when the doorbell sounded. *Ding dong, this witch is dead.* I smoothed my crazy hair and straightened my clothes before opening the door.

Chloe's wide smile looked like the "after" photo in an orthodontist advertisement. One glimpse of me, and her smile turned into a frown, creating a wrinkle between her perfectly sculpted brows. "Oh, God! Sabrina, you look awful!"

She was referring to the Audrey Hepburn movie, *not* the teenage witch. Chloe had called me that since college when she'd insisted I looked just like a young Audrey Hepburn. All things being equal, I would've preferred Rita Hayworth. But genetics being what they were, I was stuck with the "girl next door" vibe.

She brushed past me to come inside. "Are you actually sick this time?"

"Well, I've felt better, I suppose—"

"Ivie, don't take this the wrong way, but you *stink*. Really bad." She pinched her nose and moved two steps away from me. "It smells like you got sprayed by a skunk."

With her nose plugged, it sounded more like, "It spels like you got sprayed by a skuk."

I let out a quick laugh. "Yeah, well... it's a long story."

She tilted her head, a sympathetic smile on her lips, and regarded me as if I was one of those blue-haired shopping-cart ladies at the thrift store. "The farm field trip?" She patted my hand when I nodded. "It's a wonder you're still alive. That's two years in a row. You'd better tell them you aren't going next year. I shudder to think what more could happen to you. And you wanted me to go with you. Blech." She shook her head, still holding her nose, and her face puckered as if she'd tasted something sour.

Chloe had, of course, refused my ridiculous attempt to drag her with me to the farm. "There is absolutely nothing in my wardrobe suitable for farm animals," she'd argued.

She flashed her perfect smile again. "So, other than your new Eau du

Pepé Le Pew perfume, you seem to have survived. No casualties this year?"

The words "goat semen" flashed through my mind, and I covered my face with my hands.

Chloe laughed. "Oh, no. You're not getting out of it this easily. Spill."

"It's too horrible to go into this early in the morning." I stole a glance at her from between my fingers. "I haven't even had coffee yet." My teeth caught my bottom lip. I was afraid if I started talking, I wouldn't be able to stop. Chloe was my best friend, I wanted to tell her everything, but I wasn't sure our friendship was strong enough to weather witchcraft. I mean, it wasn't as if Gucci made a broomstick.

"Is something wrong? You're acting strange. Stranger than normal, I mean." She gave a cursory look around my foyer then turned her attention to the front door. "Why is Dr. Doolittle's car in the driveway?"

I blinked but said nothing. Chloe would have enjoyed the irony. She hated Matt—absolutely despised him—which was why I took almost every opportunity to remind her she was the one who had introduced us.

She arched an eyebrow. "So? What's he doing home on a Friday?"

My lips curved into a forced smile. "Oh, you know, just a bad morning." I hoped she didn't see through my inane attempt at deflection. "He's still in the bathroom. I'm trying to get him out of here as soon as possible." All true statements.

"Hmm. If you say so."

"I do. It's fine." My fake smile threatened to shatter.

She poked out her cherry-red bottom lip. "So no Coach?"

"I don't think so." My resolve had all but slipped. If I didn't get her out of there, I'd spill my guts at any moment. "They probably wouldn't let me in smelling like this. I think I might have to take a bath in tomato juice before I can go anywhere."

"Oh, that never works." Chloe shrugged and flipped her blond hair behind her back. "Too bad. It would have been fun. We could have stopped for lunch at Capers. They have the absolute best bruschetta. It's to die for, I swear." She grinned. "Next time. Now, go wash off the smell of the wild and call me later. We can have drinks before Dr. Doolittle gets home. My treat."

I opened my mouth to say something about what had happened *before* Matt turned into a skunk but closed it without saying a word. Chloe may not have blinked an eye over Matt's predicament, but she would be horrified to learn the fate of my Ralph Lauren boots. "Sounds like a plan."

She leaned halfway in, her nose twitching, and kissed the air to each side. "Don't forget to call me!"

"I won't," I promised.

Chloe turned to leave but paused with her hand on the doorknob. She tipped her head to one side as a slow smile spread across her glossy lips. "You did something different with your hair."

I combed my fingers through my tangled locks. "No, it's the same boring hair as always."

"No, it's definitely different. Maybe a little red?" Her eyes narrowed slightly. Then she nodded and gave me a conspiratorial wink. "But don't worry. I like it."

I laughed. "It must be the light in here."

"If you say so." She shrugged one shoulder. "Well, I'm off to shop. Wish me luck." She was out the door before I could respond.

With Chloe gone, the house was too quiet, and I had no choice but to face the task at hand. Jerk or not, I had to find a way to change Matt back. I continued to rack my brain for a single shred of a clue—anything from my past that even remotely resembled a real spell. I knew what I had to do. I had to call the only person who could possibly solve the mystery.

My mother.

Three

"Hi, Mom." I tried to sound chipper but only succeeded in sounding hysterical.

"Who is this?" she asked, her voice laced with suspicion.

"It's me... Ivie." I took a slow, cleansing breath to rein in my frustration. "Your only child?"

My mother chuckled. "Oh, Ivie, I didn't recognize your voice, dear."

"How many people call you and say, 'Hi, Mom'?" I paced over the plush carpet, cataloguing all the reasons why turning my mother into an elephant—or anything with a better memory—would be a bad idea.

I imagined her tilting her head like a golden retriever. "Just you, dear."

"Then why do you always ask, 'Who is this?'"

"Well, it could be anyone." Her voice became serious. "There are scammers everywhere. You really should be more careful."

"Don't you have caller ID? You could check the number, and then you'd know it was me."

I could almost hear her rolling her eyes. "You should just say, 'This is Ivie.' Then I'll know it's you." Mom always had a way of twisting things until it seemed as if *I* was the one making things more difficult.

"Never mind." I blew out a breath, summoning every ounce of courage. "Mom, I need to ask you something."

"What is it?" she chimed.

I chose my words carefully, hoping she would answer the question I was trying not to ask. "Has anything *strange* ever happened to you?"

She was silent for so long I thought I might have lost the call. Then I heard her clicking her tongue against the roof of her mouth. She did that when she was thinking. "What do you mean by *strange*, dear?" Her voice had a suspicious edge again.

I barked out what was supposed to be casual laughter but sounded more like a dry cough. "You know... *strange*. Weird, unusual, out of the ordinary... something that made you wonder." I tried to keep it light. Obscure. *Safe.*

"Well, I do wonder how your aunt Janice manages to eat like a horse and keep her figure when I eat like a bird and struggle with mine." Mom had lowered her voice to just above a whisper as if she was sharing a state secret. She let out an exasperated sigh. "You would think I ate cake for breakfast, lunch, and dinner."

"No, Mom." I took a slow, steadying breath. "Stranger than that. Something like... *magic.*" I tossed out that word as if I might have selected "alien abductions" or "astral projection" and decided at the last moment to go a different way. The line went quiet for a full minute. "Mom? Did you hear me?"

"Oh, I wouldn't be surprised if Janice has been performing some kind of magic to keep a figure like that at her age. It just doesn't seem right. She eats whatever she wants: pastry, pasta, bread..." Her voice drifted off as if she wasn't really talking to me but to the air.

I felt the crease in my forehead deepen. "No, seriously. Have you ever *done* anything strange?"

She gasped. "Ivie, dear, you shouldn't ask your mother questions like that. It's rude."

I tamped down my irritation, barely keeping it from my voice. "I mean with your mind. Have you ever thought really hard about something and then it happened?"

"That's what I'm talking about! I just *think* about cake, and I gain five pounds. Like magic!"

"Never mind," I said.

"So..." Her tone perked up. "How is my soon to be son-in-law, the doctor, doing? You should bring him by to see me. You haven't been for Sunday dinner in ages."

"He's fine."

The silence hung between us for a while, and I figured what the heck. She might know.

"Do you know how to get skunk spray out of carpet?"

My entire life lay in ruins, and I was officially Bewitched, Bothered, and Bewildered.

My best friend was an obsessive shopaholic. My mother was clueless. And I was a witch without a spellbook. Time to resort to Google.

The cat remained oblivious to all the chaos around him, and I scooped him up. "Some watch cat you are, Karma." I stroked his silky fur and his motoring purr lulled me into a state of relative calm.

I'm taking this way too well. But I simply chalked that up to my obvious state of shock.

After grabbing my laptop from the bed while balancing the cat in one arm, I closed the bedroom door and headed down to the kitchen. I settled into the window seat with Karma curled up on my lap and did a quick search on witchcraft. A vintage pencil drawing of a cat arching its back caught my attention on the main page of www. witchesRus.com.

"Oh, look, Karma. It says witches are supposed to have black cats." He opened his mouth in a jaw-cracking yawn. "In case you haven't noticed"—I leaned down and lowered my voice to a whisper—"*you* are a black cat."

I wondered if that was why I'd been so drawn to him the moment I saw him eating trash from a dumpster behind the school. He had been nearly skin and bones—a mere shadow of the plump cat in my lap—and in desperate need of a bath. The little voice in my head, assuring me good deeds were rewarded, compelled me to take him in. That's why I'd named him Karma. He was hired on, and paid in room, board, and scratches behind the ears, to bring me good fortune. Yet Matt lingered in the locked bathroom. *So much for good fortune.*

Karma reminded me of myself in many ways. His inky black coat was nearly the same shade as my hair, and our eyes were the same emerald green. The similarity was striking. A match made in witchy heaven.

"Look here, Karma Chameleon. According to WitchesRus, witches use their cats, or familiars as they're called, to draw on extra power to work spells." He tipped his face up to mine as if paying rapt attention. "Familiars are almost like a magical mirror, reflecting power back into the spell. Some people believed cats were actually powerful witches in disguise." Karma stretched out across my lap, his purr-motor revving as I stroked his fur. "Could it be you, not me?"

Matt hated my cat. The feeling seemed mutual. Could Karma have transformed Matt into a skunk? I lifted the lazy cat until our noses were inches apart, green eyes peering into green eyes. "Have you been doing magic, Karma?"

He jumped down and darted from the room. *Guess not.* The fact that he managed to remember where his litter box was most days was pure luck. The idea of him holding secret midnight meetings with a group of other witches in cat suits seemed unlikely.

Matt's cell phone rang for the fifth time in a matter of minutes. I should have left it upstairs but felt compelled to drag it around with me. At least it wasn't Ginger. I'd already spoken with *her* one time too many. I hadn't bothered to write down any of her messages. I just shouted them through the bathroom door even though I wasn't entirely sure Matt understood anything I said to him, other than his name. Then again, I never promised he would understand the messages—only that I would pass them along.

Somebody wasn't happy about being ignored. *Well, isn't that too bad.* I tossed the phone into my purse and zipped it shut. That at least muffled the sound.

My internet search took me through every website I could find referencing magic. I waded through a veritable smorgasbord of information, but most of the sites were no help at all, unless I wanted to order magical paraphernalia. For scented candles or ancient runes—made in China— the internet was the place to shop. Most accepted MasterCard and Visa, Blessed Be. But not a peep about how to transform your fiancé into a skunk... and definitely nothing about changing him back.

A hysterical laugh forced out of me. I couldn't be a witch. What did I know about witchcraft? Outside of *The Craft, The Wizard of Oz,* and *Bewitched,* I was clueless. Sure, I'd dressed up in a pointed hat and striped tights for Halloween once or twice, and I'd been known to have pretty wicked PMS. But as for the cauldron, the broomstick, or the required complexion? Hardly. Green wasn't my color... or my future last name anymore.

According to several websites, the night before fell within three days of the new moon, when it was in the final stage of waning—the last days the crescent would be visible before going dark. That was news to me. I rarely paid much attention to lunar cycles. A waning moon was evidently the best time for banishing spells and rejecting all undesirable things—like negative influences, emotional weaknesses, and bad habits. In other words, all things Matt. The new moon was also a time for purification and performing cleansings, although how conjuring a skunk could fall under that category was beyond me. I would never get the stench out of... anything.

Apparently, I also had to factor in my individual lunar month cycle—which was greatly influenced and magnified by the power of the moon—and factor in the presence of a familiar. In other words, take one part waning moon, add a black cat and one wicked case of PMS, and...

I had purified and cleansed myself of Matt.

Four

I DIDN'T HAVE ANY TOMATO JUICE, but I did have spaghetti sauce—lots of it and several varieties. So I filled the tub in the guest bath and emptied all the jars into the hot water. Dipping my toes in first, I swirled the water.

"Double, double, toil, and trouble, fire burn and cauldron bubble." I giggled. *Macbeth* was my father's favorite of Shakespeare's plays, and for some reason, quoting it made me feel closer to him. I had always figured the ties to Scotland appealed to him, but suddenly the irony struck me as funny. The legendary curses associated with the Scottish play didn't seem so silly anymore.

Before long, the tub was slick with tomato sauce and a slimy orange film floated to the top. I lowered myself carefully into the broth and then, leaning my head against the back ledge, slid down until the water reached my chin. The smell wafted up, making my stomach rumble. I still hadn't eaten, and I was soaking in a bowl of hot soup. Tomato soup.

Bathing in spaghetti sauce wasn't on my bucket list, but it *definitely* had a spot on my list of things to never do again. Bits of sausage and beef collected between my toes. I was pretty sure it would clog the drain. I didn't want to think of all the places I'd find remnants. I probably should have skipped the meat sauce.

The impulse to lick the crook of my arm was almost irresistible. Or rather, thoughts of *someone* licking their way down my arm pervaded my thoughts. Images of the sexy vet floated to the forefront of my mind again, and then I was not only immersed in what was essentially a condiment, but thoroughly turned on... again.

I'm sure Matt would have found some pleasure in my suffering. Even if I had acted out of instinct, completely unaware of the consequences, I probably deserved *some* suffering. Stewing in tomatoes wasn't my only punishment, I reminded myself as "I'm Too Sexy" played from the counter. I'd lost count of Matt's missed calls.

After marinating for almost an hour—long enough for my body to reek of an Italian restaurant—the water turned cold and the sauce formed clumps on the bottom. The piquant aroma leached out of my pores. A long hot shower followed the bath. A greasy layer of marinara had invaded every crack and crevice of my body: between my fingers and toes, under my nails, in my ears, and other more... *delicate* places. I washed my hair three times with rosemary mint shampoo and conditioner, and I nearly scrubbed off the top layer of my skin with an SOS pad from the kitchen. Between the tomato bath and the exfoliating, there was absolutely nothing more I could do.

After wrapping myself in a towel, I wiped the fog from the mirror. "Who are you, Ivie McKie?" I didn't look like a witch. I looked like the same twenty-four-year-old kindergarten teacher who didn't do anything even remotely exciting, the same girl who ate frozen dinners four nights a week and bought designer clothes from a thrift store. I used to think I knew everything about me. I was uncomplicated and, like Matt said, boring. *Maybe not so boring after all.*

Combing a hand through my wet tangles, I thought back to what Chloe had said about my hair. She had to be imagining things. I looked exactly the same. I rubbed the towel briskly over my head, absorbing as much water as I could, and then pulled it around me again, tucking my damp locks behind my ears.

Chloe's ringtone sounded at the same time the doorbell chimed.

"Hey, shopaholic." I readjusted my towel as I answered.

"Let me in."

I hung up and plodded down the stairs to the front door. "What are you doing here?"

"Couldn't wait," she said, brushing past me.

I sucked in a quick breath. "Couldn't wait for what?"

"Your explanation." She pushed her sunglasses into her hair like a tiara then crossed her arms. "You're keeping something from me, and you're going to spill *this instant*."

My heart lurched, then stopped before setting off at a thundering pace. "Keeping something from you?" *How did she know?*

"Oh, come on. You've been my best friend for almost six years. I was there the night you lost your virginity to the Brad Pitt look-alike, who *only* looked like Brad Pitt after three shots of tequila, by the way. I'm the one who talked you out of drunk dialing every guy in your contact list when fake-Brad broke your heart less than a week later, *and* I convinced you to give the male population another chance when you vowed to move to Indonesia and become a nun." She poked my arm to punctuate each thought. "I've listened to every secret"—poke—"wish"—poke—"and dream"—poke—"you've ever had without *once* breaking your confidence. And I'm probably the only person alive who's seen the underwear you *really* wear when you think no one will see you in your underwear. So don't even *try* to hide this shit from me." She gave me the evil eye. "Unless you don't trust me anymore."

"I... Of course I trust you." I trusted her, I really did, but some things were just too big.

"Then..." Her eyes scanned me, and she scrunched up her face as she leaned in to *sniff* me. "For God's sake, please tell me why you answered the door in nothing but a towel, in the middle of the afternoon, smelling like...

skunk pizza? You know, I would have never guessed you could possibly smell worse than you did this morning, but congratulations, you've proven me wrong."

"I smell like skunk pizza?" I sniffed my arm. She was right. "I took a bath in tomato sauce to get rid of the smell. You know, the... uh... farm trip?"

"Okay, so that explains why you stink, but what about the rest of it? I get why *you* ditched today, but I can't stand the suspense anymore. Why is Dr. Doolittle's car in the exact same place as it was this morning? He *never* calls in sick." She eyed me up and down. "If I didn't know better, I'd say you were getting busy with your fiancé, but since we both know *that* doesn't happen—at least not in the light of day or without several bottles of wine—I'm assuming you're keeping something else from me. You aren't getting kinky up there, are you? I'm all for a little kink, but this"—she waved toward me—"is just weird." Chloe's blank expression gave away none of her thoughts.

"Oh, my God! Chloe, no, I'm—just no." I convulsed at the thought of "getting kinky" with Matt—in any form. "I'm traumatized, you know, from my farm experience."

"Please. I may be a blonde, but I'm not dumb. You seemed fine yesterday. This is about more than a bad field trip. Start talking, girlfriend, and don't even *think* of leaving anything out."

Chloe listened as I detailed yesterday's events from the moment I boarded the bus bound for the farm until the minute I arrived home to drink myself to sleep. I stopped the story just before Matt stepped through the door. Her face went from mild annoyance to utter shock and back to unreadable as I spoke. Then both of her hands flew up to cover her mouth as she let loose with a burst of hysterical laughter.

"Oh, sure, laugh at me." I crossed my arms, pulling the towel tighter around me. And she wondered why I'd resisted telling her. Still laughing, Chloe gave me a hard nudge, and I fell into the nearest chair. "Nice, Chloe. Geez, enough already, it's not *that* funny."

"Oh, I'm sorry, sweetie." She choked back a giggle. "But you're wrong. It's *exactly* that funny. Please tell me someone got it on video."

I shuddered at that possibility. "There'd better not be a video." She cracked up again. I felt as if the wind had been knocked out of me. "Stop laughing. Do you think someone might have taken a video?"

Chloe pressed her lips together before shaking her head. "We would have heard about *that* by now." She took a calming breath, pulling herself together. "Okay, okay. I'm sorry." After a beat, she started laughing again. "No, I'm not sorry. I really need to get the whole picture here. So let me get it straight... You were checking out this deliciously sexy veterinarian across the barnyard?" She waited for me to nod. "God, he must have been something else if you wandered into a muddy pasture in your Ralph Lauren boots."

My cheeks flamed, and I nodded again. *Hot* didn't begin to cover it.

"Okay, so you tripped? And ended up on your knees in the mud? And then..."

"Yes, yes, yes," I sputtered. "Please, can we not talk about this anymore?" My face fell into my hands, and she broke into another fit of giggles.

"Oh, Sabrina, it's just too priceless. Here I am worrying about shopping for your wedding dress, and you're cheating on poor Dr. Doolittle with a *goat*."

"Ugh, I did *not* have sex with the goat."

"Admit it, that's the closest you've been to having sex in *months*. It sounded pretty hot too. Doggy style in the mud with his... paws? Over your shoulders?"

"Hooves."

"Huh?"

"They're called hooves, not paws." I groaned.

"Right." She pushed back another fit of giggles. "So he had his *hooves* over your shoulders, nibbling on your neck, bleating sweet nothings in your ear. Please tell me you were safe. You did at least use protection, didn't you?"

"For Chrissakes, I didn't have *sex* with the *goat!*"

"Semantics, Ivie, semantics." She twirled a strand of her hair. "You were dry humped by a goat in front of a busload of kids."

"Oh, God." I moaned into my hands. "It sounds so much worse when you say it like that."

"It's barnyard porn no matter how you say it." Chloe patted my head. "You must have gotten that poor goat all hot and bothered with your horny pheromones raging from drooling over the veterinarian. Speaking of the sexy vet, did you at least score a phone number?"

"What? No, I didn't get a phone number. I wasn't about to show my face again. The minute he pulled the goat off me, I ran back to the bus with my proverbial tail between my legs. What was I supposed to say?"

"Yeah, you're right. 'Thank you for saving me from the best sex I've had in months,' just doesn't cut it, now does it?" Chloe said.

"I should've never told you. You're never going to let this go."

"Nope." She popped the *p*. "Never. But at least I forgive you for ditching me and making me shop alone."

"Gee, thanks," I said.

"I do what I can." Chloe sniffed me again. "I hate to say this, but you really need another bath. Try hydrogen peroxide, baking soda, and dish detergent. That should do the trick."

"Wait, how do you—?"

"Don't speak, just listen. I really need to run, but I'll call you later. I'm sorry about the goat, but hey, at least you finally got lucky, right?"

Why does everyone say that?

Chloe froze with her hand on the doorknob and flashed a wicked grin. "Oh, and Ivie? Goats don't smell like skunk. I'll get to the bottom of your mystery odor later."

"I really hate you."

After taking Chloe's strange advice, I smelled halfway human again. My elation was short-lived as I stared at the pile of dirty clothes. They reeked of skunk and sweat. I'd worn them for too long already. I needed clean clothes.

The way I saw it, I had two choices. I could walk around in a towel all day, or be brave and go back into my bedroom to get something clean to wear. Terrycloth wasn't really an option, so I hitched the towel under my arms and took a long last breath of fresh air. I marched back into my room, and didn't breathe again until I'd opened a window. The stench from the bathroom had overtaken the space. I knew if I didn't do something soon, someone would notice.

And by someone, I meant Mrs. Camp.

Other than her, our neighborhood's resident crazy old lady, the neighbors kept to themselves. We lived on a nice quiet street made up of a charming row of late Victorian and early Craftsman-style houses. Just down the block was a crumbly old cemetery so ancient no one had been buried there in over fifty years. On Halloween, all the teenagers snuck through the gates to scare each other. And get lucky. The creepy old boneyard terrified me, so I'd never even set foot inside.

I didn't know my neighbors well. They would wave if I passed by, but no one stopped to chat. Mrs. Camp was the only one I knew by name. If I'd had to place a wager on who was the witch in our area, my bet would have been on that old biddy. *Not me.* She lived directly next door to me, and she *rarely* kept to herself. In fact, she made a point of keeping track of everyone's business—particularly mine.

Mrs. Camp couldn't find her mailbox without her glasses, but she could spot a stray cat squatting in her yard in the middle of the night from behind stained-glass windows. I suspected she hated animals. She'd probably already called animal control to round up the mysterious skunk. If he wasn't careful, Karma would find himself in a basket on the front of her bicycle. She'd pegged him as the culprit digging up her flowerbeds, and I had a terrible time convincing her he was an indoor cat, which was mostly true. He might have used her flowerbed as a litter box once. Okay, once a week.

Karma clawed at the carpet in front of the bathroom, and I shooed him away. "Karma! Get away from there. Bad kitty." I nudged the cat with my foot as I walked past.

I opened the door to my walk-in closet with a gentle push and tugged on the string to the bare bulb suspended from the ceiling. It didn't give off much light, but I'd have known my way around the space blindfolded. Thankfully, the closet was cedar-lined and far enough away from the bathroom that the smell hadn't permeated everything yet. The odor actually reminded me more of the farm because of my boots still bagged up in the corner. I forced myself to look away from the garbage bag and back to the racks of clothes. For an underpaid teacher, I actually had a fairly nice wardrobe, thanks to Chloe. I also had a black belt in thrift-and-consignment-store shopping.

I pulled out my second-favorite shirt—a navy blue pullover I'd owned almost since high school—and a pair of loose-fitting jeans. Maybe I should have worn *that* to the farm. I took my clothes back into the bedroom and discovered Karma still feverishly clawing at the carpet in front of the bathroom door. "What are you doing, kitty?"

The cat growled and went straight back to tearing at the floor. His claws dug in deep, lifting both the carpet and the pad, exposing the subfloor. With both out of the way, I clearly saw a pool of water seeping out from under the door.

"Oh, no!" I tossed the clothes onto the bed and darted to Karma, who calmly peered up at me. With a deep breath, I gripped the towel wrapped around me. "This is bad. Did you do this?" I felt ridiculous even asking. He rubbed against my bare leg and purred.

Defying my better judgment, I opened the door. Instead of searching for the little black skunk, my eyes fixated on the overflowing toilet. Inside the bowl, packed down as if Matt had been turned into a beaver, was one of my good bath towels. It blocked the water from going down, and the toilet had been flushed—repeatedly, if the water level was any indication.

"Damn it!" I yanked open the door and ran to the toilet, dropping my towel on the way, and pulled the drenched linens from the bowl. "How the hell did he—" I stopped and realized I'd forgotten to look for Matt. Even as a skunk, he'd manipulated me. The stinker.

Letting loose a string of obscenities, I splashed back into the bedroom. I would kill him. Skunk or no skunk, spray or no spray, if I could get my hands around his furry little neck, I would definitely wring it. I knew that after plotting such an elaborate ruse, he must have ventured farther than the bedroom. I'd stepped halfway into the hallway when I saw Matt, still in skunk form, at the edge of the stairs, poised to spray my cat.

"Don't. You. Dare!" I said through clenched teeth as I pointed at him. Waves of anger rose and flowed like a tangible force, surging down my arm and through my outstretched finger like ripples in a campfire. An explosion of heat—hot and bubbly—radiated from me. The moment felt right, somehow. Almost liberating. I closed my eyes, and blue light flickered behind my lids, mesmerizing me. I guess I sort of blanked out again because the next thing I knew, the skunk had vanished and in its place, reared up on his hind legs and wiggling his nose in my direction, was a huge gray rat. "Karma, no!"

The cat pounced, capturing my former fiancé in his razor-sharp teeth, and bounded straight down the stairs.

Five

K ARMA PLAYING Tom TO MATT'S Jerry happened so fast I didn't have time to react. It didn't help that my unexplainable sexual frustration had reasserted itself, further distracting me. With no time to worry about the fact that I was completely naked, I simply bolted down the stairs in a blind panic. I couldn't allow my cat to eat my estranged fiancé. How would I ever look at Karma in the same way again? Cats are supposed to eat rats, aren't they? I mean, traditionally they were raised for the express purpose of hunting rodents, right? Karma would gain immediate street cred for ridding the house of such vermin. Then again, no one would have forgiven Wilbur if he'd eaten Templeton.

"Karma! Put Matt down. Bad kitty. Bad! Kitty!" I screamed frantically. "I'll open a can of tuna. No, wait, sardines. I'll—I'll grill you some salmon! I'll even watch your back while you crap in Mrs. Camp's rose garden! Here, kitty, kitty?"

The cat cut through the dining room and ran under the table where I couldn't follow. I winced at each squeal coming from the rat as I tried to reach them. I managed to topple over two chairs before Karma darted out and cut through the butler's pantry. Swiping at his tail, I almost had him when he jumped onto the counter. I grasped at nothing but loose fur as he escaped, a muffled growl in the back of his throat. Rounding the marble-topped island, he headed straight for his bowl as if he planned to place his meal in his dish to eat.

I cornered him in the kitchen. He released Matt to lick his chops. Then, holding the rat between his two front paws and gripping him with his claws, he hovered over him.

"Karma, do not bite that rat!" I scolded then turned my attention to the gray rodent. "As for you, Matt, you've brought this on yourself. I don't know how you managed to flood the bathroom—" I froze when I heard the doorbell, my finger mid-wag. Frantic knocking followed the peal. "Oh, this is perfect. Just wonderful!" I muttered. "You see what you've both done? Mrs. Camp has probably sent animal control. I wouldn't be surprised if they scooped you both up!"

I shook a finger at the two of them, my fiancé and my pet, locked in the age-old dance between cat and mouse, and I felt my hold on reality slipping ever so slightly. Another bang on the door startled me. Karma grabbed Matt in his teeth and scooted under the kitchen table, where he must have bit down harder because the rat squealed again.

"Karma, no!" I bellowed. "Let. Him. Go!" I crawled under the table, wincing as my bare skin brushed the cold tile, and grasped the cat by the scruff of his neck. I wrestled the rat out of his teeth with as much care as I could muster. As soon as I freed Matt, Karma fled the room. "I'll deal with you later," I yelled at his retreating tail. I turned back to the twitching rodent. His heart fluttered madly, and his cool nose pressed against my palm. "If you don't behave yourself, I might not turn you back." I tried to sound confident, as if I had everything under control. Of course, I didn't know *how* to turn him back. I wondered if he knew that. Could the animal in him smell the truth?

The pounding continued at the front door, alternating with the relentless bell ringing as if someone had leaned directly on the button. I still wore nothing more than a worried expression, so I couldn't answer it. But more than bothersome, it was worrisome. Someone seemed intent on getting inside.

"Who the hell could that be?" I muttered. Matt squirmed, trying to work himself free. "What am I going to do with you?"

That's when he bit me. His tiny, razor-sharp front teeth sank into my left hand, between my thumb and wrist, hard enough to draw blood. In the same instant the bead of blood bubbled up, so did a bead of anger, just as red and viscous. With a gasp, I dropped him. As I watched him fall in slow motion, the blue heat flowed through me again.

Call it a crime of passion; I never saw it coming. I lashed out—or maybe I lashed in, because not a single word passed my lips. Okay, maybe I let loose a few choice words, but I didn't count those. Inside my head, I screamed *curses* at him. That's all it took. Stunned and nursing my wound, my thoughts were muddled.

It took several seconds for Matt to hit the floor, twisting as he fell. By the time he landed, he wasn't a rat anymore. He'd morphed into a ginormous, mostly black, diamond-patterned snake with a long gray streak down his side. *A python?* I couldn't have flown out of the kitchen faster, or screamed louder, if my hair had caught on fire. After screeching to a halt in the front hallway, I grabbed a tan overcoat from the closet and pulled it around me as I opened the door.

"What have you done with him?" the petite blonde barked as she looked past me. "Where is he?"

"Candy? What are you doing here?" Using my injured hand, I gripped the raincoat tighter, peering around her to see if she was alone.

"I'm looking for Matt. What have you done with him? I heard screaming."

"Screaming? I... I didn't hear screaming." I shrank into the depths of the coat.

"I know he's here, Ivie. His car's here. We have tickets for Las Vegas this afternoon, and I haven't heard from him since last night. He was supposed to come get his things then head back to my apartment. You can't keep me from my fiancé." She shoved her nose into the air, giant crocodile tears spilling over her kohl-rimmed eyes and creating streaks of black down her face.

"Oh, you mean *my* snake of a fiancé? I'm sure he's managed to slither off somewhere without you. Have you called Ginger?" I swallowed hard and tried to come up with a sarcastic smile. I don't think I pulled it off though.

"Why would I call his receptionist?" She turned her attention to my hand and gasped. "You're wearing my engagement ring!" She grabbed my wrist, staring at the diamond solitaire. "Why are you still wearing *my* ring?"

I tried to yank my hand back, but she wouldn't let go. "He proposed to me first."

"So! He proposed to me last. And he told me he was getting it back from you to give to me. He said he'd sooner die than let you..." Her eyes went wide, and her free hand flew up to cover her mouth. "Oh, my God... Why do you have blood all over your hand?"

Tugging out of her grip, I slipped my arm farther into the sleeve, hiding the tiny teeth marks. The blood soaked into the cuff. "The cat bit me. Not that it's any of your business." I lifted my chin and looked down my nose at her, but sounding indignant proved difficult with my heart racing. I kept picturing the giant python in the kitchen, getting into God knows what.

She shook a harlot-red fingernail at me. "That had better be *your* blood. If you've done anything to Matt..."

"You'll what?"

Candy's face went ashen as she scanned the room with her mascara-streaked eyes. "I'll call the police."

I peered behind me to take in the wreckage. Dining room chairs lay in every direction but upright, wet footprints trailed down the stairs, and the overpowering aroma of skunk permeated every square inch of the house.

And the showstopper: the large black snake slithering out of the butler's pantry. He glided over Matt's worn-out edition of *Gray's Anatomy* and headed in our direction.

I used the door to nudge her out of the house while keeping the snake in my peripheral vision. "Oops, I guess I'd better get him back in his cage. Do let me know if you find Matt. I'd like to have a word with him myself."

As soon as I'd closed and locked the door, I made a mad dash to the laundry room. I grabbed a large plastic basket, flipped it over to dump the clean clothes on the floor, and bolted back to the foyer while clutching it. Matt had coiled up, half of him on the hardwood floor and the other half on the Persian rug. I shuddered. He lifted his head, and his reptilian eyes stared at me as I slunk closer, laundry basket tucked behind my back.

"I'll bet you're pretty confused right now, aren't you, Matty? I'm going to get you all fixed up in no time. You just need to cooperate with me. Okay?" I used my sweet voice, the one I saved for my students or for special occasions at home. That qualified as a special occasion. When I got close enough, I flipped the basket upside down over him with a spontaneous shiver. Just to be safe, I reached for Matt's *Gray's Anatomy* to use as a paperweight.

I forced myself to try the spell again. I'd just transformed him twice in a matter of minutes. I could do it. I needed to strike while the magic was hot, so to speak. The power still sparked in me. I felt it from my fingertips down to the pulsating wet spot right between my legs. Just a whisper, but it was there. I strained to push the sensation out of me toward Matt. I concentrated on the same pattern that had worked before. I struggled to picture him as a human. The image shimmered in and out. Mostly out. I could only focus on the things I *knew* about him. I couldn't see his face. It was like trying to light a match in the rain. The flame flickered and went out.

The snake raised its head and struck out at me, hitting the inside of the basket with a dull crack. Plastic cage or not, I refused to spend any more time in a room with a slithering reptile. I'd been living with him for more than a year, but the word *snake* had taken on a completely new meaning. As far as I was concerned, the only *snake* I was going anywhere near was the pair of Louboutin pumps Chloe had bought me last Christmas.

Just then I noticed Karma slink back into the room. Scooping the cat from the floor to keep him from ending up as dinner, I bolted upstairs to the guest room. Karma was the perfect snack-sized treat for a predator Matt's size. Oh, the irony. Of course, I could only guess at Matt's size. I wasn't about to measure him. He was about as big around as a baseball bat and three or four times as long. *Give or take.* But where magic was concerned, there was no taking chances. I had dabbled long enough. I needed help, but didn't have a clue where to start.

Six

CRAIGSLIST HAD EVERYTHING... AND I do mean *everything*. Everything but instructions on how to change my snake of an ex-fiancé back into a human. Although, I imagined those tips would be popular the world over.

Realistically, I should have seen his betrayal coming. Matt was a snake long before he was a *snake*. Breaking up with his fiancé to marry someone else wasn't going to win him any "Boyfriend of the Year" awards, but I should have seen the writing on the wall. A gym membership for my birthday? As the resident chiropractor, he got those for free! But apparently, the right exercises would increase my bust size and add some "desperately needed" curves.

And working late as often as he did? That was number one in the "How to Cheat on Your Girlfriend" manual. Apparently, gullible was my middle name.

After beating myself up for being naïve, I settled on a nonspecific search for magic. I was amazed how many people were looking to sell a Magic 8 Ball. And something called Body Magic. Magic Chef appliances. Magic Kingdom tickets. Magic Johnson jerseys. In the tangled mess of irrelevant listings, I spotted one lonely ad for *Magician*.

Jackson Blake will amaze and astound, transforming the ordinary into the extraordinary. Not for the faint of heart but the pure of mind. Let the magic touch you where you haven't been touched before. There may be a little magic in you!

Vlad's Castle, 1142 4th Avenue, Downtown. Call for reservations and pricing.

A blurry image, most likely an Abercrombie ad photoshopped to resemble a magician, stared at me. *Interesting.* The name Jackson Blake seemed oddly familiar, though I was certain I hadn't heard it before. I contemplated the phone number for a moment then pulled my cell phone from my purse.

"This is ridiculous." I flung my phone into the pillows. "What can a magician do to help me? They don't actually *do* magic!" Neither do kindergarten teachers. Yet there I was. I looked to the cat for answers. He stretched out across the bed and yawned. I punctuated my search for the phone with a resigned groan.

I dialed the number three times before hitting send. His ringback was the electrifying tones of "Magic Man" by the rock band Heart. It gave me the chills. *Very appropriate.* I rehearsed what I would say, but my mind went blank the moment he answered.

"Jackson Blake." His voice was melted honey and sex.

My eyes darted back to the Abercrombie magician on the ad. For an instant, I feared I may have dialed one of those 1-900 numbers. I'd never heard someone so blatantly seductive before. Only two words from him and my panties had already caught fire. "Um... hi."

He chuckled. "Well, hello."

"I found you on Craigslist," I blurted before taking a steadying breath. "I'm looking for... *someone*... who can help me with magic."

"Well, magic *is* my thing," he continued in a matter-of-fact tone. "How can I help you?"

"Your ad said you could, you know, help find the magic within me? I'm desperate." I took a moment to catch my breath. *I definitely need something to touch me where I haven't been touched before.* "I can pay you."

"Find the magic within, huh? That sounds pretty intense. I think I might need more information than that." I distinctly heard a smile in his voice.

"I'd really rather not say over the phone. It's somewhat of a... *delicate* situation. Could we possibly meet in person?"

"I have a show tonight." The magician paused for several beats. "You could come." Things were sounding better and better. Or maybe that was just my wild imagination. "We can talk after. What's your name? I'll hold tickets for you at the door."

"Ivie. Ivie McKie," I said then regretted it. Did I really want a stranger to know my name?

"Okay, Ivie McKie," he said, his voice low and husky. "My show starts at nine... if we manage to start on time. I'm off the stage by ten-thirty, either way. If you aren't there by eleven, I'll be gone."

"Okay. Between nine and eleven. Got it."

"Oh, and Ivie?"

"Yes?"

"Sorry, but you'll have to pay for the ticket. I don't have any to comp," he said.

"Of course, how much will it cost?"

"Thirty for one. But you can get a pair for fifty. You can bring a *friend* along if you'd like."

He was fishing. I could tell by the way he said friend— an implication and a question rolled into one. "No, it'll just be me. Can't wait to see you tonight." As I hung up, I clenched my thighs together to fend off the ache between them. If his voice had me this worked up, I shuddered to think what would happen when we were face to face. I needed to get myself under control before I imploded.

After indulging the most extreme sexual craving I think I'd ever endured, with more self-achieved orgasms than any one person should be allowed to experience in a single sitting, I headed back to the gas chamber to find the clothes I'd abandoned. After being strewn about the bed for nearly an hour, they reeked of skunk. Since I hadn't closed the closet door, so did everything else. I had no choice but to break into the clothes Chloe had forced me to buy last time we went shopping. The bags were, thankfully, still in my car, waiting for the buyer's remorse to subside.

After dragging myself to the garage, I popped the trunk to root through the bags of clothes. I wasn't sure whether to thank Chloe or kill her for the selections I had to work with. Was anything in there even remotely suitable for a rendezvous in a magic club? What does one wear to meet up with a total stranger, anyway?

Once I'd convinced myself it was a business meeting, not a date, I selected a lightweight, black Ann Taylor turtleneck and a pair of black skinny jeans. The only time I counted myself lucky to have a waifish figure was when I wanted to wear skinny jeans. There were no curves required. Then I pulled out the bag from Victoria's Secret. I picked through several pairs of sensible, boring underwear—the kind that didn't leave lines. Then I remembered Chloe's comment from earlier. Maybe it was time I started wearing sexy underwear—*without* a reason. With an exasperated sigh, I dropped the plain panties and rooted through my choices until I came across a black, lacy thong.

I don't remember picking this. I held it between two fingers. *Chloe.* I wasn't sure if I should thank her or strangle her. Instead, I tore off the tags and stepped into the flimsy black lace. Then I snatched up the matching bra and, with more than a little difficulty, strapped myself into the too-small lingerie. The tight fit accentuated what little chest I had. In fact, I resolved to wear the bra more often. In the dim light, I looked almost curvy.

After getting dressed and making my way into the foyer, I searched the hall closet for shoes and a jacket.

I debated between a pair of low-cut black suede boots with pointy toes—very witch-like—and a pair of knee-high black leather boots with a high wedge heel. Even though the pointy-toe boots had a low heel, they were spiked. The wedge heel would be better for running. I had no intention of running, but I decided not to tempt fate twice in one week.

Grabbing the wedged boots, I struggled to pull them on. The Ralph Laurens fit better, but these looked great too. Wearing black from head to toe, I almost blended into the darkness. I stopped short, glancing at my hair in the mirror. I checked again and squinted up at the light fixture. I couldn't imagine why the bulb would cast a red glow, but it must have been. My hair couldn't be changing colors. *Could it?*

Shaking my head, I ran my hands through the layers. *When did it get so long?* Strands of red shot through it as if I'd gotten highlights. Fiery red highlights. Definitely more than what I could explain away with strange lighting. The ringing phone forced me to reschedule my panic attack.

"Ivie!" Chloe said. "I've been so worried about you that I had a hard time shopping."

"That's sweet of you. I'm sorry I ruined your shopping trip," I said, still studying my hair.

"Oh, I shopped. But my heart wasn't in it. The bag at Coach was nothing like the one in my dream. I left empty-handed." Her voice had an obvious pout. "I was positively inconsolable by the time I reached the Marc Jacobs sale. I only bought three pairs of shoes. But I have a surprise for you!"

"Really?" Her sudden glee perked me up, and I pulled my eyes from the mirror. "What kind of surprise?"

"I found a fabulous bag... for *you*." She sounded delighted.

I needed to take back every unkind thing I'd ever thought about Chloe. Maybe even forgive her for introducing me to Matt. "You didn't have to buy me anything."

"Don't be ridiculous. I didn't *buy* it; I *found* it. And it's cheap—less than two hundred. The store is holding it for you until tomorrow. It matches your Ralph Lauren boots almost exactly. I swear they were made to go together."

So much for taking things back. "How sweet of you." If it had been anyone else, I might have gotten angry.

"You're welcome. It's the cutest bag."

I bit my lip. "About the boots—"

"It even has the same gold buckles."

"Chloe. The boots are ruined." I covered my face with my hands as if that would protect me.

"No! Not the Ralph Lauren boots," she cried. "They'd hardly had a chance to live!"

"Hoof marks."

"Oh." She giggled. "That's... *terrible*. What a way to go!"

"I know." I blew out a breath. "I'm heartbroken. But what's done is done."

"You don't seem nearly upset enough over this, Ivie. You loved those boots. And they were so expensive, too! It's been two years and you *still* haven't forgiven me for making you buy them."

"I just don't think a pair of boots is worth crying over." Not when I had so much *else* to cry about.

"Are you okay?" I heard the throaty engine of her car as it accelerated. "This isn't just about the boots or the goat. I know you're still hiding something from me."

I went up the stairs to the hall bathroom to finish getting ready, glancing at a framed photo of me and Invisible Matt along the way. "It's just... I'm fine, really. But I have someplace I have to be. Can I call you tomorrow? We'll talk then."

I thought the call had dropped and said her name twice before she answered in a clipped tone. "Sure. Tomorrow."

I felt an uncomfortable fluttering in my stomach. "You're not mad at me, are you?"

"Why would I be mad?" She sounded too cheerful, even for Chloe.

"Right... Okay. Thanks, Chloe." I really wanted to tell her everything and drag her with me to the magic show, but I couldn't bear to bring anyone else into the horror my life had become. "Bye." She'd already hung up.

Not a minute later, my phone rang again. "I'm so sorry, Chloe. You're right, I have been keeping things from you, but I promise I'll tell you soon," I blurted.

"Ivie McKie?" The deep voice sounded foreboding.

A chill cut through me. My senses lit up like a pinball machine. Something was very wrong. I bit my lip. "This is Ivie."

"Are you the same Ivie McKie who was engaged to Dr. Matthew Green?"

I didn't like the sound of that. "Um, yes?"

"Ms. McKie, this is Sergeant Clark of the Roswell Police Department. We're trying to locate Dr. Green. We understand he's been missing since sometime last evening."

I laughed. Not because *anything* about the situation was funny—it definitely wasn't—but because the most horrific twenty-four hours of my life had *officially* gotten worse. "I'm sorry. I don't mean to laugh." I stopped and held my breath. What was I supposed to say?

My fiancé's girlfriend threatened to call the police because I'm still wearing the engagement ring he promised to give her, and after breaking up with me, he never showed up to meet her. Now my house smells like skunk, she noticed where the rat drew blood, and I have a giant snake slithering around my dining room. Oh, and by the way, the snake is actually my former fiancé. Ditto for the rat and the skunk.

Maybe not.

With an exaggerated whoosh, I let out the breath I was holding. "Matt hasn't called in sick in forever, so I'm sure everyone thinks he must have fallen off the face of the earth." Not bad for making it up on the spot.

"Hmmm." The scratch of pencil on paper was the only sound for several seconds. "So Dr. Green is *not* missing then?"

"Missing? No, he's definitely not *missing*." I chewed on my lip as I thought about the snake in my dining room. "Was it his receptionist? She's always overreacting. Matt wasn't feeling well, so he didn't go to work. He came home late and spent most of the night in the bathroom." Sort of true.

"Would it be possible for me to speak with Dr. Green?"

Sure, if you're a Parselmouth like Harry Potter. "I'm sure that would be fine." I struggled to keep my voice even. "Have you tried calling his cell phone?"

"Yes, ma'am. I've tried his cell phone numerous times. It goes straight to voice mail."

"That's strange. I could have sworn I heard him on his phone not long ago." I was getting better at lying. At least, I hoped so. "Let me see if he's still here." I placed the phone on the counter and stepped into the hall for effect. "Matt? Matt, honey, someone's on my phone for you." I waited a full minute before walking back into the bathroom to retrieve my phone. "I'm sorry. He must have gone out to the pharmacy. If you'll leave your number, I can have him call you when he gets back."

"Yes, please do," he said and rattled off his number.

I didn't write it down. I only hoped I could stall long enough to reverse what I'd done. After disconnecting the call, I threw my phone into my purse. Candy had made good on her promise to call the police. A thought hit me. *Matt's red BMW!* I held my nose and bolted into the bedroom to fish through his pockets for the keys. I had to get rid of his car—at least until I could change him back.

How did this happen to me? I didn't mean to turn him into a skunk, and I really did try to change him back. The fact that he ended up as a rat and then a snake was purely accidental. It wasn't as if my new... *thing* came with an instruction manual.

After shutting Karma in the guest room—just in case—I went downstairs to check on the enormous snake one more time before heading out. Still coiled up under the clothes basket, Matt flicked his tongue at me. I piled a few more heavy books on the top of the basket. I didn't want to come home to find him slithering around the house.

With a flip of my wrist, I checked my watch as I walked out the door: already after nine. I needed to hurry if I was going to make the show before meeting Jackson Blake— the one person who might be able to help me work my faulty magic.

Seven

FTER EXAMINING THE ADDRESS SCRAWLED on the back of my hand and the display on the GPS, I shifted my attention to the building. The nondescript structure could have housed any number of businesses at one time or another, although—judging by the outside—it didn't appear to have been in use in a long time. While searching for any sort of sign out front, I noticed random bits of graffiti—museum-quality spray paint art depicting phallic-looking snakes, among other things—but no illumination and no apparent entrance. The edges disappeared into the long-fingered shadows.

So of course, I pulled into the parking lot to get a closer look. Why not? What could be scarier than the day I'd had? The building may have looked abandoned, but the parking lot teemed with what appeared to be escapees from DragonCon, queuing to enter through a side door.

Jackpot.

Once I'd parked the BMW under the only working streetlight, I eased out of the car and pressed the remote to set the alarm.

Before that day, Vlad's Castle was the absolute last place I would've *ever* gone on purpose. Especially alone. I had an urge, bordering on a need, to confide in Chloe—and beg her to ignore the speed limit all the way there. *But too late for that.*

I approached the leather-clad bouncer—black pants, black vest, black hair, no shirt—aware I was ridiculously overdressed. His muscles bulged under his Edgar Allen Poe-inspired tattoos. A raven spread its impressive wings across his chest. A thick coat of pale makeup hid his natural skin tone, and the bottomless pits of his dark eyes, fenced off by heavy kohl liner, roved over my new curves. I had once thought my pale skin and dark hair made me look Goth. I was sadly mistaken. That guy... *that place...* was Goth.

"Jackson Blake left a ticket for me?" I fidgeted, scavenging my purse for money. "Ivie McKie?" I pulled out a few bills and held them tightly.

"Thirty dollars," he droned. He took my two twenties and moved to the person behind me.

I stayed put, tapping my toes on the pavement, and he turned to stare at me, his face a stone mask.

"We don't give out change." His black-painted lips pressed into a hard line.

I planted my hands on my hips. "You're joking."

"We don't give out change," he repeated in a monotone. "Flaunting your hot little body won't make a difference."

"Of course." I forced my lips together to keep from saying something that could get me in trouble and zipped my purse shut, tucking it tightly under my arm. Coach did *not* belong in that place. Not even when it was just a clever knockoff.

"And just a bit of advice? If you're gonna go with the Wiccan look, you need to commit to it. Don't half-ass it." As if he'd suffered a spontaneous flash of chivalry, he held back the dark tarp that doubled as the door. Then it fell behind me, bathing me in darkness.

I shoved through the faux-undead crowd until I made it all the way inside. The show had already started, and the sole source of light came from a single spotlight focused on the man on stage. My feet froze, and I stared at the magician as if I'd been fitted for a pair of concrete boots.

Barely visible under his elaborate costume, he still caused my insides to clench. Only his lips were exposed beneath his white, featureless mask, and I fixated on their slightly parted fullness as he drew in a quick breath. *Those lips would feel so good against mine.*

Whoa, wait, what? I shook my head to clear the illicit thoughts, squinted into the darkness, and stumbled around in search of a seat. The same song that had played as Jackson Blake's ringback filled the room, setting an ominous tone. Finding a spot with a decent view of the stage proved difficult, and I chanted *excuse me* like a mantra. I settled into a seat near the front, closer than I would have liked, but it afforded me the best view of the man I came to see.

He wore all black except for his crisp white button-down shirt and the red satin lining of his cape. I watched as he shifted his lanky frame from side to side. He reached toward the audience while turning a deck of cards over and over in his hands. His long fingers shuffled the cards before singling out the ace of spades. With a loud clap, his hands came together then he held them open, revealing... *nothing.* The card had disappeared. He bent forward and pulled it from behind the ear of a woman in the front row. With a stupid smile, I clapped like a demented seal along with the rest of the crowd.

As he pulled a large box from just offstage, his mouth tipped up slightly before pressing into a tight line again. My stomach spun like a front-load dryer.

Placing the box at his feet, he addressed the audience. "Ladies and gentlemen, if you would be so kind, please remain very still. What I am about to do is highly dangerous." He thrust his hand into the velvety box and pulled out a white dove. Struggling against the flapping wings, he presented the bird to the audience, sweeping it from one side of the stage to the other. "For this next part, I need complete silence." He laid a dark scarf over the bird then waved his hand above it and recited words I couldn't comprehend. With a grand flourish, he propelled the bird over his head, releasing it into the air. A bright flash of white light momentarily blinded me as the little dove appeared to explode into an enormous black snake.

Recoiling, I screamed, drawing unwanted attention from the audience. That was no parlor trick. That was serious magic—something I knew a little bit about. Very little, but still. My heart skipped a few beats then skittered at a new pace as I gaped at the python twining around his shoulders. I'd just witnessed almost the same thing that had happened in my kitchen, right down to the flash of light and the snake. I wanted to jump up on the stage and hug him. He wasn't kidding when he advertised his magic as being "not for the faint of heart." Mine was beating out of my chest.

The toe of my boot tapped out his theme song as I waited for Jackson Blake to exit the stage through a curtain in the back. Once he disappeared, the lights brightened, and I got my first chance to examine my surroundings. The club resembled a drafty medieval dungeon, complete with torture devices. What had I wandered into? Princess Leia in her gold bikini lay draped over an antique-looking banquet table with another large snake coiled around her. I'd almost convinced myself the reptile was fake when it lifted its head and rippled its tongue in my direction. Her snake didn't scare me. I had my *own* snake to worry about.

I navigated through the crowd of tattooed and pierced bodies, forced to brush against their sweaty flesh as I passed. In my last life—the time before I found out I was a witch—I would have been too paralyzed by fear to move through the room. My newfound knowledge bolstered my confidence just enough to propel me forward. Even though I had no idea how to use my powers, I definitely had them.

The overwhelming stench of patchouli and pyrotechnics made my nose tingle, but all things considered, I still preferred it to the skunk. Thanks to the nods and prodding of several people, I found my way behind the stage and knocked on the door marked with a red pentagram.

The man who greeted me looked as if he was made of Silly Putty and had rolled in the Sunday comics. Colorful ink covered his shoulders and chest. Black flames swirled over his bald head like hair from hell. A combination of images and words were scrawled across his cheekbones and chin. Inked black chain link and barbed wire arched above his eyes. He had multiple piercings through his eyebrows, lips, and even both cheeks. Steel dimples. He towered over me—at least seven feet tall—and hovered closer than would be considered polite in my usual circles.

He glared and spoke in a deep, resonating tone, not unlike Lurch from *The Addams Family*. "Can I help you?"

I opened my mouth but barely a squeak emerged. "Jackson Blake?"

"Who's asking?"

"Me?" I cleared my throat and managed to create more sound. "I mean, Ivie McKie?"

"Well, Ivie McKie, are you here for the after-show entertainment?" He flashed a toothy grin as he studied my new attributes.

I felt my cheeks flame. "Um... no. I called earlier with a bit of a *situation* I needed help with."

"How can I help you?"

"*You* aren't Jackson Blake." I crossed my arms. No way would I mistake *his* voice for the panty-melting voice I'd heard on the phone.

"A good magician can be whoever he wants." He smacked his lips.

"I've got it covered, Alex." I recognized that honeyed voice.

"Whatever you say, boss." The tattooed man lifted his bare shoulders in a slight shrug and slipped back inside the door, leaving it ajar.

"You can come in," Jackson Blake said.

I pushed the door open with a weak shove and stepped into an old-fashioned dressing room. Along the back wall, rows of dim, round light bulbs framed a wide mirror that reflected my image back at me. My newly red-streaked hair lay tucked behind my ears, and I wore minimal makeup— just mascara and a bit of berry lip gloss. I looked out of place even dressed all in black. Like a kindergarten teacher in a Goth club.

"Hello?" I said to the empty room. Even the tattooed giant had disappeared. A chill ran up my back, and I wondered if it was due to the damp air or a frisson of fear. I twisted the gold circle on my left hand then stopped as I realized I still wore my engagement ring. "Shit." I tugged on the ring, but it wouldn't pass my knuckle. Plunging my finger into my mouth, I bit down and pulled until the ring slid into my mouth.

"I hope you're planning to share with the *whole* class." He stepped from the shadows, a lopsided grin lighting up his face.

I turned so my back was to him as I spat the ring into my hand. I slipped it carefully into my pocket before facing him. Younger than I expected and unmistakably handsome—like a male model ripped from a Halloween costume ad—the man in front of me was obviously Jackson Blake. He had artfully tousled chestnut hair and light stubble framing his jaw. Not a single tattoo marked his perfect face, and his clear blue eyes sparkled. He still wore the black trousers and white shirt under the black velvet cape, and topped it off with a stovepipe hat and a cane.

"You must be Ivie." He extended his hand, and I hesitated before taking it.

"Jackson Blake?"

"Jack." His touch sent a ribbon of heat up my arm. "You'll have to excuse the theatrics. It's all part of the act." His lips quirked up at the corners. "Don't let Alex scare you. He's a pussycat."

I resisted the urge to say, *I might be able to arrange that.* "Thank you for agreeing to meet with me."

He shrugged. "Oh, sure. I'm always willing to help another member of the magical community." He motioned to a red velvet settee and waited until I sat before joining me. "You said it was a matter of urgency. What could be so important on a Friday night?"

With a deep breath, I launched into an abbreviated version of the past twenty-four hours. To his credit, he didn't flinch once. Nor did he laugh or roll his eyes. He did crack the easiest smile as I recounted chasing the cat with my fiancé in his mouth. But when I finished with the large reticulated snake, his face took on a serious expression.

"I see," he said once I'd skidded to a halt. "Have you spoken to anyone else about this?"

I let out a nervous laugh. "No. Most people would call me crazy."

He nodded.

"How long have you been doing magic?"

He threw his arm over the back of the settee and I shivered at his proximity. "Since I was six or seven. My family is quite magically inclined."

"Oh!" I didn't know what to think about that comment. What did *magically inclined* mean? Did they sit around a cauldron whispering incantations at night? Pull coins out of one another's ears for lunch money?

"Did you see the show?"

"Yes, I got here right before it ended." Tilting my head, I took in his appearance. "Do you have a second show this evening?"

He laughed. "I didn't want to disappoint you by wearing my regular clothes." He grabbed the brim of the hat in both hands and spun it end over end with a dramatic flourish before tossing it into a trunk in the corner.

"So do you think you can help me?" I perched on the edge of the seat.

"I think I might be able to help you, yes."

The tension drained from my shoulders, and I sank back into the smooth red velvet.

He counted something on his fingers then smiled. "I think I can work you into my schedule sometime next week."

"Next week?" I blurted. "I can't wait until next week! It has to be now. *Tonight.*"

"Tonight, huh?" He flashed a quick smile then stood and clapped. "I'm starving. Let's go get a midnight snack and a cup of coffee, and we'll talk about your predicament."

As a rule, I stayed away from the Great American House of Waffles—known in my circle as the Awful Waffle. It wasn't that I had anything against waffles. In fact, I loved waffles. I just tended to shy away from creepy people, and the Awful Waffle's major claim to fame was its assortment of creepy people after midnight—like the guy cooking my food. His previous jobs might have included biting the heads off chickens in a traveling carnival, barker for the circus big top, and rock-breaking in a chain gang.

The magician didn't look at all creepy. In fact, he was completely delicious—way better than the waffles, if I was any judge. He'd shed his costume before we set out to get food. His street clothes, as he'd called them, drew more attention than his elaborate getup. Matt always wore khakis or a suit, never denim. Jackson Blake should never wear anything but.

The way he wore a pair of jeans should've been illegal. They weren't nice, really—the knees were ripped out, they were worn across the seat, and they probably needed to be washed—but I couldn't tear my eyes away from the way they clung to his body. He'd paired them with a wrinkled, off-white, long-sleeved Henley, all the buttons undone. He hadn't shaved in at least a day, maybe two, and his messy brown hair hadn't seen a comb in just as long.

Matt was always clean-shaven, his hair always combed, and his clothes freshly laundered. But he wasn't sexy. Not even a little. What had I been thinking? Jackson Blake rocked the sexy so hard it bordered on dangerous—for me anyway—and it thrilled me as much as it terrified me. No way in hell was I his type.

"Did you hear me, Ivie?" He waved a hand in front of my face.

"Hmmm?"

"I asked if you'd studied magic anywhere."

"Study? Like at Hogwarts? No." I swallowed a giggle. "I'd never attempted magic before. Never even *thought* about it. I didn't actually attempt it this time, either. I just lost my temper and... *bam*!" I slammed my hand on the table and bit back a grin when he flinched. "He was an animal. Totally unplanned."

"So you don't practice witchcraft or belong to any Wicca groups or covens?"

"Me? No. I'm a teacher. I belong to the PTA. I don't have a crystal ball, a broomstick, or even a broom—I have a Swiffer. I've never mixed a potion, other than the rare margarita, and I don't mix a very good one of those either."

"Were you drinking last night?" He grinned.

Did I look like a lush? Did my breath smell of alcohol? I think not. "I had a few glasses of wine. I wasn't drunk if that's what you mean."

"Sorry. I had to ask." He looked at me from under thick lashes.

I leaned in and started to place my hands on his. I let them fall on the table instead. "I need help. That trick you did with the snake, could you teach me to do that?"

"Sure. I can help you." His face lit up as if he held back a smile. "Have you ever heard of a convergence of magic?"

Eight

C*ONVERGENCE OF MAGIC, MY ASS!*
Tamping down my anger as well as could be expected, I climbed into the driver's seat of Matt's red BMW and slammed the door. I had stuck around long enough to hear his explanation, but if Jackson Blake thought I would trek into the woods with a complete stranger to attempt some sort of spell in the middle of the night, he had another think coming. *How gullible did I look?* I'd seen enough slasher movies to know better than that.

But oh, my God, what a way to go.

I narrowed my eyes at him, still sitting in the booth, a forkful of waffle poised at his kissable lips and flashing that damn sexy grin at me through the plate glass window. He waved one last time, and I shifted, averting my eyes from his smoldering stare. No more crazy ideas. I needed to regroup and try something else. There had to be another way. I'd gotten myself into that mess; surely I could get myself out. So what if brushing against Jackson Blake's leg under the table was the closest I'd been to the tingle I felt when doing magic? That didn't mean *anything.* If I was being honest, I would admit I was more afraid of myself than the stupid hot magician. Hell, it had taken everything in me to keep from straddling him right there in the booth.

Time to go home and try the spell again. After all, I'd managed to change Matt three times without help. Focus. That's all I needed. Right. *Focus.*

I spent the better part of the drive home *focusing* on how Jackson Blake smelled, like clean sweat and spicy deodorant, all musky and manly and... I squirmed against the seatbelt. I needed to focus on something else—like being on the rebound. I should be getting over a horrible breakup and downing gallons of Ben and Jerry's while listening to Air Supply, not trying to get a hold of Jackson Blake's magic wand.

Besides, could I even call it a breakup? I didn't give him back the ring, even if he had asked for it. But I doubted his first words when he resumed his douchey humanness would be, "Let's try again!" So I guess *technically*, I was single. There's nothing wrong with a single girl lusting after an attractive guy, and holy Houdini was he beautiful. But that's entirely beside the point. No matter how gorgeous Jackson Blake was, I would not—under any circumstances—go into the woods with him.

I took the highway off-ramp a little too fast, and my tires screeched. Damn Jackson Blake and his stupid panty-melting grin for distracting me from miles away. I'd known him all of two hours and I already liked him better than my snake of an ex-fiancé.

The streets on my side of town were deserted, and I contemplated running the red light. *Who would know?* Instead, I fiddled with the radio. My fingers froze on the classic rock station as the crescendo of "Magic Man" blared through the speakers. If I had been standing, my knees would have buckled. Incredibly bad timing? Or a sign from above? Either way, I was screwed.

I gunned the engine a split second before the light changed to green and turned left onto the main drive. I wasn't going home. Despite my better judgment, I headed straight back to the stupid Awful Waffle and the ridiculously hot magician eating eggs and waffles in the booth where I'd left him. I only hoped he would still be there.

An icy gust of wind swirled my hair around my face, and I pushed it back with an unsteady hand as I struggled to follow Jackson Blake through the underbrush. It had been a short drive from the diner—maybe twenty minutes in the opposite direction from home—but we'd been trekking into the thick of the woods for several minutes since parking our cars. Keeping up with him was brutal.

He seemed unaware of the dropping temperature. Even dressed in jeans and a turtleneck, I felt the wintry air soak into me and shook like Bruce Banner in the throes of a temper tantrum. "Why is it so damn *cold*?" I muttered. He didn't answer. I didn't really expect him to.

I tripped over a tree root and narrowly avoided genuflecting at his feet. Jackson Blake threw me a disapproving scowl and rolled his eyes when I pointed to my wedge heel boots. What did he know about trudging through the woods in heels? Nothing, that's what.

All he'd told me was he knew the perfect place for some kind of magical ceremony. A convergence, he called it. I would have to take the professional magician's word for it. What I knew about magic would fit on the inside of a bubble gum wrapper.

An owl hooted in the distance, and I flinched. At least, I *hoped* it was an owl. The damn farm was looking positively civilized now. Not a good sign.

There aren't any wild goats in the woods, are there? "Remind me again why we're wandering through the woods on the coldest night of the year," I demanded through chattering teeth.

"You're exaggerating. There have been worse nights than this," he argued with an audible grin.

I grumbled out my dissent. "When?"

He laughed and kept moving forward, his path illuminated only by his cell phone. He didn't seem to have trouble navigating the obscure path.

Why do I suddenly feel like the Blair Witch? "Do you even know where we're go-*oh*-ing?" I stumbled over a loose rock.

"Just try to keep up."

Really, I *was* trying. The wedge heel boots were officially a regrettable choice. They wouldn't have been good to run in either, as it turned out. "So Jackson Blake..." I half-jogged to catch up to him, moving with the unsteady gait of a drunken baby learning to walk.

"Jack," he said over his shoulder.

"Right. Sorry. J-Jack. You said your family was magically inclined, so I'm guessing you've done this convergence thing before?" I tried to gauge his expression in the dim light.

"Not exactly," he said with a quick sideways glance. "I've read about it though. Piece of cake. You'll see."

He lengthened his footsteps until he was a stride and a half ahead of me again and we walked in silence for another several minutes.

We'd hiked for ten minutes past the point where I felt comfortable when we finally stepped into a small clearing. A blackened spot in the center marked where a fire had burned in the recent past. The charred-wood smell, acrid and unmistakable, hung in the frigid night air.

"Where are we?" I searched for a possible, yet nonexistent, escape plan. Without shelter from the trees, the gusts of frozen air whipped freely around us. The biting wind made me wonder if it might snow. It rarely did in Atlanta, even in the dead of winter. October shouldn't be so cold. "Do you come here often?" I swallowed a nervous giggle at my unintentional pick-up line.

He smiled and muttered under his breath as he dug through his pockets.

Surely, I must have heard him wrong. I shivered as much from his ridiculous suggestion as the chill. I was crazy to be out without a jacket and he wanted me to...

"Take off all my clothes?" My voice came out in a strangled squeak.

He nodded, pulling a lighter from his pocket with a satisfied grin.

"You're joking, right?" I stared at him, gnawing on my lips. *They're probably a lovely shade of cornflower blue by now.*

He stared back. I shuffled back and forth in a feeble attempt to generate heat and waited for him to crack a smile or laugh. He did neither.

"It's crucial," he said.

A glance at his serious expression set my heart on a collision course with my throat. I couldn't speak for a full minute. "Why? Why... *naked*?" I whispered the word as if it had power.

"Ivie, you told me you did research. Surely you learned that witches do their best spells when free of constraints."

"Like clothes?" I asked, sarcasm dripping from my voice.

"Exactly. Like clothes."

I *had* read that. But I'd chalked it up to silly superstitions, not fact. Tightening my arms over my chest, I tried to tuck myself into a fetal position while still standing. "Look, I don't know you." My teeth chattered as I spoke. "A few days ago, if anyone had told me I would be wandering deep into the woods with a total stranger—a club magician no less—I would have laughed at them. Hell, I probably would have had them fitted for a straitjacket. So if you think, for even one fraction of a second, I'm stupid enough, or crazy enough, to strip out here in the woods with *you*, well then you're—"

He stopped fidgeting with his lighter and folded his arms, a self-satisfied grin on his handsome face. "The only guy who knows how to help you with the spell you're trying to do?"

He had me there. "But it's c-c-cold outside," I complained. "I can't feel my toes."

He glanced to where the moon would be if it wasn't hiding behind the clouds. "We need to draw our powers together where they can supercharge. Our clothes will block the connection." He gazed at me, and his blue eyes looked almost black in the dark. "You don't want to impede the power exchange, do you?"

I exhaled. "No." I covered my face with both hands and peeked at him through my fingers. "But we're going to freeze to death. You know that, right? Can we at least leave our underwear on?"

"I think that would be okay," he conceded. "But if there isn't a power surge, we may need to take them off."

I groaned. We really needed to have a power surge. I had less than three days to change Matt back or I'd be calling in sick again on Monday—*from jail.*

He stalked away and gathered up loose limbs and twigs, throwing them into the burned-out center of the circle. "Help me. We need to build a fire."

I helped him collect enough leaves and branches to start a pathetic fire that didn't give off much heat. The illusion was almost enough to propel me to take the next step though. I pulled my hands into the sleeves of my turtleneck and stopped to glare at him. "Turn around. This is hard enough without you watching me."

"Sure." He turned his back to me.

Before lifting my shirt over my head, I edged closer to the pitiful flames and waited until I felt a flicker of warmth. Then I folded the turtleneck and placed it on a large flat stone by my feet. Jackson Blake pulled his white Henley over his head and dropped it, letting it puddle at his feet.

He had a nice back. His muscles bunched when he moved, like a swimmer's. Then he unbuttoned his jeans, and my mouth dropped open.

He chuckled. "Now who's watching who?" he said with his back still to me.

My teeth clamped down on my bottom lip, and heat moved from my chest to my hair. "Sorry, sorry, sorry." I spun away from him. "I don't usually do things like this."

He chuckled again. "Things like what?"

"Take off my clothes in an open field," I replied with a nervous giggle. "With a total stranger." I pulled off my boots one at a time and slid them under my folded shirt.

"Well, if it makes you feel any better, I don't do this either."

"No. It doesn't make me feel better," I mumbled as I finished undressing.

Of all the nights to wear a slinky thong, I chose the one night I end up naked in the woods. Once my jeans were folded and added to my pile of clothes, I said, "Okay, now what?"

"Now we have to get closer. Our bodies need to come in direct contact," he said.

I shuddered at the thought.

"It'll channel the magic, and it'll help keep us warm." I wasn't sure, but I could have sworn he sounded nervous. I spun around to see his expression. "I'm freezing my ass off." He blew a white cloud into his hands with an obvious shiver.

Right. Cold. Not nervous. "So do I come to you, or do you come to me?" I asked with a tremor that was most definitely *not* from the weather.

"That all depends. I can come to you... if you trust me to turn around."

"I'll come to you. Don't turn around," I blurted. He stood about six feet away, facing the dark woods, and I tiptoed across the moist grass until I stood behind him, close enough to feel his body heat. "Okay. Now what?"

"Put your arms around me. We need to be as close as possible."

I wrapped my arms around his waist and tucked myself against him, pressing my cheek against his warm back. It felt good—strange but good. I couldn't remember the last time I'd been that close to Matt. "Now what?"

"Now we concentrate on drawing our magic together. You focus on mine, and I'll focus on yours. It should cause the convergence to occur. We should be able to feel it."

"*Ooooh*-kay."

"Close your eyes," he whispered.

I squeezed my lids shut and concentrated on drawing the magic. "They're closed." I should have felt the magic surge. I knew that much. Even in bitter cold, I should have felt the warmth. "I don't feel anything. It should be growing. Do you feel anything?"

"I definitely feel something growing," he choked out in a husky voice.

"It's not working." I pouted. "Can we get closer to the fire?"

"We can try that."

We moved together until we were less than a foot from the crackling flames.

"Still not working," I huffed, watching my breath swirl.

"Maybe we need to..."

I held my breath, waiting for him to say we needed to remove the thin layer of undergarments still between us.

"Maybe..." He cleared his throat. "Maybe we need to be face to face. So we can see into each other's eyes."

I bit down on my lip. That sounded so personal. As if what we were doing wasn't personal enough. But desperate times... I tipped my face up to the night sky where the thick clouds hid the moon. "Okay." I lowered my arms and closed my eyes as he turned around to face me.

"You can open your eyes," he whispered, his warm breath in my hair.

"I'd rather not."

"Please, open your eyes."

"Jackson Blake—"

His fingers cupped my chin, pulling my face upward. "Ivie, we're standing naked in the woods. Do you think it would be okay to call me Jack?"

I opened my eyes, peering into his. "Jack." As I whispered his name, the heat surged in.

"Give me your hands," he murmured, taking mine and turning his palms up, twisting our fingers until only the tips were touching.

A glimmer of electricity prickled over my skin. "It's working. I'm starting to tingle. Can you feel it?"

His breath wheezed out in a jagged rhythm. "Mmmm. I do."

"It's magic." I giggled, giddy with excitement.

"Definitely magic," he agreed.

Then the blue heat penetrated my core like shock waves. An electric ripple tore through me, and just like the other times, a rush of something completely different followed close behind. With no outlet for the surge of magic, an intense static charge sparked off the tips of my fingers and toes before rushing swiftly to my blazing hot center.

A soft whimper escaped me as Jack pressed his mouth to mine. He tasted of maple syrup, butter, and passion. With gentle pressure, he nibbled on my lips as his warm hands skimmed up my arms and over my shoulders to cup my face. His touch thrilled me to my toes. Not just his touch... his sweet flavor, his clean boy scent, the warmth radiating out from his delicious body. A simple kiss would never be enough to satisfy the three-alarm fire raging inside me.

I wanted to devour him, and no one had even come close to eliciting feelings so carnal in me before that moment.

My fingers inched up the solid planes of his chest until I reached the light stubble on his jaw, forcing him away from me. "I can't..."

"What? Why?" He panted, resting his forehead against mine.

"No. I don't mean I can't do this... I mean, I can't get *enough*. I want more." I crushed my mouth against his again, my fingers tangling in his hair. "I want you. Here. *Now*." My body burned for a total stranger, and I no longer had the willpower to stop.

He groaned, his hands sliding down my back until they cupped my behind, pulling me tighter against him. "You have no idea how much I want to, and I can't believe I'm actually going to say this, but..." He chuckled. "I *can't*."

My lips stopped moving against his, and he lifted his head just enough to look into my eyes.

"Don't look at me like that." He held my face, a pained expression on his. "It's really cold, Ivie. I... I literally *can't*."

My breath came out in little white puffs as I stood there blinking at him. Understanding dawned on me and I sneaked a peek at the flat front of his gray boxer briefs. "The car." I pushed away from his warmth to search for my things. "Put out the fire and grab your stuff. We need to get back to the car."

Hopping from one foot to the other, I yanked on my boots then scooped up the rest of my clothes. I reached for his outstretched hand, letting him drag me through the woods. As we stumbled over the underbrush, giddy anticipation consumed me. I barely noticed the bitter cold or the sting of jagged vines clawing at my skin.

"Christ, Ivie, you're freezing." Jack hugged me, kissing down my neck as he tugged me toward the BMW.

"No! Not mine. Yours." I shoved him toward the silver SUV and latched my lips to his while he fumbled for the keys. The last thing I needed was bodily fluids discovered in Matt's car, and there would *definitely* be bodily fluids exchanged.

Who the hell are you, Ivie McKie? I'd wandered into the woods to perform a spell and ended up unearthing a side of me I had no idea existed. *If only Chloe could see me, she'd be so impressed.* And Matt—boring, my ass! Not that either of them would believe me if I told them. Magic was one thing; sexual exploration was quite another.

"Wait," Jack said into my mouth as he uncurled my fingers from the rear door handle. "I have stuff in the backseat."

I nodded as he steered me to the front of his vehicle without detaching his lips from mine.

I nuzzled into his shoulder as he opened the door and lifted me into the front passenger seat. He climbed in behind me, scooting under me until he had me straddling his lap, then pulled my face to his for a searing kiss that literally took my breath away. As he kissed me senseless, I let my hands explore his warm skin. They skimmed over his shoulders, across his chest, and reached between the seat and the door to pull the lever, hurling our bodies backward as we moved into the fully reclined position.

"Better?" I giggled.

"Much." His lips curved against mine before taking his tongue on a journey over my chin, down my throat, finally reaching my chest. His teeth grazed my lace-covered nipples, making me moan as the muscles between my legs clenched. "You like that?" He unhooked my bra before sliding the straps down my arms and tossing the flimsy fabric away.

"So good." I wriggled above him, snaking a hand between us to cup his growing erection. "You're not so cold anymore?"

"No. Not anymore." He grinned as his fingers slipped into the waistband of my thong, making me tremble as he teased the top of my sex.

"Just rip it," I whispered, still caressing him through his boxer briefs.

He pulled his face back, searching my eyes. "What?"

"My thong. Just fucking rip it. I can't wait." I ground my hips into his, pressing my hand harder against him.

"Fuck." He shuddered, tore the tiny scrap of fabric from my body, and slid a long finger deep inside me. "You feel so fucking good."

My head fell back as a second finger slid into me. "Oh, God... Inside," I ordered, fumbling to set him free as I coiled my fingers around his hot, velvety length. "I need you inside me *right now*."

"I can do that." Jack nodded, gripping my hips as I slid my wetness over him.

All I had to do was raise up and impale myself on him, and he would be buried inside me. But before I could take matters into my own hands, he shifted away slightly. "God, will you just fuck me already?"

He twitched beneath me, screwing his eyes shut as he repeatedly slammed his head against the headrest. "Damn it." He groaned. "What about protection? Shouldn't we use some sort of protection?"

"Oh, shit, protection. Do you..."

"Yeah." He leaned forward to open the glove box and pulled out a strip of condoms.

"You keep condoms in your glove box?"

He tore a foil square open with his teeth and held it out to me. "Are you really going to complain about that right now?"

"No, not complaining." I snatched the latex, smiling when he let out a low hiss as I slowly unrolled it over him. "Okay, Houdini, time to make it disappear."

"Oh, hell, yeah." He thrust his hips, and I gasped as he plunged into me with a deep growl. "So fucking tight."

"Oh, God... Never had anything so... like this." I held my breath as my body adjusted to his thickness. Every upward stroke reached places I didn't know existed. "Mmmhmm... right there. God, I fucking love magic." My fingers bit into his shoulder as he pounded into me.

"Fuck *magic*. I love being inside you." He grunted, sucking my nipple as I bucked my hips into his.

My hand flew against the cold glass, and condensation pooled between my fingers as I balanced myself. "Jesus, fuck... do that again. I think I'm going to..." My entire body shook as I exploded, tightening and convulsing around him.

"Me too, baby. Me too." With one last violent tremor, he slammed into me, squeezing his eyes shut.

My arms wrapped around his neck. I panted as I nibbled the shell of his ear. "How long... before... we can... do that again?"

His face broke out in a wide grin. "How long does it take to get to your house?"

Nine

J ACK MISSED THE EXIT MORE than once, prolonging the ride, but I didn't mind. I relished the chance to catch my breath before reentering my private nightmare. I slid my key into the lock then turned to face Jack in all his rumpled goodness.

"This may seem a little strange to you, but I promise my life isn't normally this bizarre," I said.

He beamed at me. "Are you kidding? After tonight, I can only *hope* the rest of my life is this bizarre."

"Trust me, I have no doubt it will be. You look very"—my eyes swept over his bare chest—"*sexy* in nothing but a pair of ripped jeans."

"Well, you, my little witch"—he bent down to capture my bottom lip between his teeth and brushed a stray piece of hair from my face—"look fucking *hot* wearing nothing but my shirt."

We stared into each other's eyes for what seemed like forever before the cold seeped into my consciousness, making me shiver. "We should go inside."

Jack reached around me to open the door, ushered me inside, then closed and locked it.

I flipped on the lights and noticed the clothes basket—though still over the big black snake—wasn't where I'd left it. Matt had managed to wedge it against the hall table. He raised his head to stare at us through the slats in the plastic.

"Interesting cage you have there." Jack tilted his head and frowned. "Not the most secure thing I've ever seen."

"It's all I had." I shrugged and peered at Matt. Even though I wasn't cold anymore, looking into his beady eyes sent an involuntary chill through my bones. "I'm not exactly keen about having a snake in the house. I'd much rather just turn him back straight away." Jack made an unintelligible sound, and I spun around to find him still scrutinizing the snake—his body tensed. "You aren't afraid, are you?" I was mystified. He'd seemed perfectly comfortable with a snake earlier.

"No. I don't know. I'm—" Jack scratched his head as he studied Matt. "*Confused*, I guess. When you say 'turn him back'..." He searched my eyes.

"Yes, of course, I need to turn him back." The thought of leaving him like that any longer than I had to was *laughable*.

"So the..." Jack waved toward the basket.

"Is he not as big as I described him? I'm sure I exaggerated. Like the old fish story. 'I once caught a snake *this big*.'" I stretched my hands as far apart as I could and forced a laugh, but it came out a little hysterical. "He seemed pretty big as he slithered in my direction this afternoon."

Jack looked away from the makeshift cage, his eyes roaming the rest of the house. "You've gone to a great deal of effort here, haven't you?" He cracked half a smile. "Is this even real?" He tapped the laundry basket with the toe of his leather shoe, and Matt reared up and hissed at him. "Pretty real."

"He wasn't always a snake. I told you, that's my fiancé. Well, ex-fiancé." I dipped down to look at Matt, and he struck out at me, ramming his head into the slats again. "Gah!" I flinched.

"Is it my imagination, or does he really not like you? Like, *at all*." Jack let out a nervous laugh.

"It wasn't an amicable breakup." I remembered the look on Matt's face when he had asked for his ring back and rubbed the spot where the rat had bitten me. "I don't think he's very happy with me. I can't blame him really, not after, you know..." I held my nose for an instant then wriggled it like a rat before slithering my hand through the air. "Anyway, are you ready to try the magic again?"

"Absolutely." Jack's posture relaxed, and he flashed a wide smile. He stepped toward me and gripped my hips to haul me against his growing erection. His warm breath fanned over my neck. "I'm more than ready to make more magic with you."

Without speaking, I locked my fingers with the handsome magician and dragged him into my kitchen.

Trying to draw on the power from where our fingers laced together, I concentrated on the heat from his skin. "This is exciting," I whispered, stepping closer to him until our faces were only inches apart.

"Exciting," he repeated, his lips curving up at the corners.

I could only imagine what he was thinking. How often had he worked magic with someone as inexperienced as me? I rested my forehead on Jack's shoulder as the sensations washed over me. "I'm starting to tingle," I said with the giddy excitement of one of my kindergarteners. "I can feel the heat coming from you."

"I'm *definitely* hot for you." Jack groaned, pressing his lips against the hollow behind my ear.

"Not yet." I wriggled away and struggled to contain my enthusiasm.

Straining against the blackness of my memories, I tried to pull up an image of Matt. His face still eluded me, so I concentrated on what I *knew* of him. His aura perhaps. Vague impressions flickered in and out of focus, and they were nothing nice.

Jack raised our linked hands up over our heads, dragging me closer until our bodies pressed together. I let my head fall back and closed my eyes, too caught up in the new feelings building inside me to notice anything other than Jack nuzzling my neck, rasping his stubble against my shoulder. I definitely felt something deep down. I didn't know if it was magic, but I wasn't interested in stopping.

"Ivie..." he whispered as he feathered light kisses along my jaw.

The familiar tingling moved from my outstretched fingers, through my arms, and down my torso, heating me in places that had nothing to do with magic. My lips searched for his, starting at his jaw and working across to devour his mouth, while I still tried to conjure Matt in my thoughts. It grew more and more difficult as the power that was Jackson Blake drew me in.

I didn't know how long I'd been distracted, but it was long enough for the black snake to tangle around Jack's legs and up his body, poised to wrap tightly around Jack's throat. When I heard the faint flutter of snake tongue flicking near my ear, I opened my eyes. Jack was frozen, his face twisted in terror. He'd noticed just before I did that he was about to be suffocated by my former fiancé.

I swallowed a scream as fear replaced arousal in a single horrifying shudder. One heat replaced another. The new emotion burned me from the inside out. As if a big bubble had burst, the buildup of energy ruptured, sending shock waves out from my body in swells. The lights went out. Or maybe they didn't go out as much as they were swallowed up by the dark. In the time it took me to take a single breath, the light had returned.

Jack sat on the floor as if he'd just casually plopped down for a rest. The snake was gone. A graying Scottish terrier sat in his place.

We stayed quiet for a minute. From his spot on the floor, Jack stared between me and the dog. Then he stood slowly, running his hand through his hair until it stuck up. The sight of him, combined with the residual magic pulsing through me, drove me into a frenzy.

"Jack." I grabbed his face roughly, tugging him to me. "I need you to fuck me."

That seemed to shake him out of whatever spell he was under.

Jack's fingers bit into my shoulders as he shoved me against the refrigerator then used his hips to keep me pinned. He slid his hands down my arms and lifted up the bottom of my shirt... *his* shirt... to sink a finger into me.

"God, you're so wet. Is that for me?" He groaned.

"Just for you." I slipped one hand into his waistband as the other struggled with the button.

He shoved my hands away, unzipped his jeans, and pushed them down to set his erection free. "I'm going to fuck you standing up. Right here against the refrigerator. Do you have a problem with that?" His growl sent Matt running out of the kitchen and made my thighs tighten in anticipation. I shook my head before he hauled me up, wrapping my legs around his waist, and slammed into me. "So. Fucking. Hot." He grunted, his hips grinding against mine at a punishing pace.

"Oh, God," I said, in a shaky breath.

Jack continued his merciless attack, pounding into me over and over again. "Come on, baby, come for me. You know you want to."

I was so close, every nerve ending within me on fire. My body shuddered each time he hit that spot that no one before him even knew existed. Arching my back as if responding to his spoken command, wave after wave of pleasure spiked through my body, making me cry out. I'd never climaxed so many times at once, and I'm certain if he wasn't holding me up, I would have collapsed to the floor in a puddle.

"Hold on to me, baby." He wrapped my limp arms around his neck, shifting me for a better angle. A light sheen of sweat beaded across his forehead as he thrust deeper, then again, stretching me a little more each time as he swelled within me. "You feel so good. Oh, baby, I'm gonna... ahhh." He froze, squeezing his eyes shut, his mouth open in a silent scream.

He jostled me, trying to shake me awake, maybe. Perhaps just to get a better grip so as not to drop me; I didn't know. My body was boneless against him.

"Jesus." Jack blew out a breath and shuddered hard. "I just fucked you without protection."

My eyes opened, taking in his horrified expression. "I... um... it's okay. I'm on the pill."

He relaxed slightly and nodded but still looked shaken. Then the little dog barked, and Jack's face turned an unflattering shade of green.

"Holy shit, you turned that snake into a dog," he choked out. His grip loosened until I slid gently from his grasp to stand on my feet. His hands went back to his already chaotic after-sex hair.

My lips tipped up into a smug little smile. I may not have done the spell I'd intended to do, but I had certainly channeled the magic. "I told you I was a witch. You didn't believe me?"

Jack pulled his jeans back up and fastened them before pacing the kitchen. "Hell no, I didn't believe you. I thought you were just one of those"—he waved his hands around—"magic groupies."

My mouth dropped open. "*Magic groupies*?" I didn't like the image that conjured up.

"Yeah, the girls who hang around after the show." He seemed to struggle to keep his thoughts together. "It's a Goth club. We see a lot of strange characters there."

I didn't understand how he would make such an assumption about me. "But you do magic. You said your whole family was magically inclined. Surely you have to realize other people can do magic, too?"

He looked down, suddenly interested in the tops of his shoes. "Ivie, I have a confession to make..." Jack pulled on his hair so hard I feared it might come out.

His discomfort made my stomach twist and I tugged on the hem of my—*his* shirt to cover myself. "Well?"

"I'm a fake."

A fresh surge of heat flowed through me, as if the energy hadn't fully left my body and churned just below the surface. "A fake?" I narrowed my eyes. "What do you mean a *fake*?"

"I mean, I don't really do magic. My tricks are just *tricks*. There is no magic involved whatsoever. But I am a really good illusionist who learned from a skilled magician." He didn't show the least bit of remorse. Like a spoiled child caught stealing cookies from the cookie jar.

"I don't understand. You *lied* to me?" My face must have been a mask of shock.

I didn't know why I was surprised. People lied to me all the time. Matt hadn't told me the truth about anything. But Jack? I'd known him for only a few hours, and I was completely taken aback. We had a...

"What about the magical connection we shared?" I gasped. "What about our merging with nature and drawing upon the strength within us?" I lowered my voice to a whisper. "What about the *sex*?"

He winced, his eyes filled with guilt. "Ivie, you're very sweet, and I'm sure you know you're beautiful, but I honestly thought you were just playing a game. I've heard about girls who like to pretend they're Wiccans and spend a night roleplaying the whole magic thing in the woods. So I made up the convergence to play along."

My face flamed, and I was unable to raise my voice above a whisper. "We took our clothes off in an open field. We had sex. *Twice!*"

He bit his lip and blushed, his guilty face almost apologetic. "The sex was amazing."

Somewhere deep inside me, deeper than I knew existed, a tap opened. No... a pipe burst. Like a raging river or an underground aqueduct, it flowed through me into every nerve ending in my body. As if I'd harnessed the electric current running through the house, the lights dimmed as I pulled the current from the outlets into me. Faint sparks radiated from my fingertips. I knew I should be afraid, but I was too angry to register fear.

Matt, in his new form, let out a sharp whine and cowered against the wall.

"Ivie," Jack said in a shaky voice, "Ivie, you're... *glowing.*"

That tamped down my anger somewhat, as I was almost instantly enthralled by my power. I caught my reflection in a dark window, and Jack was right. I was glowing. I couldn't take my eyes off myself. That was the first time I'd seen what happened when the magic surged in me. Faint blue sparks shot out of my outstretched fingertips, and I saw my eyebrows knitted together in angry concentration.

"Christ, your hair... This isn't *possible.* None of this is possible. I think you should try to calm down. Didn't you say you turned your fiancé into the snake when you were angry?"

His question pulled me further away from the rage pulsating through me. "Not a snake." I shook my head, still watching my every move in the window. "A skunk."

"What?"

Even as I turned toward him, I couldn't quite tear my eyes away from my reflection. "I didn't turn him into a snake that first time. He was a skunk." I watched his reaction in the glass, certain he was afraid. "I was angry." I forced myself to look directly at his face. "So angry I tingled with heat. I burst with it." As I said the words, for the first time since I'd felt the initial rush of electricity flow through me,

I remembered what had happened that night. I'd been out of control with rage, pointing my sparking fingers at Matt and shouting at him. Shouting that he wasn't a man, that he was a... "Oh, my God! I did this!"

The anger rushed out of me, and with it went the electricity, the power that could possibly reverse the spell I'd cast on my unsuspecting dog of a fiancé. Plopping down to sit cross-legged on the floor, I rested my face in my hands. I was exhausted, and frustrated, and nearly on the verge of tears. Every bit of energy I had had been sucked out of me by that last bit of magic. I needed sleep, and at that moment, I didn't care if I slept right there on the cold tile.

Drawing in a long, steadying breath, I looked up at the wide-eyed magician. "I think you need to leave, Jackson Blake."

"Ivie, please give me a chance to explain." He sputtered out the words, but I wasn't listening.

I just wanted to climb into bed and rest. It was almost daylight, and I had wasted the entire night on his foolish, dangerous game. I'd never be able to turn Matt back, and I would probably be locked up for the rest of my life for killing him when he was—I stared into my four-legged fiancé's sad eyes—right here.

"Please just go," I begged with what little energy I had left. "Let yourself out if you don't mind. I'm too tired to get up."

"Let me help you." Jack knelt beside me and tried to help me up, but I brushed his hand away. I didn't need any more of what he had to offer.

He stood and nodded before walking out of my kitchen. I heard the faint click of the front door as he went out.

That was the last thing I remembered.

Ten

SUNLIGHT STREAMED THROUGH THE WINDOW, burning a hole through my eyelids. At least, that's what it felt like. That, or the marching band inside my head carried torches to burn their way out of me while I froze my ass off on the cold kitchen tile, still wearing nothing but Jack's Henley. If that wasn't bad enough, Matt stood over me, barking in time with the ringing of the doorbell.

"Go 'way!"

The last thing I wanted to do was answer the door. It was probably Jack, back with another excuse or another scam to get me into bed... again. Not that we'd *actually* made it to a bed. But the idea did intrigue me.

And oh, God... Whether I wanted to admit it or not, if I saw him again, I would definitely cave.

I gripped my head and staggered over to the cupboard. I refused to fall for his tricks. Again. I dug through the array of over-the-counter medicines until I found aspirin and choked down two without water.

"Shut it, Matt." I scowled at the small dog. Judging by the continued ringing, whoever was at the door was in it for the long haul. "Just a minute!"

I ran to the laundry room and dug through the pile of clean clothes on the floor, settling on a pair of Matt's green gym sweats. After tugging them on, I dashed to answer the door and caught my reflection in the hall mirror. I wiped at my raccoon eyes and ran my hands through the tangled mess of flamboyant Jessica Rabbit hair, failing miserably in taming it even somewhat. With a deep breath, I pulled the door open. Two uniformed policemen stood there.

"Can... can I help you?"

The taller of the two stepped forward. He towered over his much shorter partner, reminding me of Penn and Teller. I almost expected him to ask me to pick a card. I forced the magician reference from my brain. "Is Dr. Green in?" he asked.

"Umm... no, he's not home. Is something wrong?"

"Dr. Green has been reported missing, and his car was found abandoned this morning."

"His car was *abandoned*?" My voice went up an octave. I'd almost forgotten I'd deserted the car in the woods when I left with Jack. "What makes you think he's missing?"

"Dr. Green's fiancée called in a missing person's report."

"His *fiancée*?" I'd officially become a parrot.

"Yes, ma'am. We're just following up. If he isn't here, we'd like to have a few words with his former fiancée, Ms. Ivie McKie. We understand she was the last person to see Dr. Green before he disappeared. We'd like to ask her a few questions. Is she available?"

Things were getting better and better. They didn't know who I was. My hand shot up to my hair, and I played with it until it spilled over my forehead a little more. I was torn between lying and coming clean. I wondered if they'd arrest me outright or just drag me in for questioning. Seeing me led out in handcuffs would make Mrs. Camp's year.

"Um... no. He kicked her out. I'm Matt's... um, cousin... Sabrina. Matt asked me to, um, dogsit. While he went out of town. I think he went to Las Vegas."

The Scottie barked at the officers, clearly trying to rat me out.

The shorter of the two policemen—Teller—took out a small notepad to write down everything I said.

"When did you last speak with Dr. Green?" Penn asked.

"Oh, um, sometime yesterday?" I scrambled to think up my next lie. "In the morning. He left a key for me under the mat."

"And did he seem fine when you spoke with him?"

"Fine?" Define fine. "He sounded extremely excited to go to Las Vegas and marry his lovely new fiancée." The bitch. "In fact, he couldn't wait to pack his bags and hit the road."

I had no idea what came over me. I'd given false information to the police. I was going to jail. No, worse...

I was going straight to *hell*.

"Do you mind if we have a look around?"

"Oh... um. A look around?" My knees threatened to give out. "I'd have to ask Matt before I let strangers into the house." That's what Mom always said, so it sounded good to me.

"It shouldn't be a problem to get a warrant. We'll at least need your information and a contact number," Penn said.

Teller tapped his pen against the pad and waited for me to give him my fake name and Chloe's address and phone number.

Correction, *she* was going to kill me... and then I'd go straight to hell. I had to call her and fill her in. *Immediately.*

"And ma'am?"

"Yes?"

"If you happen to speak with Ms. McKie, please tell her it would be best if she didn't leave town."

I watched through the window until the police pulled out of the driveway before I sprinted to the kitchen to grab my cell phone. It wasn't there. After pulling apart the entire downstairs searching for it, I realized it must still be in the pocket of my jeans... in Jack's car.

"Damn it!" My fingers wove into my hair, tugging painfully as I tried to think. "Matt's phone!" I darted up the stairs and grabbed it from the bathroom counter. I fiddled with the drawstring on Matt's sweats while it powered up, then I dialed Chloe's number. "Chl—"

"Ivie! Where the *hell* have you been? I've been trying to call you all morning. I've been worried sick! Who's Jack, and why does he have your phone?"

I paced over the cold tile. "I don't have time to go into the whole story, but I need your help!"

"Not so fast," she said. "I need answers."

With a groan, I switched the phone to speaker and shouted as I ran to the master bedroom, grabbing Matt's clothes and stuffing them into the bag he'd started packing. "I'll tell you everything, I promise. I need you. Can you come over right away?"

Matt barked at the phone, and I heard Chloe gasp. "What the hell was that? Was that a dog? When did you get a dog?"

"That's why I need your help. Please! Oh, and if the police call, tell them your name is Sabrina and..." I zipped up the bag. "Better yet, don't answer your phone until I have a chance to explain."

Her silence was completely uncharacteristic.

"Chloe?"

"The police? Oh, my God, Ivie... What have you gotten yourself into? Did you steal the dog from the guy who has your phone? Does Matt know?"

The dog growled, and I bit down hard on my bottom lip as I glanced his way. "Yeah, I'm pretty sure he knows." I picked up the phone and clicked off the speaker. "Please hurry. I'm in a lot of trouble, and I really need your help."

"Okay, okay. Should I stop off for a latte on the way there?"

"I'm not in the mood for a latte. Just *hurry.*"

"Cinnamon dolce skinny decaf? It's your favorite," she said with a teasing lilt.

"It's *your* favorite... and I don't think my stomach could handle anything right now."

"Fine," she huffed. "I'll be there in ten. But this had better be good if I'm giving up the gym *and* a cinnamon dolce latte!"

"I don't think *good* even begins to cover it."

Eleven

"Do you have any idea what this means?" Chloe stared into my eyes with a look of wonderment. "Ivie, you're a witch!"

"Tell me something I don't know," I said before dropping my face into my hands.

After initially freaking out over my ever-changing hair—currently flaming red and shoulder length—Chloe sat quietly on the edge of my bed while I went through the entire story—from the part where Matt came home to say he was leaving me to the part where Jackson Blake walked out my door and the police showed up. I didn't leave anything out. Not that any of that mattered in comparison.

"I knew something was going on. I just *knew* you were holding out on me. My best friend... a witch! Oh, my God. That's so cool." She yanked off her designer jacket, flung it behind her, and plopped down on the bed again. "I still can't believe you let that hot magician leave. Who does that? And I don't get how he ended up with your clothes, your purse, and your phone."

"Weren't you listening? We had *sex* in his car."

"You say that like it's a bad thing." Chloe waggled her eyebrows at me. She'd obviously tuned out the part about Jackson Blake tricking me into getting naked in the woods.

"It *was* a bad thing. Unlike you, Miss Impulsive, *I* don't do things like that."

She smirked. "Well, maybe you should."

"Stop right there." I threw up a hand. "I don't want to talk about the magician anymore. Besides, you didn't even see him. How do you know he was hot?" I dismissed her silly thoughts with a flick of my wrist but caught myself thinking about him again.

Chloe rolled her eyes. "Ivie McKie, I've known you my entire adult life, and there is one thing I am absolutely sure of. If you had sex with the guy in his car after knowing him for less than two hours, he was *hot*."

If there was one thing *I* was absolutely sure of, I wasn't going to admit she was right. "Please, forget about the magician."

She jumped up as if the bed were on fire and paced across the carpet. "Have you tried to conjure anything?"

It was my turn to roll my eyes. "I've been pretty occupied with trying to turn Matt back."

"Ugh, Matt." She shook her head, waving as if swatting a bug. "He deserves what he got. I'm talking about something good. Like…" Chloe ran to my closet and came back with the black garbage bag containing my destroyed Ralph Lauren boots. She dumped the boots on the floor in front of me. "There."

I held my nose as the smell wafted toward me. "There what? They're toast."

"That's what I'm talking about, genius." She planted her hands on her hips and raised one carefully arched eyebrow. "Fix them."

"Fix them *how*?"

Chloe let out a groan. "Do I have to spell it out for you?" She giggled. "Get it? *Spell*?" She hesitated, obviously waiting for me to laugh. I didn't. "You're a witch. You turned a man into a *dog*."

"A skunk," I interrupted. A minor detail, but I was nothing if not a stickler for details.

"Well, he's a dog now, and I'm pretty sure you were the one who did that. If you can turn a skunk into a dog, you can surely get mud, manure, and—are these claw marks?" She inspected my ruined boots more closely.

I lifted one shoulder in a weak shrug. "Hoof marks."

"Right." She bit back a grin. "Well, I'm sure a witch who can turn a man into a skunk and a skunk into a dog can fix a silly little pair of Ralph Lauren boots."

Chloe had a point. I had managed a few different transformations already. Maybe I could restore my boots.

"Hey, it can't hurt to try," she said.

"It might. I have no idea what I'm doing. I could accidentally turn the boots into a crocodile and it could bite your toes off." I had to laugh at the ridiculousness of the entire situation. Chloe laughed along with me, but I heard a subtle tremble in her voice.

"Okay, I'll give it a try."

"Excellent!" She took several steps backward to get out of my "spell range" and shrugged. "Just in case."

I nodded then turned my attention to the boots.

I tried to remember the sensation I'd felt when I initially turned Matt into the skunk—the heat that flowed through me, the static tingle of the electricity—and the sensation I felt when Jack had been in the kitchen and the blue light sparked from my fingers. I tried to tune into that feeling and focus my energy on restoring my favorite boots.

"It's not working," I whispered.

"Should you say something? Like a spell?" she asked.

"I don't know any spells."

"Just make something up." She was quiet for a second. "Oh, and it should rhyme. Spells *always* rhyme."

"Because you know so much about spells all of a sudden?"

"Just think of something."

I thought back to some of the spells I'd found in my Google search. Chloe was right; the spells were written like creepy nursery rhymes. "What rhymes with boots?"

"Toots?"

I turned to gape at her. "Toots? Really? That's all you could come up with?"

"Hey, I'm not the kindergarten teacher. You are." Chloe motioned for me to turn around to the task at hand.

"Okay. Okay." I rubbed my temples, racking my brain for the perfect words. *Boots, scoots, loots, hoots... roots!* "I think I have something." I drew in a jagged breath. "Drawing my powers from earth, plants, and roots, I channel my energy to restore these boots." I stared down at the boots.

Nothing.

"They still look like crap." Chloe huffed. "Maybe that wasn't the best spell. You're not trying hard enough."

I grunted. I felt a slight tingle in my fingertips. Nothing like what I'd felt before, but still something. I reassessed the information I'd discovered in the past twenty-four hours. I had to be missing something.

"Get the cat!" I pointed to the sleeping ball of fur curled up on my bed. "According to everything I've read, cats are supposed to reflect energy into the spell. If we're going to try this, we need to do it right!"

Chloe scooped up Karma. "He's a hefty one, isn't he?"

"Trust me," I snorted, "it's a good thing he's so well fed. He tried to eat Matt yesterday."

Chloe barked out a laugh. "That would have solved a lot of our problems, wouldn't it?"

"Hardly! His *fiancée* is already convinced I killed him and hid the body. If I don't change him back soon, someone might believe her."

Chloe sobered up and shoved the cat into my arms. "Right. Try the spell again."

I hugged Karma with one arm and extended the other, fingers outstretched toward the ravaged boots. Directing all of my attention into drawing the energy into myself like I'd done before, I closed my eyes and visualized the zigzagging current rushing away from the outlets and into my body. I took a deep, cleansing breath and opened my eyes.

The tingling started deep inside my core. I felt it coursing through me quickly, like a million tiny ropes pulling toward my fingers. Concentrating on what I was trying to accomplish, I switched up the words a little, letting my voice drift out with the incantation.

*"Drawing the power
from the earth, plants, and roots,
I channel my energy
to restore youth to these boots."*

Karma squirmed, a low growl emanating from his chest. The lights dimmed and a bluish glow extended from my fingers down to the floor. The boots shimmered in and out of focus for a quick moment then everything returned to normal.

Almost everything. I still heard Matt scratching on the bathroom door.

The boots I'd been ready to toss in the trash were nowhere to be found. In their place was a pair that looked brand new—as if I had just pulled them out of the box. My fingers hummed with the remnants of the power, and my head spun. The cat struggled until I released him, and he hurried out of the room.

"Holy crap!" Chloe seized my arms, her fingers digging into my flesh. "Can you make a purse? The buttery leather one from my dream?"

I heard what she said, but at the same time, her words didn't register. I was too absorbed in the pristine pair of Ralph Lauren riding boots.

I tugged away from her and crouched down to run my fingers along the shaft of one, feeling the supple softness of the Italian calfskin leather. They were perfect. I could even see my reflection in one of the gold tone buckles.

They were the very same boots I'd purchased over two years ago.

I mean... the. Exact. Same. Boots.

Chloe snapped her fingers in front of my face. "Hello? Anyone in there?"

"Shh." I waved her away. "I'm thinking."

"Think purse, Ivie. *Think. Purse.*"

"Later," I muttered, still distracted by the boots.

Chloe couldn't contain her excitement. "You did it! You did magic! On purpose this time. Snap out of it." She grabbed my shoulders, shaking me until she practically knocked me to the floor. "If you can fix your boots, you can change Matt back!"

That brought me out of the spell I was under, and I beamed up at her shining face. "I can change Matt back."

"That's right. Think positive." She pulled me up. "You think up a spell; I'll go get the dog. Oh, and Ivie?" she added as she practically bounced to the bathroom.

"Hmm?"

"Don't look in the mirror just yet. I need you to stay focused."

Twelve

"I DON'T THINK I LIKE HIM even like this. The little shit peed on my shoe." Chloe scowled at the dog by her feet. "Ivie, are you listening to me? These are Jimmy Choos!" She shook her foot as she dragged Matt behind her, using my last pair of new pantyhose as a leash. "And I think he has fleas."

I pressed my lips into a hard line. "Let's hope he still has them after."

We both laughed at that.

"Here." Chloe handed me the makeshift leash and stepped back again.

My concentration shifted to the dog. I worded the spell to make him new again, like the boots, but stopped myself. Did I really want Matt like new? Absolutely not. I wanted Matt back to his old miserable self. I couldn't afford to have him turn into a baby. I reworded everything in my head while Chloe forced the cat into my arms.

"Ready?" she asked.

"Ready." I drew in a long breath and let my eyes flutter shut as the words flowed out of me.

> *"From man to beast in error changed,*
> *this spell I now undo.*
> *Your situation rearranged,*
> *and change you back to you."*

"Nothing happened," Chloe said.

"Was I glowing?" I opened one eye to peek at her. "Did you see sparks?"

She shook her head. "Nothing. Not a flicker. I don't understand. That was a way better spell than the one you used for the boots."

I dropped the cat and pressed my face into my hands. "What am I going to do? I'm going to get the gas chamber."

"I don't think they use the gas chamber in Georgia. I'm pretty sure it's lethal injection."

My eyes snapped up to meet hers. "You're not helping."

"I'm sorry. I'll keep trying, but I don't know anything about magic. What about the hot magician?"

I glowered at her, using my best intimidating stare. "I don't want to talk about him."

"You can't really afford to be picky at this point. Matt is still a dog, and"—she looked down at him curled up on the floor—"as cute as the little jerk may be in this form, you can't leave him like this forever. *Someone* might actually miss him eventually."

She was right. Someone *did* miss him and she'd already gone to the police.

"Believe me, Chloe, there is absolutely nothing Jackson Blake can do to help me."

Chloe watched Matt and packed a bag for me while I took a quick shower and changed into the fresh clothes she'd brought me. I wasn't sure where we were going, but thanks to my stellar idea of giving her address to the police, we couldn't go back to her place. I'd seen enough movies to know I couldn't use my credit cards. Those could be traced. I was practically a fugitive.

Like Harrison Ford.

Since Matt wasn't dead, they had no real evidence. But I couldn't prove he was alive, either. I would gladly drag him by my pantyhose straight to the police station and say, "Here he is, officer, my scoundrel of an ex-fiancé." I'd be locked up for sure—in a padded cell. Maybe I *was* crazy.

With my eyes closed, I tipped my head back to rinse out the shampoo, imagining the red washing down the drain with the suds. If only I could wash that dog right out of my hair, too.

I twisted the knob until the water only dripped from the showerhead and pushed open the curtain. Even through the fogged glass, I plainly saw the harlot red that had overtaken my hair. And it had grown... again. Hair doesn't grow that fast, yet mine had.

I'd never thought I was beautiful, but I liked the way I looked. I wasn't so sure anymore.

I swiped my hand across the mirror and blinked back tears. Not a single dark strand remained. I could no longer disappear in a crowd. My hair practically glowed. And for clarification—the carpet definitely matched the drapes.

I look like Ronald McDonald's slutty younger sister. "Would you like a happy ending with that value meal?"

"Are you okay?" Chloe shouted through the door. "You've been in there for a long time."

"I'm fine." I wiped my cheeks with the backs of my hands. "Be right out."

Scrubbing my hair with a towel, I hoped the red would rub off. I knew it wouldn't, but I could hope, couldn't I? As I wrapped the towel around my head like a turban, my thoughts drifted back to Jack. Why did I have to have sex with a total stranger?

Jackson Blake is nothing to me.

I would tell myself that over and over until I believed it. I needed to concentrate on what I was doing, and what I needed to do was get dressed. Except my clothes didn't fit. Well, my jeans slipped on with ease, but my bra was tight. *Really* tight. As if it had shrunk in the wash or I'd gone up a whole cup size.

My entire life was coming unraveled like a cheap sweater. Every time I did magic—I stared at my new breasts and my new hair—took me one step closer to transforming into a Victoria's Secret model. Everything had turned upside down. I looked more like Ginger than myself. Matt would surely find me stunning.

How ironic.

After several minutes of struggling, I gave up trying to strap myself into the lacy deathtrap. Frowning at the fitted red shirt Chloe had brought me, I pulled Jack's loose Henley over my head instead. It still smelled like him—*like us*—and I sucked in a lungful of his intoxicating spicy scent. My eyes closed as I stuffed my feet into a pair of comfortable sneakers. I was in deep trouble. With one last lingering look at my reflection, I flew out of the bathroom and down the stairs.

"What happened to the shirt I gave you?" Chloe scowled and pressed her hands onto her hips. "And why aren't you wearing a bra? Did your boobs—"

I shook my head. "Don't ask."

"Whatever. Take him; I think I might be allergic." She rolled her eyes as Matt barked at her. She shoved the pantyhose leash into my hand. "And next time he needs to potty, you're taking him. I don't need to see *that* again—ever."

"Grab the cat," I urged, tugging Matt's makeshift leash as I dragged him toward the door.

Chloe gaped at me. "Oh no, we can't take Matt *and* the cat in my car. I have leather seats. Do you know what cat claws do to leather seats?"

"You can't expect me to leave him here."

Chloe stared at me in that way that made me feel as if I was back in high school.

"Ugh, fine. Pour him a big bowl of food and fill his water. He'll be good for a day or two." I hoped so anyway.

She didn't move. She stood there, hands on her hips and one eyebrow arched up in defiance.

"*Really?*" I swallowed the impulse to turn her highlights green. "Take Matt. I'll feed the cat." As I handed her the pantyhose and turned to dart into the kitchen, the doorbell rang, freezing me. My eyes locked with Chloe's. "The police?" I was on the verge of hyperventilating.

Chloe didn't look nearly as terrified as she should have been. In fact, she looked contrite. "I don't think it's the police." Her smile wavered. "But don't get mad, okay?"

"Why would I get mad?" I asked, trying to slow my thundering heart.

"Well..." She twirled a lock of hair. "I *may* have called your phone while you were in the shower."

My mouth fell open as I dragged in a jagged breath. "You *what?*"

"I asked the magician to bring back your stuff." She shrugged. "Honestly, he sounded pretty happy to do it. Don't turn him into a rabbit or anything. At least, not until I've had a chance to really check him out."

Before I could stop her, Chloe pulled open the front door to reveal a reserved, penitent Jackson Blake. He stood with my clothes and my cell phone in his outstretched hands, bowing his head in what could only be surrender.

My mouth opened then closed again. He'd obviously showered and changed but didn't look as though he'd slept any better than I had.

"I'm so sorry, Ivie. I know I'm a total asshole, and I wouldn't blame you if you didn't forgive me, but please forgive me." Sincerity dripped from his lips like honey.

"Why should I forgive you? How do I know you're not just trying to make sure I don't turn you into something nasty like... like... a *white rabbit*? Then you'd have to live in your stupid hat."

"I deserve that, I do." Jack glanced at Chloe, and I swear I saw her wink at him. "Please let me make it up to you." He lifted his pleading eyes to mine, like a little boy trying to charm his way out of trouble.

I stomped over and snatched my clothes from his hands. Matt's grandmother's ring dropped to the wood floor with a pronounced *clank*. I scooped it up and debated putting it back on. Matt growled at me from his spot at Chloe's feet, so I stuck my tongue out at him and jammed the ring onto the third finger of my right hand. *Take that!*

"Can you please get in here before the entire neighborhood hears your conversation?" Chloe grabbed the front of Jack's shirt, dragging him inside before slamming the door. "I'm getting a serious headache from all the barking."

Matt yapped once at Chloe then went back to snarling at Jack.

Chloe elbowed Jack. "He really doesn't like you."

"He, umm... I'm sure he's not happy about what happened in the kitchen last night," I said, feeling a blush spread from my face down my chest. "You know how Matt feels about his kitchen."

Chloe crouched down to speak to the dog. "Serves you right after what you've done." Then she stood to address me. "Too bad we can't dose him with Valium or something."

"You could give him a Benadryl. If you have any," Jack said with a shrug. "That would calm him down."

"Oh, good idea." Chloe turned to me. "Benadryl?"

"Upstairs medicine cabinet." I waved toward the stairs but never took my eyes from Jack's.

"Perfect! I'll drug the dog. You feed the cat." Chloe dragged Matt up the stairs behind her.

"Don't give him more than one," Jack yelled as she disappeared into the upstairs hallway. He tilted his head, scrutinizing me with an odd expression.

"What?"

"Your hair. It's even redder. And you're still..." He gave me a thorough once-over, his Adam's apple bobbing as he swallowed. "You're wearing my shirt." He ran his hand over his face and mumbled something I couldn't make out.

"What did you say?" I glared at him.

A slow smile spread across his face. "God, you're so..."

A leftover surge of heat burst in me. I seized the front of his blue button-down with both hands, yanking him toward me until our lips connected almost violently.

Jack's arms slid around me, pressing me against him as he kissed his way down my neck. "I can't stop thinking about you."

Teetering on the edge of my senses, I shoved him away and crossed my arms. "Were you thinking about how you tricked me out of my clothes in the woods? Or perhaps how you had sex with me under false pretenses?"

Jack held out his hands like a shield. "Hey, you're the one who initiated—" He flinched as I threw hate balls at him with my eyes. "That's not—I'm doing this all wrong." Jack scrubbed his hands over his face and avoided eye contact as if I were a dangerous predator. "Look, I know what I did was terrible, but I really do like you and I want to help."

"Well, I don't have time for *your* kind of help. I need to feed my cat. Then I have someplace to be."

As if he knew I was talking about him, Karma chose that moment to flit down the stairs and march over to rub against Jack's legs with a cheerful meow.

My mouth fell open. "Traitor." I stomped into the kitchen, with Jack and the cat close on my heels, and pulled the large bag of cat food out of the pantry.

"Ivie, please, I'm begging here." He placed his large hands on my shoulders, making my skin pebble with goose bumps.

"*Jack.*" His name came out as a groan.

He spun me around, tipping my face up until I had no choice but to stare into his eyes. "I know you don't believe me, but I'm really not that guy. I don't drag defenseless women into the woods to take advantage of them, and I don't have sex with girls I don't care about. But with you... rational thought went straight out the window."

His breathing picked up as he glanced at the refrigerator, the scene of our most recent crime. With one flash of his damn sexy crooked grin, my panties were wet. The bag of cat food slipped from my fingers, spilling all over the tile.

Smashing my lips against his, I backed him into the white marble island, fumbling with the button on his jeans.

"This doesn't change anything," I said before he bit down on my bottom lip, sucking it into his mouth.

"Mmmhmmm," he purred as his tongue found mine.

My senses were on high alert as his hands slid under the Henley, inching up toward my breasts. He paused when he realized I wasn't wearing a bra, and his face broke into a wide smile.

"Do *not* smile at me." I forced a scowl. "I'm furious at you."

"I deserve it." His face morphed into a serious expression as he teased my nipples, making me writhe against him.

"Let's just be clear about one thing. This"—I waved a hand between us—"is simply a by-product of the magic. It has *nothing* to do with—" I gasped as his hand slid to my waist to push my jeans down my thighs then made its way to the wetness between them.

"Right, nothing." He nodded, kissing a trail down my neck.

"I don't want you. I just want your... *you know.*"

He chuckled. "My cock?"

"Exactly." My hand snaked into the front of his jeans and wrapped around his length.

"Well, you're in luck." He thrust into my hand. "My cock happens to be happy to comply." He hitched my leg over his hip and slipped a finger into me as his mouth found its way back to mine.

"Ivie," Chloe called from upstairs, "I can't find the—"

"Look in the other bathroom!" I shouted in between kisses.

"You're kidding, right? It smells like skunk and pee in there. You so owe me for this."

"Hurry," I said to Jack.

He nipped my chin. "You can't rush perfection."

"Try. Try *really* hard."

"Oh, it's hard, baby. It's really, *really* hard." His lips smiled against mine as he entered me, fast and deep.

Jack grinned as he buttoned his pants and ran a hand through his just-been-thoroughly-fucked hair. I had to fight the urge to grab him and have my way with him again. "Please let me help you, Ivie."

"For the last time, how can you possibly help?" I yanked my jeans up my legs, zipping and snapping them quickly. "You're a fake, remember?"

Despite myself, I genuinely liked him, and I wanted to believe he liked me too. How could I ever trust him though? How could I be sure what I felt was real and not just excess magic brimming over?

"Most magicians are just very skilled imposters, but I happen to know someone who's the real deal. Surely you've heard of Jonathan Blake?"

"The famous magician? Who hasn't?" A light went off in my head as it dawned on me why Jack's name was so familiar. "Other than being the guy you stole your name from, what does Jonathan Blake have to do with anything?"

"Did you see his last TV special, the one where he transformed a woman into a tiger and then back again?"

"Yes, so what? He did a neat trick. Big deal. You turned a white dove into a python. Although I wouldn't mind hearing how you did it, knowing won't help me."

"Maybe not, but Jon can actually do that trick. He doesn't use smoke and mirrors. It's real magic," he said.

"How do you know it was real?"

"Jonathan Blake taught me everything I know."

"Watching someone on YouTube doesn't make them your teacher," I snapped, shoving past him to fill a bowl of water for Karma. I contemplated pouring it over Jack's stupid head before setting it on the floor where the cat grazed on scattered food.

He scowled. "I didn't learn by watching him on YouTube. I actually studied with him. *Closely.* We were even in the same room. Listen, I've seen him do that trick. It looked a whole lot like your spell with the snake. There was no trap door, no folding screen."

"How does that help me? We tried this last night, remember? You're good at a lot of things"—I felt my skin flush—"but magic isn't one of them."

He cocked his head to the side and smirked.

"Okay, the dog is drugged and I'm ready to get the hell out of Dodge..." Chloe skidded to a stop as she stepped into the kitchen. Her eyes darted from Jack to me then to the cat feasting on the kibble I'd spilled. "What the hell happened in here? Why do you two look like you were just joyriding with your heads sticking out the window?"

Jack blushed as he tucked a lock of my hair behind my ear.

"I, um, dropped the bag, and Jack was helping me clean it up," I said, feeling as if my face was as red as my hair.

"I'm not sure if you noticed"—she pointed to the mess—"but you didn't do a very good job."

"Yeah, well. I figured there really isn't any point. Besides, that's not important. Jack was telling me about a magician he knows."

"Another magician? Do tell." Chloe crossed her arms and leaned against the refrigerator, the same spot Jack had taken me the night before.

Jack glanced at me, his head tilted toward where Chloe stood, and I felt the blush spread. "I was just saying *I* might not be able to do real magic, but Jon could help. I could... *we* could go ask him together."

Chloe pouted. "Jon?"

"Jonathan Blake." We answered her at the same time.

"Why would world-famous magician Jonathan Blake want to help us?" Chloe beat me to the question, and my lips twisted into a resigned frown.

Jack pulled himself up to his full height, rolling his shoulders back. A grin split his face. "He'd better. Or I'll tell our mom."

Thirteen

CROSS TOWN IN JACK'S REMARKABLY spacious and impeccably tidy townhouse, I paced in front of the expansive plate-glass windows. My nerves were so shot, I half expected someone to slip *me* a few of the Benadryl pills that had knocked out the dog.

I'd managed to convince myself a squadron of police cars would pull up at any minute with lights flashing and a disembodied voice announcing the jig was up over a loudspeaker. Crossing my arms behind my back, I closed my eyes and imagined what it would feel like to have cold steel clamped over my wrists. Then the thought of Jack handcuffing me to the bed had me restless for an entirely different reason.

The whole sex thing had gotten out of hand. I felt as if I'd been reborn as a porn star or something. Just sitting in the front seat of his SUV on the ride over had brought back delicious memories. Keeping the magic at bay and my hands to myself took every drop of my will. Then my dirty mind raced with ways I could get Jack by himself... and out of his clothes. Unfortunately, Chloe's constant presence made that next to impossible.

While my dog of a fiancé lay snoring and curled up over the heating vent, Chloe explored her surroundings. "So, Jack..." She fingered loose change in a shallow jar while picking through a stack of mail. "How is it a club magician can afford such a nice place?" She caught me watching her and smiled as she glided to the bookcase to fan through the pages of random novels, dislodging an occasional dollar. I'd seen Chloe's snooping act before, and it was always amusing.

"I do all right," Jack answered, startling me as he passed behind me. "I have a pretty decent day job."

"Day job, huh?" Chloe abandoned the books to focus on Jack. "I don't know why, but that disappoints me. Does that mean we're not going to the magic club tonight?"

"No. I, uh, just do the Friday night show." Jack carried Karma around like a newborn baby, stroking his fur and having what appeared to be a conversation with him. My traitorous cat seemed to be enjoying the attention.

I caught Jack glancing at me every few minutes, but I wasn't going to let him off the hook so easily. I was still mad at him; at least, I was trying to be. I was glad he came back, but I would rather turn *myself* into a dog than admit that to him. My official stance was to stay angry until he found a way to make up for all his lies. I had to give him credit; he was certainly making a valiant effort.

"You never told me why you look so different." Jack sank into the worn cushions of his leather sofa and motioned for me to join him. Instead, I leaned against the arm, trying not to look awkward. "It's just, your hair..."

I knew exactly what he meant. I'd seen it.

"And your..."

I felt his eyes studying me, but he didn't finish the thought. He didn't have to. The once-waifish Audrey Hepburn look-alike appeared to be channeling Rita Hayworth. For the record, I didn't love the new me.

"It would appear to be a 'side effect' of the magic," Chloe piped in with a sour expression, making quotation marks in the air. She'd given up her treasure hunt and sat gracefully on the floor, her legs crossed at the ankles.

Her sarcasm didn't get past my radar. My life was falling apart faster than a badly set-up game of Jenga. My best friend was annoyed she had competition in the "hot body" department, my ex peed in corners and ate kibble, I'd developed a moderate case of nymphomania, and my cat liked the stupid magician better than me. What more could possibly go wrong?

"Did you call him?" Chloe asked for the fourth time.

Jack groaned. "I already told you I left him a voice mail, three texts, and a message on his Facebook page. He'll call me." He shifted his weight, resting against the opposite arm of the sofa and still stroking Karma absently. "Jon doesn't have the same sense of urgency as other people. He's more of a 'fly by the seat of your pants' kind of guy."

"Then what good is he? We're sort of on a time crunch here." Chloe flipped her blond hair behind her and turned to me. "Doesn't your *magic man* understand we're on a time crunch here?"

"Yes, Chloe, I get it. Time is of the essence." He grinned at me, and I bit back a smile.

"Well, no one is acting like it. The police have called me three times this afternoon. Three times." Chloe waved three insistent fingers and stood to pace around the room, wearing her own path in the carpet. "I had to turn off my iPhone. Did you hear me? I turned it off. I never turn off my phone. *Never*."

"Chloe, believe me, I'm more worried than anyone. I'm afraid I won't be able to change him back. What if he's stuck like this forever?" I looked at Matt, sleeping peacefully as a little Scottish terrier. "How would I possibly convince anyone he just disappeared without a trace and I had nothing to do with it? I definitely get how bad this situation is, but I need you to be calm. If you freak out on me, I have no idea how I'll hold myself together." I slid down the arm to sit on the end of the sofa and covered my face with my hands.

"Oh, come on, don't cry," Chloe said. She came over to pat my shoulder. "It'll be fine. We'll figure out how to turn Matt back, and everything will return to normal." I looked up just in time to catch her staring at my hair with an awkward grin. "Well, maybe not *everything*..."

"See? Nothing to worry about," Jack said as he slouched deeper into the cushions.

Chloe pursed her lips and stared at him. "Maybe *you* can get all comfy and relax, but we can't sit here all day doing nothing." She turned to me. "You need to try again. Come on..." She pulled Karma out of Jack's arms and shoved him at me. "Take the cat. I'll get Matt. You"—she pointed at Jack—"take off your clothes."

Jack snapped upright and did a double take. "Take off my clothes? Why?"

"I want to see you naked," Chloe deadpanned, barely pausing before she fell into a fit of giggles.

"Very funny, Chloe." I shook my head and put the cat down. "We've tried the spell so many times, I'm exhausted."

Jack's phone buzzed, and he whipped it out of his pocket.

"Is it Jonathan?" Chloe scooted to look over Jack's shoulder as he checked his text messages.

"Yes, it's him." He scowled at his phone. "Damn it."

"What? What's wrong?" Chloe and I asked in unison.

He looked up. "He's in Las Vegas through the end of next month."

"Oh." I plopped back down on the couch and played with a loose tendril of my hair. "Well, that's that, I guess. Do you think the red will clash with the orange jumpsuit?"

Chloe swatted the hair out of my hand as though there was a bug in it. "Don't be ridiculous. It's hardly the end of the world. We just need to hop a plane to Vegas."

I stared at her for a minute before pulling my thoughts together enough to speak.

"Are you forgetting that little detail about me not being allowed to leave town?"

Chloe's face split in a wide smile. "Trust me."

Fourteen

"WOULD YOU PLEASE SIT? AND stop fidgeting. You're making me nervous." Chloe lowered herself into one of the black vinyl airport chairs.

My eyes darted around the room as I folded my arms. "Too keyed up."

"Ivie, no one will recognize you. I seriously doubt your own mother could pick you out of a lineup looking like this." She motioned toward my vibrant red hair and new D-cups. "Although, I've got to say, I wouldn't mind standing in line for one of your magical boob jobs. And my hair is desperate for a highlight. I was supposed to go this weekend, but as you can see, I won't be making *that* appointment."

I was in danger of being arrested and had been "advised" against leaving the city—which I was about to do with stolen airline tickets—and Chloe wanted to whine about her highlights. I almost laughed, but I couldn't relax enough to make the sound. I wouldn't be able to relax until we were on the plane and taxiing down the runway. Scratch that... until we were safely in the air.

I'd reached a new low, and I feared I wasn't at the bottom yet. Nervous energy and residual magic coursed through me, making me squirm.

"I can't believe you talked me into this." I shifted my weight and lowered my voice to barely a whisper. "I'm breaking the law just being here."

"Please..." Chloe rolled her eyes at me. "You're only breaking the law a little." She brought her thumb and index finger together until they were almost touching.

"I don't think there's such a thing as breaking the law a little. That's like saying someone is a little pregnant. It's all or nothing."

"That's ridiculous. Besides, you didn't steal Matt's airline tickets; I did. You just worked an itty-bitty spell to fix your ID."

"Shhh. People can hear us, you know." I forced a smile at an old lady with a neat helmet of blue hair and thick glasses sitting a few seats away. She scowled at me then went back to her book.

"It's not like he was going to use them," Chloe whispered. "They're non-refundable tickets. And the little beast still gets to go to Vegas." She nodded toward the Scottie in the red carrier. "Which reminds me... Tell me again why *I* have to sit with him for five hours while *you* get to sit with Hottie Houdini?"

I'd lost count of how many times Chloe had complained about sitting with Matt. I'd tried to convince her to stay at Jack's house and dogsit. Of course, she refused. It was her idea to bring Matt, and despite my objections, she did have a compelling argument. If Jonathan Blake were somehow able to help me change him back, it would be convenient if he were actually in Las Vegas.

Chloe had even splurged for the original Sherpa doggy carrier—approved for use on most major airlines—in red. It matched her Louis Vuitton luggage. For reasons unbeknownst to me, that was important to her. I didn't really care either way. I'd stuffed my clothes into a leopard print overnight bag from Avon. It didn't match anything.

Chloe elbowed my ribs. "You didn't answer me. Why do I have to sit with the dog?"

I leaned in. "Because one, you had the bright idea to bring him. And two, I'm not the one sitting in first class."

"We have to bring him. You can't change him back if you leave him in Atlanta." Her lips curled into a smug smile.

"What about Karma? He should be here too." I felt my voice ratcheting up and had to force myself to whisper. "What if I can't work a spell without him?"

"Oh, please. You said yourself the cat wasn't even in the room when Matt went from a snake to a dog, and he was sunning himself in a window when you fixed your license. That proves you don't need him."

"It proves I got lucky. All the other times, he was right there." Just thinking about the magic made my skin prickle.

"Well, we couldn't have brought him even if we'd wanted to. They had room for one onboard pet, and Matt needs to be on that plane." Chloe nudged the carrier with her toe. "Though I don't know why he needs to sit with me."

"If you don't want to sit with him, we could swap seats." I didn't really want to change seats with her, but I knew she would never agree. My seat was located in the only "coach" Chloe wanted nothing to do with.

"Never mind. I'll sit with the stupid dog." She sighed, eyeing him through the mesh panels on the carrier. "But he'd better behave himself, or I'll let them stow him with the rest of the luggage."

Matt barked an objection, and we both laughed.

"I need to run to the ladies' room before they call the flight." I glanced around the room. "Where's Jack?"

"Since when do you need Jack to go to the..." Chloe's mouth fell open. "You're planning to have sex with him in the restroom, aren't you?"

"Don't be ridiculous. I'm... That's just... *gross*." My attempt at righteous indignation was pitiful. "I just don't want him to wander too far and miss the flight. That's all."

Chloe's lips quirked up, and she settled back in her seat. "You keep telling yourself that."

"There he is." My hands trembled as I shoved my bag against her seat. "Just watch my stuff. Please? I'll be back in a few minutes."

Moving as quickly as I could without breaking into a full-on run, I crossed the crowded space, stealing an OUT OF ORDER sign from a janitor's cart, and hooked my arm with Jack's. I dragged him toward the ladies' room.

"Is something wrong?" Jack's heavy brows furrowed as he looked at the plastic sign then at me. "What's the matter?"

"Nothing's wrong," I said through my teeth as I gave a quick smile to a woman leading her young daughter out of the restroom. Once the two of them were safely out of earshot, I propped the sign in front of the door and pulled Jack inside. I spun him around and held his face in both hands. "That *itty-bitty* spell Chloe had me work has me wound up so tight I'm about to burst. I can't sit still; I can't relax. My heart feels like it's about to beat out of my chest, and if you don't take me into a stall and give me at least one orgasm, I won't be responsible for what happens to the rest of the people in this airport."

"Christ, Ivie." Jack looked at his crotch and adjusted himself. "You can't say things like that to me in public."

"You're right. I'd much rather do things like that to you in public." My fingers gripped his shirt as I hauled him into the closest empty stall, locked the door, and shoved him onto the toilet seat. "Well? Take off your pants."

Jack sucked in a breath. "You're serious?"

My hands trembled as I unbuttoned the front of my jeans. "Hell yeah, I'm serious. Why do you think I dragged you in here?"

"As much as it pains me to say this, we can't do this in an airport restroom."

I lifted one shoulder, trying to appear nonchalant. "Well, if you're not interested, I saw this sexy soldier leaning against the wall near the newsstand. He might be—"

"Fuck that," he growled just before crashing his lips against mine.

Once I'd shimmied my pants down my legs until they pooled around my ankles, I went to work on his zipper. Slipping a hand inside his boxers, I wrapped my fingers around his hardened length. "I knew you'd see it my way."

He let out a hiss as I straddled his hips, lined him up, and sank down onto him. "This is so... wrong."

"Shhh... Not wrong. Good." My lips trailed across his exposed throat. "But we need to hurry."

"Mmm..." As I ground my hips into his, he curled his fingers around my shoulders for leverage, punctuating each word with a thrust up into me. "Always. In. A. Hurry."

We'd barely made it back to the gate when they called our flight.

Chloe pushed my bag toward me. "You couldn't have hurried?"

"Um..." I fiddled with a loose button on my shirt as a flash of heat spread across my face. "We did." *They don't call it a quickie for nothin'.*

"They just called first class, so I need to go. I'll see you on board." She leaned in as if she was going to kiss my cheek. "You reek of sex."

I bit back a smile, and she smirked at me.

"Who are you, and what have you done with my shy, kindergarten teacher friend?" We both laughed as she grabbed the dog carrier and skipped to the gate.

Matt had used his frequent flyer points to purchase one ticket in his name and one in Candy's. Jack was flying with Matt's ticket and Matt's ID. They never gave the picture a second look.

I was flying with Candy's ticket and my own ID. Like Chloe said, it was "just an itty-bitty spell" to change my name to Candy's on my driver's license, but pretending to be someone else had me on pins and needles. My pulse wouldn't return to normal until we safely reached the ground in Las Vegas and stepped clear of the airport.

A few minutes later, Jack and I were settled into our seats waiting for the plane to taxi down the runway. After the flight took off, an attendant came around with a cart, and I gladly paid for a miniature bottle of rum to go with my miniature Diet Coke. The minute the Fasten Seatbelts sign went dark, Chloe's head poked through the curtain separating first class from coach. As soon as she saw us, she marched straight to our seats.

"Is something wrong?" Jack asked her.

She folded her arms. "It's Matt. He keeps staring at me and whining, and it's pissing me off."

"Don't look at him," Jack said. He closed his eyes and leaned his head back.

"I can't just ignore him." She looked at me, giving me the same pathetic expression I'd seen on the faces of my kindergarteners at the end of recess. "You know he never liked me."

Jack popped one eye open. "Well, you could always put your sweater over the carrier so the bad doggy can't see you anymore."

"Whatever," she huffed, spinning on her heels and stomping back to first class.

She was gone less than five minutes before I heard her shoes clacking toward me.

"She's back." Jack chuckled.

"I need your sweater." Without waiting for a reply, she snatched it from my lap.

"What happened to *your* sweater?" I asked.

"It's Michael Kors. I'm not putting *Michael Kors* over the dog."

"Mine's Ann Taylor!" I argued.

"No comparison," she said, spinning around with my gray cardigan under her arm.

I couldn't fall asleep. Even after two miniature rum and Diet Cokes, I just lay there, running through everything that had happened over the past few days. Jack was out cold, but based on his whimpers and the bulge in the front of his jeans, I felt certain he was dreaming things we'd try later.

I didn't know how much time had passed, but I'd know Chloe's breathing, even with my eyes closed. I turned my head to see her standing there, out of breath and wild-eyed, clutching the red dog carrier in both hands.

She was about to say something I wouldn't like.

"You have to take him." She thrust the carrier toward me. "I'm done with this... dog."

"What has he done now?" I groaned.

"He has gas. I know he's doing it on purpose. It's horrible and disgusting, and I want nothing to do with him. People are going to think it's me!"

I swallowed a laugh. "What am I supposed to do with him?"

"I don't care what you do with him, but you have to take him." She plopped the carrier down in my lap.

"Excuse me." A flight attendant with jet black hair pulled back in a French twist almost as severe as her frozen facial expression interrupted my best friend's mini-tantrum. I imagined the older woman was beautiful several face-lifts ago. "You can't have your dog back here. You need to take him to your seat."

Chloe opened her mouth to say something, and the flight attendant scowled, waggling a finger. My pissed-off BFF pouted before stomping back through the curtain with Matt.

I felt my seat shaking before I realized Jack was laughing quietly. "How do you do it?" he asked.

"Do what?"

Jack turned to face me. "She's a handful, that's all I'm saying. You're a good friend."

"She's been a good friend to me." I had no idea how I'd managed to put up with all of Chloe's eccentricities for so long, but then again, she'd put up with mine. Tears welled up in my eyes.

"Things were bad for you even before all this hocus pocus stuff came about." It wasn't a question.

"Yes."

"The *dog*?" He nodded toward the first-class curtain.

I had to laugh. Matt was a dog long before he was, well, a dog. "Yes. He hasn't really changed much."

"You deserve better," Jack said with a little smile.

My lips tipped up slightly. I couldn't have agreed more. "Meet me in the restroom."

"What?" Jack's head tilted, his expression wavering somewhere between excitement and confusion.

"Five minutes." I shot a glance toward the lavatories in the back of the plane then brushed my knuckles against the growing bulge in his jeans. "Meet. Me. In. The. Restroom. In five minutes." I climbed over him, with a quick kiss on his nose, to scurry down the aisle.

I hurried inside the empty lavatory and locked the door, pressing my ear against it to listen for Jack. I waited five minutes, then five more before I gave up, grumbling the entire way back to my seat.

Jack stood to let me in, and I glared at him.

"What happened to you?" I scooted past him and flopped into my seat.

He ran both hands through his already messy chestnut locks and sat down, shooting a quick glance over his shoulder. "The flight attendant."

My mouth fell open. "What were you doing with the flight attendant?"

Jack groaned. "I wasn't doing *anything* with the flight attendant. She saw me get up to head back there, and she stopped me." He threw another glance behind him. "You've seen her. She's scary."

"That's it?" I scowled at him, folding my arms. "She *stopped* you?"

"Yes, she stopped me." He stared at my pissy expression before blowing out a breath. "She gave me a nasty look and shook her head. I'm guessing this sort of thing happens a lot."

"So let me get this straight... One nasty look from a harmless little flight attendant prevented you from a sexy rendezvous with a *witch*?" I mouthed the last word, glancing around me to be sure no one was paying attention.

Jack laughed. "Yes, Ivie. At the moment, I was far more concerned with being arrested by an Air Marshal than you turning me into a little white rabbit."

A growl I didn't even know I was capable of emanated from my chest. "Well, that's just stupid."

"It may be stupid, but we already have enough to worry about without adding an indecency charge to it." He leaned in to kiss me, and I turned my head so he got my cheek instead.

"You had your chance, Houdini." I shifted toward the window and watched him out of the corner of my eye.

Jack shook his head with a smirk. "I'm going to the restroom."

I spun my whole body to face him and narrowed my eyes.

"I really need to go, okay?"

"Whatever." I dismissed him with a wave.

He laughed the entire way to the restroom, and I swear I heard him even after he closed the door.

Trying to focus on anything other than my recent string of bad luck, I scrutinized the clouds. It's funny how I can never find a silver lining when I need one.

Chloe plopped down in Jack's seat. "What are you pouting about?"

"Where's Matt?"

"Oh, I left him in first class snoring away. I'm telling you, Benadryl is a wonder drug. So spill. What's got your panties in a bunch?"

"It's nothing. I tried to convince Jack to meet me in the bathroom for a little... you know, and he wouldn't do it."

Chloe's eyes popped open wide. "What the hell has gotten into you lately? I'm beginning to think you really are in heat. First the sexy vet, then the goat, and now the hot magician. You've gotten more action this week than in the rest of your entire life." She giggled.

"Ugh." I groaned. "Please, never mention the goat again."

"You're just mad it was the goat humping you from behind and not the hot vet." She fanned herself with her hand. "Only you could get lucky on a kindergarten field trip."

Just as the words spilled out of her mouth, I heard Jack choking behind her, and I spun around to see his face turning a bright shade of red.

Holy humiliation! "Oh, God! Please forget you heard her say anything. I swear it's not what it sounds like." I pushed Chloe from his seat. "You go back to first class before you cause any more damage."

Jack blinked a few times, shifting his attention from Chloe, snickering behind her hand, to my horrified expression. "You were... um..." Jack swallowed hard, and lowered his voice to a whisper. "Humped by a goat... on a—a kindergarten field trip?"

I gave a weak nod.

Jack's head bobbled a few times like a gift shop toy before he burst out in loud laughter, drawing stares from all over the plane.

"It's not that damn funny." I faced the front again, my arms pulled tightly across my chest.

"You're right. It's absolutely *hilarious*," Chloe said with a smirk before heading back to her seat.

Beside me, Jack continued to shake with quiet laughter. "This has got to be the strangest few days of my entire life."

Preaching to the choir.

Fifteen

"**P**ICK UP THE PACE, CHLOE," Jack shouted as we dragged our luggage through the Las Vegas concourse.

The wheels on Chloe's carry-on squealed against the hard floors like Matt had in Karma's mouth, but at least she was still moving. I'd pried her away from a slot machine more than once already.

"I'm moving as fast as I can!" Chloe yelled, trying to run in a pair of Ferragamo wedge-heel strappy sandals.

"Those shoes are ridiculous," Jack said to no one in particular.

Her feet clacked against the floor as she huffed from behind us.

"They match her bag," I whispered, throwing a look over my shoulder to be sure she was still moving forward.

"Of course they do." He shook his head.

I was never more relieved I'd refused Chloe's pleas to check her luggage. We didn't have time to wait for the carousel to bring our bags around. We were already late.

Jack reached the sidewalk and flagged the first in a long line of yellow cabs while Chloe and I caught up. I waited for her so she wouldn't do something foolish like go off on another one of her spoiled-girl rants. Or worse, swipe her card in another slot machine.

"Sorry," she said with half a smile as she jogged to catch up. "I probably should have worn the other shoes."

I forced a smile. "You think so?" I would have snatched the Ferragamos off her feet if I thought it would make her move a little faster.

Once Chloe reached the yellow taxi, Jack grabbed her red Louis Vuitton suitcase and heaved it into the trunk with our much smaller bags. The three of us, plus one irritable dog coming down from a Benadryl high, piled into the back seat.

"Ivie, can you please shut him up?" Jack asked as he punched a number into his cell. He sank a finger into one ear while pressing the phone to the other.

Leveling my scariest scowl at Matt did nothing to stop the noise. "I'm trying." I shook the carrier and whispered to my furry ex-fiancé, "Shut up, or I'm going to stop trying to turn you back. You can stay a dog forever for all I care."

He whimpered for a second then went back to barking. I guess he didn't believe me. I suppose under the circumstances, I didn't blame him. We both knew I'd change him back the instant I figured out how.

"I'm serious, Matt, you'd better behave. I'm the only chance you've got of being normal again." As normal as a classic narcissist could ever be, anyway.

The barking quieted, and Jack hit the redial button to connect his call again. After several tries, he threw his phone into his lap and scrubbed a hand across his face. "I can't get a hold of him. Damn it! This is just like him. Unreliable son of a—"

"So we just get tickets to the show and flag him from the audience," Chloe suggested.

Jack bobbed his head and scowled. "Sure, we could do that. If the show wasn't already sold out."

"Oh," Chloe and I said at the same time. I almost added, "Jinx," before remembering I didn't need any more bad luck.

"Can't we just, I don't know, wait outside for him? Stalk his room, maybe?" Chloe said.

"That would be a great idea if my brother didn't have an entourage worthy of Elvis. We'll never get anywhere near him if he doesn't know we're coming." He picked up his phone to dial again.

"Anything?" I asked.

Jack's jaw clenched, and he shook his head.

Great. We have to wing it. Not usually one to go off without a plan, I'd done more than my share of improvising over the past few days.

"Oh, I have the perfect idea." Chloe beamed.

I knew that smile. We were headed for trouble.

I tugged on the tiny black lace skirt riding up my fishnet-covered thighs. How she'd convinced me to wear something no self-respecting kindergarten teacher—or novice witch, for that matter—would be caught dead in, I would never know. There was no way we would get away with her ridiculous scheme.

Chloe leaned forward and wiggled her shoulders until her cleavage swelled over the top of her stolen bustier. "Stop thinking so hard. I told you before, this will work."

Easy for her to say. *She* didn't teeter on her five-inch platform stilettos. Mine threatened to give me nosebleeds. Chloe might have looked the part, right down to her identical tutu hanging perfectly still across her thighs, but with my streak of bad luck, I was in the wrong city for playing the odds.

Chloe giggled. "Ivie, it's not that bad. You're a redhead now. Start acting like one."

My face screwed up in disgust. I didn't want to act like a redhead. I didn't want to *be* a redhead.

"I wouldn't go that far." Jack wrapped an arm around my waist, tugging my body against his, and kissed the top of my flaming head. "We need to get in and out with as few people as possible seeing you like this."

The sweet gesture caught me off guard.

"Stop with the sour faces, both of you. I think this will be fun. I've always wanted to be a magician's assistant." Chloe smeared another blob of red gloss over her already shimmering lips and then turned the tube on me, making me feel as if I'd just kissed a beehive.

I made myself a promise that I would dye my hair dark as soon as we got home. If we ever made it home. "Tell me again why we're doing this?"

"Because we've tried everything else, and you won't use your hocus pocus to get us where we need to be." Chloe fluffed her already fluffy hair. "Now just stick to the plan and don't fidget."

I didn't need to remind her what happened when I used my "hocus pocus." We had a living, breathing example with us wherever we went. "Nobody's going to believe we work *for* the hotel. We look like we're *working* the hotel. As in prostitutes. We look like hookers."

"Speak for yourself, Sabrina. I look hot."

Jack released me, shooting Chloe a stern look. "Ladies, please. Quit the bickering. If we're going to have even half a chance of pulling this crazy plan off, you two have to work together."

She pouted out her bottom lip and nodded.

"Fine," I said then snapped my mouth shut.

"Okay, good. Now we need to get backstage to catch Jon's attention. Once he sees us, we'll be golden. We can wait out the show in the wings and talk to him after." Jack went over the plan for what was probably the twelfth time.

It sounded so easy, but I knew better. Nothing in my life was easy.

"We just have to get past security and maybe a few crew members and probably his manager." He planted a quick kiss on my sticky lips, sending a spark of desire through me that had me wishing we had time to sneak off to the closest bathroom or broom closet. "Piece of cake."

Piece of cake. Sure.

"Now what?" Chloe asked as we made our way down the darkened corridor.

"Left. No, right. No. I'm not sure." Jack scratched his head.

"Brilliant plan, Houdini." Chloe jammed her hands onto her hips.

Jack shrugged. "I've never been here before. I figured it would be a straight shot once we got through the employee-only checkpoint."

We were easily within shouting distance of the backstage area but had no idea which way to go. I heard music, but with the echo, I wasn't sure where it was coming from.

"We could split up?" Jack offered.

"No!" I practically tackled him to stop him from taking a single step away. "I definitely don't want to split up."

"No, Ivie's right," Chloe said. "Jonathan doesn't know us. We need to stick together."

"Fine. We can try—"

"What are you doing back here?" a deep voice echoed from the shadows. A large bald man in a black T-shirt with *Blake* emblazoned across the front in bold red letters came out of nowhere. He was easily twice Jack's size, and that was being conservative. He looked Chloe and me up and down, shaking his head.

If I thought I could control it, I would have tried a little magic. Instead, we had to rely on Jack's powers of persuasion.

"Oh, I'm so glad you found us. We were lost. We're part of the show. First night," Jack lied convincingly. Of course, I already knew he was a good liar.

"I'm going to be sawed in half," Chloe said, flashing her perfect teeth in a wide smile. She was good. *I* almost believed her.

I watched the man's face carefully, and it looked as if he was about to point us in the right direction. Then Matt barked and snarled inside the poorly disguised carrier.

"Sorry." Jack laughed. "Dog acts. Always temperamental."

"Mr. Blake doesn't have a dog in his act," the man said as he reached for something at his hip.

Matt's wriggling threw me off balance. I snapped off the heel of my stupid borrowed shoe and tumbled backward, shrieking. I let out a string of obscenities as my scantily clad bottom hit the cold floor.

"Are you okay?" Jack leaned down to pick me up, and the guard grabbed his arm, pulling him to his feet.

"You need to back up and stand still," the man said, unholstering a gun.

My eyes popped open wide when I saw a glint of light reflecting off the shiny metal. "Don't worry about me, I'm fine. I'll just stay down here if that's okay."

"No. Off the floor and against the wall with your friends," he said.

"Really, it's okay. I'm Jonathan Blake's younger brother. He's expecting us. Here, look." Jack reached for his wallet, and the man pointed the gun at him.

"Hands where I can see them," he ordered.

Jack held up his hands with his palms facing the man. "I was just going to pull out my driver's license to prove who I am."

"You can show them at the police station."

"You can't arrest us!" Chloe shrieked as she yanked the collar of Jack's shirt. "This is Jonathan Blake's brother." She grabbed his chin. "Look at his face. See the resemblance?"

The man seemed to run Chloe's words through his head and scowled. "Where's the ID?"

Jack turned and motioned to his rear pocket.

The large man pulled out Jack's wallet and looked at his ID then spoke into a walkie-talkie clipped to his collar.

"Jim, will you ask Mr. Blake if he has a brother named"—he looked at Jack's ID again—"Jackson."

Another voice—Jim, I suspected—interrupted the crackle on the walkie-talkie. "No one told me about a brother coming to town. He has a brother?"

"That's what I'd like to know. Some joker has a pair of hookers out here, and he says they're for his brother. So go ask Mr. Blake if he has a brother named Jackson."

"I'm on it," Jim said.

Chloe leaned in as close to the walkie-talkie as she could safely get. "We're not hookers."

"Ma'am, you can't talk into this," the man said to her.

She let out a nervous giggle and mouthed, "Sorry."

The radio squawked again. "Mr. Blake said his brother's in Atlanta."

"Well, you heard the man," he said, corralling us against the wall again.

"Jon! It's me, Jack," Jack shouted.

"Mr. Blake, please! Don't let them arrest us!" Chloe and I took turns screaming. Once again, I was imagining handcuffs slapped around my delicate wrists when I heard a voice behind me.

"I guess you'd better let them go, Cal."

I spun around to see a taller, darker version of Jack leaning in an open doorway.

Jonathan Blake smirked. "My mom would be pissed if I had my little brother arrested."

Sixteen

TWO HOURS AND ONE OVER-THE-TOP magic show later, we were ushered into a lavish dressing room in the Luxor Hotel. The moment the door swung open, the stench of stale beer and lavender soap pricked at my nose. My shoes sank into the thick gold shag carpeting as I spun around, trying to take it all in.

I didn't know where to look first. Egyptian murals in shades of red, gold, and black covered three of the four walls. Red silk curtains framed the fourth, a solid wall of windows that showcased the glittering lights of the Strip below. An enormous button-tufted sofa in blood-red mohair anchored the center of the room, and my fingers itched to touch it.

"Were you scared, Jacky?" Jonathan smacked Jack across the back.

Jack's brother didn't look much like him. He was attractive and I couldn't miss the family resemblance, but he was darker, less friendly. I wouldn't have walked alone into the woods with *that* Blake brother, for sure.

"Hell yeah, I was scared. Why didn't you answer any of my calls?"

"You know"—he shrugged—"got busy. First we hit the casino for a few hours—totally lost my shirt throwing dice—then one of the guys suggested a day trip to the dam. Can you believe in all the times I've been out here, I've never been? We lost track of time, just tooling around." Jonathan took a long pull from his bottle of imported ale.

"Tooling around? Are you serious?" Chloe pulled herself up to her full height beside the towering Jonathan Blake. "We've been chased, manhandled, almost shot, and Ivie ruined one of my absolute favorite pairs of shoes." She counted off each item with her fingers. Even *I* had a hard time taking her seriously in fishnets and lace.

Jonathan stuck his thumb in Chloe's direction. "So what's with the hooker?"

"Hooker?" Chloe shrieked. "Why does everyone think I'm a hooker?"

Jack coughed back a laugh. "No, it's not like that. This is Chloe, Ivie's best friend."

"She's a little pushy, isn't she?" Jonathan said.

Chloe's mouth dropped open, and she turned to me. "Did you just hear him call me pushy?" Her voice ratcheted up an octave. "First I'm a hooker, now I'm pushy?" She made a move toward Jonathan with her hands balled into tight fists, and I had to snag her skirt and yank her back. "I hate this guy already."

Jonathan leaned in to whisper in Jack's ear. I only caught part of what he said, but based on the way they were looking at Chloe, it was about her.

Chloe, drawing from her years of practice, pulled out her best debutante impression—arms folded neatly, long blond hair elegantly tossed over her shoulder, nose slightly in the air, and beautiful face set in a graceful scowl. "I don't care how much money he makes. He's a jerk."

"Come on, Chloe, he could help. Flash that perfect smile I know you have hiding in there, and be nice."

Her delicate features morphed into an appalled expression. "Are you really asking me to be nice to that ass?"

"Geez, I'm not asking you to marry the guy... just be nice to him." I bit back a smile. "That's all."

"I can't promise anything."

My mouth snapped shut before I put my foot in it.

Jonathan sat on the arm of the plush sofa and leaned forward. "So what's this big secret that had you flying all the way to Las Vegas?"

"We—or rather, I—need your help with some magic," I said, tugging on the ridiculous skirt riding up my thighs again.

"You came all this way for me to teach you a magic trick?" He laughed.

"Not exactly a trick," I said. "What I need is some help channeling energy so I can do the spell myself."

Jonathan scoffed and turned to Jack.

"Ivie's a witch," Jack said.

Jonathan held a straight face for a minute before barking out a laugh. "So tell me, Jacky, does Mom know you're taking drugs?" He stood up, downed the rest of his beer, and grabbed a pair of small wooden balls from the table. He rotated them in his hands, making one then the other disappear and re-appear. "Whatever you're on, pass it over. I've had a really long day."

"Such a busy life you lead," Chloe scoffed, practically vibrating with annoyance. "The Amazing Jonathan Blake, blowing money at the craps table and making drunken trips across the desert. Your mother must be so proud."

Jon's face broke out in a wide smile. "This chick's a trip." He may have been darker than Jack—darker hair, darker eyes, much darker humor—but they had that same sexy smile.

"Listen, I'm not on anything. I'm serious." Jack snatched one of the balls out of Jon's hand. "Ivie really is a witch."

"Come on, bro, you didn't fly all the way from Atlanta to jerk my chain, did you?" He grabbed the ball back, slapped Jack across the shoulder, then pulled him in for a bear hug. "Why didn't you tell me you were coming? I would have set something up for you." He winked then shot a cursory glance my way. "So what's the deal with Ann-

Margret over there? A witch, huh? Too bad, she's cute."
He winked at me. I couldn't stop myself from shuddering.

"Not that kind of witch." Jack laughed. "She does magic. Could probably teach you a thing or two."

Jonathan smirked and nodded in my direction. "So show me."

My nose wrinkled all on its own. Smile or no smile, I was with Chloe. I definitely didn't like the elder Blake brother very much.

As usual, Chloe came to my rescue and hauled up the dog carrier until it reached her eye level. "See this?"

Jack's brother peered into the carrier. "What's with the pooch, Jacky? Bringing your work home with you now?"

Chloe let out an exasperated sigh. "This *pooch* is Ivie's fiancé."

"*Ex*-fiancé," I said.

"Right." Chloe nodded. "Ex-fiancé. I didn't much like him as a human, but now the police think he's missing, so it's sort of important she change him back before someone arrests her."

"You people are either crazy or drunk." Jonathan shook his head and tossed the wooden balls into a silk duffel bag on the floor. He pulled another beer from the mini-fridge and cracked it open on the side of the table. "I, for one, hope you're drunk. Just give me a minute. I'll catch up."

Jon's flippancy irritated me, and I let that annoyance fester into something more tangible. Though not quite the same intensity of fury as the other times, I still felt tiny bursts of energy rippling under my skin. I closed my eyes and tried to relax, letting the heat flow through me, and concentrated everything to the tips of my fingers. The sensation started as a light prickling just beneath my fingernails. Not strong enough to hurt, but enough I couldn't ignore it. When it was ready, like water just reaching a rolling boil, I opened my eyes, stretched my hand toward Jonathan Blake, and brushed his sleeve lightly.

He flinched away from my touch as if I'd burned him then stood frozen in a pair of loose-fitting SpongeBob boxers and nothing else. His eyes went wide, and his mouth hung open. "What the hell was that?"

A surge of pride rushed through me, and I giggled. "That's a little something I like to call... *magic.*"

"Nice SquarePants." Chloe nodded to Jon then nudged my shoulder. "Told you you didn't need the cat."

"What the fuck happened to my clothes?" He spun around as if they might be on the floor behind him.

"I'm not exactly sure." I sort of wondered that myself, but in the grand scheme of things, Jon's clothes were the least of my worries. "I have no idea where things go. I may have actually disintegrated them."

With a fresh batch of butterflies in my stomach and a deep ache in my core, I stared at the remarkably well-built and almost completely undressed Jonathan Blake—until Jack cleared his throat. I'd almost forgotten he and Chloe were in the room.

"How the *hell* did she do that?" Jonathan gaped at Jack.

Jack smirked. "You should have seen her turn a snake into a dog." He pointed to Matt in the carrier.

"So you really are a witch?" Jonathan slowly backed away until his calves hit the huge sofa, and he fell into the cushions without spilling a drop of his beer. Then he downed the entire bottle without taking a breath and wiped his mouth with the back of his hand. "Like a witch witch? Broomstick, cauldron, black cat? That kind of witch?"

"I have a black cat." My thoughts did a hasty about-face from images of Karma to visions of broomsticks dancing in my head.

I'd never actually considered flying, but I couldn't help imagining the possibilities. I'd have to conquer my fear of heights. Would that even be feasible? What if I did start zipping across the Atlanta skyline? Would the FAA arrest me? Were other witches out there whizzing around on broomsticks, turning unsuspecting fiancés into wild animals or household pets? Were there even other witches out there? Did they know about me? Should I be worried about that?

"Is she even listening to us?" Jon asked.

"Hmmm?" I shook my head to bring myself back to reality. "I'm sorry. I was thinking about—it doesn't matter. What did you say?"

Jonathan zipped a pair of black jeans with shaky hands. "I said I don't know how I can help you. Your magic is in a totally different league from mine."

"What do you mean?" Hit with an unexpected wave of panic, I spun around to confront Jack. "You said he was the real deal."

"Real deal, yes. Some sort of wizard? No," Jonathan said. "You're looking for Harry Potter. What I do is illusion. It's magic, but not out-of-this-world magic. You can actually conjure, my dear. That's something so far above me, I'm embarrassed to even admit it."

"What are we supposed to do now?" The residual prickling took on an uncomfortable edge, transforming the butterflies in my stomach into bats. I looked from Jonathan to Jack.

"What you're going to do now is exactly what we came here to do—channel his energy and try the spell again." Chloe pushed past Jonathan then opened the dog carrier. Matt rubbed against her legs, and she rolled her eyes. "The sooner we change this little idiot back, the better. I think I'm starting to like him."

Seventeen

"OH, NO, JONATHAN BLAKE." I spit out his name like a sour grape. "I may have fallen for that line once"—I glared at Jack as a shudder ran through me—"but that does not mean I'll fall for it again."

"Jacky, I'm so proud of you. You were paying attention. I don't think even *I* would've had the balls to strip in the woods. I mean, dude... shrinkage?" Jonathan put his hand up for a high five that Jack had the good sense to ignore. "Hey, whatever, man. I just can't believe you pulled that off. Impressive."

Jack approached me slowly, both hands shielding his package as if I were a rabid dog or something. "Of course you don't have to take your clothes off." He turned to his brother. "Does she, Jon?"

"Seriously, it couldn't hurt." Jon winked.

Jack shot him a death glare that shut him up fast then turned his eyes back to me. He cupped my chin, and for a second, I thought he might kiss me. "Just channel his energy. Nothing more. Try to pull whatever power you can from Jon and focus it on Matt."

With a nod, I sucked in a deep breath, struggling to remember the last time I'd tried that spell. It hadn't worked then, but I'd gotten a better handle on controlling the energy flowing through me, so maybe it would work.

My eyes closed as I ran the words through my head a few times for practice. "From man to beast in error changed, this spell I now undo, your situation rearranged, and change you back to you."

"What the hell is she muttering?" Jonathan whispered to Chloe.

"Shut up, it's a spell."

Jonathan laughed. "That's the most pathetic excuse for a spell I've ever heard."

I popped one eye open. "You two are not helping me concentrate."

"Sorry," Chloe mouthed. She put her thumb and forefinger to her lips, twisting them sideways, and pretended to throw a key over her shoulder. "Lips are sealed."

Closing my eyes again, I cracked my neck to one side then the other and gave my hands a good shake before taking three deep cleansing breaths. Energy pulsated in the air around me, and I stroked the pads of my fingers with my thumbs, trying to build up the charge. I felt a bit like a boxer preparing for a fight.

"Does she always do this?" Jonathan asked.

"*Shhh*," Chloe warned.

"You know, it's almost a shame to change him back," Jonathan prattled on. "He's pretty cute. At least he's small. Seriously, he could have ended up as a big, drooling St. Bernard or a Great Dane or something. Can you imagine?"

A gust of breath blew past my lips. "Would you please shut up?" With a quick shake of my head, I struggled to push the image of Matt as a giant dog out of my mind and concentrate on the ripple building in my fingertips. I opened my eyes just in time to see the faint blue light glinting from them.

"Hey, I'm just saying," Jon interrupted again. "A Great Dane would be a lot harder to tote around."

Chloe's hand connected with the back of Jon's head just as *my* hands reached toward Matt's furry form, and he whimpered as the static charge crackling between us made his fur stand on end.

I cleared my throat and spoke slowly.

"From man to beast in error changed,
this spell I now undo.
Your situation rearranged,
and change you back to you."

Like blowing out a candle—as I'd seen it do so many times already—the light vanished and returned just as quickly.

"Oh shit," Chloe exclaimed.

"N-no way," Jonathan stammered.

Jack leaned in to whisper in my ear, "Houston, I think we have a problem."

I blinked a few times, unsure if I really saw what I thought I saw. It couldn't be. *Not again.*

"Everyone else saw that too, right?" Jonathan choked out as he pointed to the spot where the Scottish terrier had been. "Seriously, is that a—"

Did I really just transform Matt into..."A Great Dane?" I sputtered, choking on my own saliva. *Yep. A giant, drooling, black Dane with a gray muzzle.* Once my coughing fit died down, I turned around and narrowed my eyes in Jon's direction. "Yes. As a matter of fact, it is. Thanks to *someone* putting the idea in my head while I recited the spell."

Chloe exhaled without a single drop of her usual grace and picked up the red Sherpa dog carrier. "He's not going to fit into this for the ride home."

"Okay, let's not panic." Jack shot a quick glance at Jon as he ran his hands through his hair so vigorously I thought it might fall out.

"Oh, I'm not panicking. I'm just going to kill your brother." I pointed to the huge dog lolling his head to one side, big sloppy tongue hanging out. "How are we going to get that... *thing* on the plane? He's as big as a person."

"Just put him back. Back to the little dog size. We can at least cart him around like that." Chloe shook the carrier as if it she expected me to pull a terrier out of it.

"Just let me think." My head throbbed as I sat on the spongy carpet. I tried replaying the spell in my mind, rewinding each scene to find exactly where I'd gone wrong—a futile exercise that yielded zero results.

Matt lumbered over to me and barked out one thunderous objection.

"I don't want to hear it. This is your fault. You were the cheating, lying dog in this relationship, not me."

He growled and bared his teeth.

My self-control snapped, letting loose the torrent of emotions I'd worked so hard to contain. "You'd better behave, Matthew Green. One bite, and I don't *ever* change you back. Do you hear me? This time, I'm serious. You can live out the rest of your days chained to an engine block in someone's back yard for all I care."

He whined and dropped to the floor beside me, his wet nose nudging my knee until my jeans were damp.

A twinge of conscience pinched me. "Enough with the guilt trip. I'm doing the best I can."

How did I end up responsible for a dog nearly twice my size? And how would I possibly find my way out of that predicament? *Isn't this a fine mess you've gotten yourself into?* Exhausted, I let my face fall into my hands. My stomach growled, giving the dog a run for his money. I couldn't remember the last time I'd eaten. Worst of all, I was all kinds of horny again.

The air shifted around me, and I knew I wasn't alone.

Jack squatted beside me and smoothed my hair away from my face. "It's going to be okay. We'll figure something out. Maybe Chloe's right. You *could* try to turn him into a little dog again."

"No." I shook my head so hard, I saw stars. "I don't want to try again. I'm tired of trying. Besides, I don't think I can concentrate anymore. The magic makes me so, umm, you know... *tense*." With every touch of Jack's fingers, I grew more and more aroused, but I wasn't about to say that. "I don't even want to ask about my hair, and my bra is so tight it hurts." I forced a laugh when all I wanted to do was cry. "I must be the only woman alive to complain about a free boob job."

"It's definitely made things more interesting." He nudged me with his shoulder.

"Jack, can I, um, talk to you in private?" I peeked over my shoulder and tried to keep my voice low. Chloe gave me a weak smile then went back to bickering with Jon.

"Uh, sure." Jack stood then pulled me to my feet. "Do you want to step into the hall for a minute?"

"No!" My hands shot up to cover my mouth as I struggled to regain some of my runaway self-control. "I mean, no, I'd rather not go where someone can hear us." Or see us.

Jack's eyebrows pulled together for a minute until my meaning sank in, then they shot up and his eyes went wide. "Oh! Yeah, um..." He turned to look around the room. "The bathroom?"

Pulling my bottom lip between my teeth, I nodded. Slipping my hand into his, I let Jack lead the way.

Much like the main room, the bathroom was a study in extravagance. Gold-tone faucets and a stack of thick red terrycloth punctuated the black marble fixtures. The walk-in shower for two—or more—displayed a mural more fitting for King Tut's tomb than a vacation mecca.

"Over the top," he mumbled as I closed and locked the door.

I shoved his shoulders, knocking him off balance enough to make him stumble against the wall.

"Damn, Ivie, what the hell?"

"We don't have much time before they wonder where we are and what we're doing, so off with the pants and get with the doing." My fingers worked the laces on my stolen outfit, and I released the stranglehold on my growing breasts with a groan. "God, that feels so much better."

Jack zeroed in on my heaving bosom and licked his lips. "They've, umm... wow."

With my best come-hither grin, I wriggled out of the hooker skirt. "Come on, Houdini, get your pants off."

Jack closed his eyes and rested his forehead against mine. "Ivie, no. We can't."

I heard him speaking, but his words made no sense. Both his tone and the bulge straining against the front of his jeans told me he didn't mean it, but he'd said it nonetheless. "What do you mean we can't?"

"God, I can't believe I'm saying this." Jack pushed a hand through his hair and exhaled in a gust. "I don't want to have meaningless sex with you."

My stomach plummeted at his confession.

My expression must have changed because he put his hands up in front of him and shook his head. "No, wait, that's not what I meant. I don't mean sex with you is meaningless. It's not. Dammit..." He groaned. "The thing is, I want to have sex with you. Lots and lots of sex. I just want it to mean something, and not just as a way for you to blow off steam after a spell."

"Oh." I stared at his serious expression. Was I ready for a *meaningful* relationship? I hadn't even recovered from the *meaningless* one. Mr. Meaningless himself was drooling all over the carpet in the next room. But Jack was different. I knew that much after spending less than twenty-four hours with him.

He cupped my face. "Please don't think I don't want you. Because, truly, I do."

After taking a long moment to process what he'd said, I gave him a shaky smile and a quick kiss. "I appreciate what you're saying, but..." Meaningful could wait. My fingers found their way to his zipper. "What I really need right now is this." I cupped his hardness and leaned in to capture his lips again, lingering as I worked his pants down his legs. "Please?"

Jack let his head fall back and banged it against the wall repeatedly. "Why can't I say no to you?"

The sweet taste of victory flooded my senses, and I wrapped a leg around his hips, lining myself up to where I wanted to be. "Just take me, Jack. Fast and hard. In fact, the harder, the better."

After expending every drop of energy within me—twice— Jack tugged his shirt over my head. He grabbed a pair of sweatpants from my bag and helped me step into them before joining the others in the main room.

"Told you." Chloe held out her hand, and Jon slapped a twenty into her palm. He turned to Jack, holding his hand up for a high five.

Jack shook his head. I think even the dog rolled his eyes.

"I need to lie down." I leaned into Jack, craving his touch like a drug. I was certain it was him, not simply the magic, making me feel that way.

"Come on, we need to find you a bed. Jon, do you have a room in this hotel?"

Jon fell into a chair and pulled his knees to his chest as he stared at the huge dog. "We can't take that *beast* to my room."

"Can't we stay in here?" I asked. "I just want to go to sleep for a little while."

"Here, lay on the couch." Jack gave me a little shove, and I sank into the scratchy mohair. "Sleep."

The last thing I remembered was Jack's lips whispering against my forehead.

My stomach rumbled with the ferocity of Mount Vesuvius, interrupting the strangest dream I'd ever had. I wrapped my fingers around the silky sheet, tugging it up to my chin. The tinge of pyrotechnics and sweat stung my nose. Instead of four-hundred-fifty-thread-count Egyptian cotton, I had Jonathan Blake's red satin cape wrapped around me like a blanket. *Guess it wasn't a dream after all.* Other than the glow coming from a muted television, the room was dark. For all I knew, it could have been day or night. If the vibrations in my stomach were any indication, I'd slept for days.

I blinked the sand out of my eyes and cleared my throat. "Do I smell food?" *Mmm, bacon and eggs.*

Jack leaned over the back of the couch to look at me. "Are you hungry?"

"Are you kidding? I could eat a horse."

We looked at the oversized dog sleeping on the floor beside me.

"That's one way to take care of him, I suppose," Jack said.

"Not funny." Memories of Karma practically acting out a MasterChef Mystery Box Challenge flooded back to me. "Where're Chloe and Jon?" I pulled myself up when I realized we were alone.

"Interesting you should ask that." He shoveled a forkful of omelet into my open mouth, effectively stopping my next question.

My mouth was full of food, and he wasn't forthcoming with any information, so I poked him.

"Watch what you do with those fingers. They're dangerous." He grinned at me as I chewed and swallowed.

"Are you going to tell me where your brother took my best friend or not?"

He stabbed at another bite of egg and held it up like a weapon. "What makes you think it was my brother doing the taking?"

"Because Chloe hates Jonathan." I carefully dodged his attempt to feed me.

"You've been sleeping for several hours. Things change."

My mouth dropped open just long enough for Jack to shovel in another bite of eggs.

"While you were playing Sleeping Beauty on the couch here, your best friend managed to work her own brand of magic on my brother." He held a glass of orange juice to my lips. "Sip."

I gulped down a mouthful of sweet pulp. "But she didn't like him, like, at all. Not even a little."

"He can be very charming when he wants to be. He taught her a magic trick and, apparently, succumbed to a little feminine enchantment himself."

Classic Chloe. "So where did they go?"

"I have a hunch, but it would be ungentlemanly of me to say." He winked.

"No," I mouthed.

"I think so, yes." He bobbed his head, sucking in his cheeks.

I felt around in the cushions. "I need to text her right now."

"You can't. You left your phone, remember?"

I fell back into the couch. The eggs settled like a lead weight in my stomach. "I almost forgot." *I'm a fugitive from justice.*

"Come on." Jack tugged my arm until I sat up again. "You need to eat."

"I'm not hungry anymore."

"You need your strength." He waggled the forkful of eggs in front of my nose, and I opened my mouth.

"I'm not a baby, you know," I said as I chewed.

"Didn't your mother ever tell you it's not polite to talk with your mouth full?" His lips curved into an easy smile, but I wasn't in the mood for his teasing.

I narrowed my eyes and pulled my lips into a dark scowl as I chewed. The more I thought about my predicament, the more my anger morphed into despair. I felt the familiar sting of tears welling up in my eyes.

"Hey." Jack abandoned the plate and sank into the sofa beside me, tugging me into his arms. "I know this is hard, but you're stronger than you realize. And you're not alone. You have Chloe... and you have me."

Jack's words hit me like a wrecking ball, and big fat tears bubbled out of me like a fountain. I fisted his shirt with both hands as I curled into him and sobbed against his chest. The weight of the past few days lifted a little with every fresh wave.

Jack rubbed soothing circles on my back as he held me and pressed soft kisses against my hair. He let me cry until my shuddering breaths slowed to a smooth rhythm. "Please let me be here for you? Can you do that? Can you just try to let me in?"

I gave a jerky nod, wiping my runny nose on his shirt.

He chuckled. "Is that a yes?"

"Yes," I whispered, wiping my face with the corners of Jon's smelly cape.

"Now drink your juice." He grabbed the half-empty glass and handed it to me. "Go ahead and finish your breakfast. The shower's all yours when you're ready. Just forget about everything else for the next hour, and let me figure out how we're getting home."

Home. I couldn't even imagine how we'd get back with that horse of a dog. He certainly wouldn't fit in the carry-on luggage compartment. And once we figured out how to get him back to Atlanta, what would I do with him? I was no closer to changing him back than I'd been a day earlier, and I was no closer to explaining to the police what had happened to my fiancé. *Ex-fiancé.*

I'm so screwed.

Jack handed me the fork, and I shoveled in another heaping bite of egg, choking it down when I thought of a new question. "Has Matt eaten since we got here?" I may have disliked him, but I couldn't let him starve. I found I had much more compassion for him as a dog than I ever had as a person.

"He ate a bowl of oatmeal and four hamburgers. I think he's fine. He's been out like a light ever since."

"Did you slip him another Benadryl?"

"Nah. At his current size, it would take a few more than that to knock him out. Besides, we need to conserve what little we have. I'm pretty sure he's just tired from all the excitement."

All I could do was nod. I may have had one less thing to worry about, but there were still far too many to count, and the day was young.

Eighteen

"SO AS IT TURNS OUT, Jon has a private jet." Chloe twisted a lock of her blond hair around her finger and let a loose curl fall as she stared into Jon's eyes across the table. I think they were holding hands under there.

"Would you stop that? You're making me lose my appetite." I tried in vain to avert my eyes from the train wreck in front of me. Watching Chloe shove big, juicy grapes into Jon's mouth was more than I could bear. It didn't seem fair for Chloe to be blissfully happy while my life careened out of control.

"Oh, be quiet, Ivie. It's not like you don't have your own magician," she said with a pronounced wiggle of her fingers in our direction.

Jack shrugged at me, but I saw his smile threatening to come out.

"Yeah, Ivie, you have your own magician," Jon said and punched Jack lightly in the arm.

"Ouch." Jack rubbed the spot.

Maybe not so lightly.

"Can we get back to the important stuff?" I drummed my fingers on the side of the table. "What were you saying about a private jet?"

"Oh right. I have a private jet." Jon plucked another grape from the bunch and popped it in his mouth. Then he leaned in and whispered something in Chloe's ear, setting her off in a fit of giggles.

My breakfast threatened to make a reappearance. "Hellooo?" I banged my fist against the table, making the flatware clank together. "You actually own a jet?"

They stopped canoodling to gape at me.

"Let's just say it's at my disposal." Jon shrugged. "How else am I supposed to get to shows?" He went back to popping grapes into his mouth.

"Private jet means no problem getting Matt home. We don't have to fly commercial," Chloe said.

"For today's purposes, the dog is part of my act," Jonathan added.

"Perfect," Jack said with a wide grin.

"Not perfect." I forced a smile. "But not bad."

Jack took my hand and squeezed. "We're going to figure something out. Don't worry."

For the record, I did worry... a lot. So much that my hair seemed to be falling out. I had left a clump of bright red strands in the shower drain, like the remnants of a Ronald McDonald wig. "When do we leave?"

"What's the rush?" Jon tossed up a fat, purple grape and caught it in his mouth. "Nothing waiting in Atlanta but a firing squad, right?" He smirked as he chewed.

"Jon!" Chloe smacked his hand and scowled at him. She turned to me. "Sorry."

"I'm glad you find my situation so funny all of a sudden." I pushed away from the table, tipping my empty water glass onto a plate with a loud clatter.

"Oh, Ivie, he's just trying to add a little humor to the mix." Chloe followed me across the room. "I've been thinking a lot about what's happened, and I have an idea. You can't remember what Matt looks like anymore, right? Can't picture him in here?" She tapped a French-manicured finger against my forehead. "Well I think that's the whole problem. You imagined your boots the way they looked brand new, then you did the spell and they were brand new again. You can't picture Matt as a person because all that's left of him is his betrayal and the names you gave him when he called off the wedding. A skunk, a rat, a snake, and a dog... or two. But this time, he's at least a person-sized dog. You're getting closer."

I had to give it to her. Her theory made more sense than anything I'd heard in days. "Chloe, you're a genius." I hugged her and planted a kiss on her cheek while she wiggled free.

"Let's not get carried away." She snorted.

"I need to find some way to imagine Matt the way he was. We need to get to Atlanta and find a picture of him somewhere. There has to be one at the gym. He practically lives—*lived*—there." Tingling started at my toes and worked up my spine to my hair. For the first time in days, I had hope that my life might actually get back to normal. I glanced at Jack in his rumpled clothes with his perpetually messy hair and heart-stopping smile. Maybe not normal, but better. "So when can we leave?"

Jon juggled a handful of grapes. "Right after tonight's show. I'll ask the pilot to set a flight plan."

Jack shook his head. "That ridiculous thing isn't going to hold if he decides to bolt."

Chloe gripped the thin, rhinestone-encrusted strap and clipped the other end to Jack's belt, looped around Matt's neck. "It wasn't ridiculous when he was a Scottie. It was cute. I had big plans to take him out for 'walkies' with this leash!"

Jack laughed. "If you say so."

"Matt won't bolt." I grabbed his gray muzzle between both hands and stared into his puppy dog eyes. "Will you?"

Matt whined, shaking his head to extract his face from my grip.

I wiped my slobbery hands on my jeans. There were worse things. Like skunk spray or rat bites—or snakes.

All of them put together still trumped the actual guy, and yet, I couldn't wait to change him back. I actually looked forward to seeing his stupid, smug grin and listening to his condescending voice. For all of five minutes, that is—just long enough for me to walk out of his life for the last time.

"He knows what'll happen to him if I don't change him back. Don't you?" I watched his tail plant itself firmly between his legs.

"Not so scary now, are you?" Chloe teased.

Matt growled at her.

She stepped back. "I really don't like him."

Jon swooped in behind her and wrapped her in his arms. "Are we ready to go?" He rested his chin on the top of her head.

She giggled. "I'm ready."

I wasn't. A niggling sense of foreboding clung to me like summer sweat. "Okay, let's get this show on the road."

One by one, we boarded the Cessna Citation as if queuing up for a funeral procession. Our time in Vegas had been an all-too-short reprieve from the grim reality waiting for us in Atlanta. Well, waiting for me. The rest of them were merely spectators. And just being with me was disrupting their lives.

Chloe flopped into the window seat and bounced a few times. "This is better than first class! I don't know if I'll be able to slum it on a commercial flight ever again." She giggled. "Oh, speaking of commercial... I left a message with my boss. I'm clear through the end of the week."

"You think we'll need all week?" I squeaked.

She shrugged and glanced at Jon. "Either way, my time's freed up."

"I told the guys I'd be back in a few days. They aren't happy, but hey, family emergency, right?" Jon settled into the cream-colored leather seat. That was the third time he'd reminded me that he'd left his usual entourage behind. "They can call Copperfield if they need someone. I'm pretty sure his agent owes my agent a favor."

"It's so nice of you to come with us." My cheeks ached from holding the fake smile.

Chloe beamed. "It is nice, isn't it?"

"Oh, you know, I thought maybe I could help." Jon squeezed her hand, and I translated that to mean he'd tagged along for the booty factor. "I usually travel with a whole entourage, but I figured you were trying to come in under the radar." Make that four times.

I imagined turning Jon into a little gray hare. "Yes, it would be best if I did."

"Hey, Jack, you remember the guys from that summer I toured Hamburg?"

Jack's eyes snapped up from the text message he was sending, and he choked out a laugh. I suspected there was more to that story.

"Oh, man, great bunch of guys. Lenny still can't look at a redhead without throwing up." Jon stared at my hair and blinked twice. "Oh, hey, sorry, Ivie." He flashed a quick smile.

I won't turn Jon into a rabbit. I won't... "Don't worry about it. I'm not really a redhead."

"She isn't. You should see what she looks like when she's not all juiced up on magic. Very Audrey Hepburn." Chloe beamed at me as if she were doing me a favor. As if maybe I didn't look my best as a redhead.

"I'm going to check on Matt." I moved to the back of the plane where he slept.

Jack had slipped him the last of our remaining Benadryl capsules, knocking him out cold. I worried he'd still be sleeping when we got home, but Jack assured me it would wear off by then. I really hoped so, because I wasn't going to carry him if it didn't.

I knew I should be sleeping too. It was after midnight and we would be arriving in Atlanta early, but as usual, nervous energy twisted my stomach into knots.

Sliding into what reminded me of a buff-colored leather recliner, I pulled out my notebook to start a to-do list. The top of the list? *Do not get arrested.* That seemed obvious, but I scrawled it out anyway. *Find picture of Matt. Get dark hair dye. Buy new bras. Call in sick. Change Matt back.* If I had time, *Get refill for birth control pills.*

I needed to move calling my boss higher on the list since I wasn't going to show up at work looking like *this*. I ran a hand through my tangled mass of cherry Kool-Aid hair. At that point, I wasn't sure if I had a job at all. Especially if the police had already been there. My head pounded just thinking about it. With my aching head resting against the seat, I listened to the drone of the engines and drifted off.

"Ivie. Ivie, wake up." Jack's voice broke through my amazing dream.

"Jack?" Dream Jack, in his magician suit, had me bent over an airplane lavatory, slamming into me from behind. Reality Jack jostled me awake on a plane heading for a date with a lethal injection. *All things being equal, I'd rather be asleep.*

"Hey, we're almost there."

The pilot's voice came over the intercom like a bad cliché. "We're starting our approach into Atlanta's Hartsfield-Jackson Airport. The Fasten Seatbelt sign is on, so please move your seats into the upright position and remain seated until we have safely landed and taxied to the gate. We should be on the ground in ten."

Ten minutes 'til touchdown. My stomach flopped around like a carnival goldfish, and a faint prickling ran over my skin. The thought of returning to the scene of the crime gave me goose bumps. The worst part? Not knowing what waited for me back at home.

Matt panted at my feet but I found it hard to drum up any sympathy for him. It was his fault we were in that mess in the first place.

My stomach plummeted along with the plane's descent, my knuckles whitening from my death grip on the armrests as we dropped toward the runway. The heavy thump of rubber hitting asphalt, along with the resulting shriek of wind as the spoilers flew up to slow our approach, sent my heart careening into my throat.

I tried to calm my racing pulse by combing my fingers through my hair and tucking it behind my ears. Then my shaky hands struggled to straighten my clothes. *One should always look her best when walking into a firing squad.*

Jack grabbed my hand, lacing our fingers together, and brought it to his lips for a quick kiss. "Time to go." His gentle touch calmed me.

"No turning back now." I blew out a breath.

He smiled and leaned in to nuzzle my neck. "I'll be right beside you the whole time."

"Okay, kids. Everybody out of the boat." Jon's voice shattered our moment. He pulled his bags from the overhead compartment. "Chloe, what the hell do you have in here?" He strained to lift Chloe's bag with one hand.

"Oh, no, I'll take that." Chloe blushed and wrestled the handle away from him. "This is as light as I travel, I'm afraid."

Jack gripped Matt's rhinestone leash and reached out to clasp my hand.

I threw my leopard print bag over my shoulder. "I'm as ready as I'll ever be. Let's go."

The moment my shoes met the tarmac, the hair on the back of my neck stood up. A strange, unexpected aura permeated the air around me, like the shifting barometric pressure before a storm, and I didn't like it. Not one bit. I tipped my face up to the sky and closed my eyes. A heavy force pressed down on me. "Something's... off," I told Jack. "Wrong."

"Hey, look at me." I turned toward him and he smiled, squeezing my tense hand. "Everything's fine."

"No." I shook my head, fixating on the curious hum of static energy. My insides wound up like pantyhose in a dryer. I'd never had a premonition before, but without question, I was in the midst of one. "It's not."

Jon and Chloe came down the stairs arm-in-arm, oblivious to the supercharged ions. "Seriously, woman, how many pairs of shoes do you have in this bag?" Jon teased as he set down the heavy bag.

She waved him off. "Just a few." Her bright smile faltered as her eyes met mine. "What's wrong?" She swept the area with her eyes. "Ivie? What is it?"

I was detached from my surroundings, trapped in the dark aura. *Maybe I'm dreaming.* "I don't know." I cleared my throat. I didn't recognize my voice. The unfamiliar feeling had me wound up. "Someone's here. They're looking for me. I have no idea how or why, but I can *feel* them thinking about me. They have my picture..." I spun around to gape at Chloe. "The one you took of me ice skating in the park last Christmas!"

The color drained from Chloe's face. "You're scaring me. What do you mean someone's here and they have a picture I took of you?"

"Don't ask how I know, but I'm sure. They've been to my house." I shook my head to clear the cloud surrounding me. "It gets worse. They have a picture of me taken two days ago when we checked in for our flight. It's grainy but definitely me."

"Can I get my hand back?" Jack winced, and I released the stranglehold I had on him.

"Sorry." My fingers tingled as blood rushed back into them.

A frown darkened his features as he scanned the area. "If you're right, we need to get out of here."

"I guess it's a good thing I ordered a limo." Jon motioned to the black stretch SUV pulling around the back of the plane.

"Really?" Jack's lips pressed into a tight line. "A Hummer limo?"

"Thank you!" I threw my arms around Jon's neck and plastered a big sloppy kiss on his stubbly cheek.

Jon shrugged, a perma-smirk etched across his face.

The Blake brothers passed the bags to the driver as I followed Chloe and the enormous dog into the limo.

"Where to?" the driver asked.

Everyone looked at me for an answer. I didn't have one. I was just as lost as lost could be, powerful magic flowing inside me or not.

"My house," I said and leaned forward to give him the address before flopping back against the seat.

Nineteen

AT LEAST A DOZEN POLICE cars lined the airport exit ramp. That wasn't out of the ordinary for the country's busiest airport, but I just knew they were all there for me. The inexplicable sensation that had washed over me on the tarmac lingered.

"What do we do if the police are at your house?" Chloe asked, shattering my already fragile composure.

"I don't know." I stared through the blacked-out windows. "We still need to find a picture of Matt. So the gym?"

"That would be a good start." Jack squeezed my hand. "We can swing by your house first, and if it's not safe, we'll head there."

I nodded, watching the trees go by.

The ride to my house was longer than I remembered. Or maybe I was just anxious to get there. But as we approached the historic street, the prickling sensation was back.

"Wait," I said to the driver, "can you drive past the house? Go all the way to the cemetery."

Jack held my face and stared into my eyes. "What is it?"

"Trust me."

Several cars were parked outside of my house as we drove by, and I flinched away from the glass. I knew they couldn't see me, but I wasn't going to take that chance.

"Oh, shit." Chloe stared out the window. "What are we going to do?"

It was local police and a few unmarked cars, but yellow tape stretched across my front walk like a barrier. I could only imagine who was in the house.

"We're going to head to the gym," I said and turned to the driver to give him the address. I only had one chance of fixing my situation, and that meant I needed to get a picture of Matt.

Matt's office was located in a high-end gym a few miles away in the town's modern business district. I asked the driver to pull around to the side to avoid the packed parking lot. A Hummer limo would stand out, even there.

"You can't go in there," Jack said.

"I have to." I stiffened my spine, ready to argue with him. "I need that picture."

"Everyone knows what you look like. The red hair won't fool anyone. I'll go." He unbuckled and grabbed the door handle, but I pulled his hand back.

"No, wait. We have no idea who or what is waiting."

"I can go," Jon suggested.

"That's really sweet of you to offer, but you tend to draw a crowd." I thought back to the hotel lobby in Las Vegas and the crowd of people clamoring for his autograph.

Chloe gasped. "Me? You want me to go in there? Everyone knows me."

"No, you aren't going, Chloe," Jack said. "I am." Before I had a chance to argue, he put a finger to my lips. "I'm the only one who makes sense. No one knows me. I'm not a celebrity. And as far as anyone knows, I have no connection to you or Matt."

My leg bounced as I gnawed on my battered thumbnail. He had a point, as much as I hated to agree. "Okay. But you have to promise to be careful."

He smiled and kissed the tip of my nose. "Of course."

"You need to go to the chiropractic office. Matt has photos of himself hanging in the waiting area—several of them. It doesn't matter which one you grab. Just don't get caught."

"I won't." He reached for the door handle, and I yanked him back to smash my lips against his.

"Be careful."

He nodded and kissed me again then got out of the limo and disappeared around the side of the building.

My pulse jumped the minute I lost sight of him. Every possible scenario imaginable ran through my head. Several minutes ticked by, and Jack had yet to appear.

"He's been gone too long," I said.

"It hasn't been that long, Ivie," Jon assured me. "He's probably just being careful. The guy was an Eagle Scout."

"Oh, my God!" Chloe blurted, stopping my heart for a split second. "What if you did away with every picture of Matt, even the ones here?"

"Don't even say that." I shuddered. I'd already thought of that. What if I *had* banished every picture ever taken of Matt? What would I do?

"There he is." Jon pointed to the lanky figure coming around the side of the building.

"Oh, thank God." I clutched my chest.

Jack climbed into the Hummer and slammed the door. "Got it. We need to get Ivie out of here fast. There's a cop talking to a redhead in the lobby outside Matt's office, and I overheard him mention Vegas and your new hair color. They know you're back in town with a blond woman and a couple of handsome guys."

"Handsome guys, huh? You got all that while you were in there?" I asked.

"The receptionist likes to talk." He flashed that cheeky grin of his.

"That's not *all* the receptionist likes to do," I snapped.

Jack tipped my chin up to look me in the eyes. "Do I sense a green streak forming in that stunning red hair of yours?"

"Do I have a reason to have a green streak, Houdini?"

"Not a single one." He kissed my parted lips then pulled away. "But we really need to go."

The driver put the limo into gear just as I heard sirens in the distance.

"Tell me that isn't what I think it is," Jon said.

"Gah!" Chloe screamed. "The police."

"Shit, I was afraid the receptionist recognized me." Jack pushed a hand through his hair.

"Ginger," I said through clenched teeth. *Perfect.*

"How did they know who you were?" Chloe perched on her knees to peer out the back window.

"They had a stack of pictures from the airport," Jack said.

Stupid clown hair.

Matt growled and battered the inside of the windows with his nails. I could only imagine what he must have thought.

"Matt, shut up," I yelled.

The wail of the sirens grew louder. The jig, as they say, was up. I thought my heart had come to a standstill.

"Ivie, what are you going to do?" Chloe shook my arm.

My eyes squeezed shut as I concentrated on breathing. *In... Out. In... Out.* With each breath, I tried to shoot sparks from my fingertips like some cartoon witch, but I had nothing. Even if I had a jolt of energy building somewhere down deep, it wouldn't be enough to take out the approaching black-and-whites.

"Ivie, get out of the car." Jack opened the door and thrust a folded-up photo and his cell phone at me. "Head for the woods. They can't hold us on anything. I'll call you as soon as it's safe."

"I can't leave you." My attention shifted between the three of them and the dog.

"Go." He shoved me, and I stumbled out of the limo. "Before the cops get close and it's too late."

After one last glance at Jack's face, I ran as fast as I could for the safety of the tree line. From my spot behind a gnarled oak, I watched the limo pull around the corner. They hadn't even made it out of the lot before the police surrounded them. My pulse thundered in my ears as an officer rapped against the glass and the limo driver rolled down the window.

Before long, my friends filed out and lay face down on the pavement. A policeman struggled with Matt's flimsy leash until it broke, and Matt launched himself in my direction. He took long, bounding strides as he closed the distance between us. The police gave chase, and I knew I needed to disappear before Matt led them to my hiding place.

In a state of panic, I ran through the woods with Jack's cell phone clutched in my hands like a life preserver. I had no idea where I was going or where I would end up. My brain conjured up horrible images of Jack, Chloe, and Jon carted off in handcuffs and locked in cold, dark prison cells with overflowing toilets and real murderers.

I braced myself against a tree, panting as I caught my breath and listening for footsteps or the dog's deep bellow.

I didn't realize I'd dialed my mother's number until I heard her cheery voice. "Hello?"

I'd forgotten how much I missed the sound of it. "Mom?" I blinked back tears.

"Yes?" she asked.

"It's me, Ivie."

"Well, of course it's you, Ivie." She chuckled. "I only have one daughter."

"Mom, I need your help. My friends have been arrested."

"My goodness, dear. What on earth did they do to get arrested?"

"It's a long story."

I paced the sticky floor of the ladies' restroom at a Chevron gas station on the outskirts of town. The smell of vomit and other bodily fluids permeated the small space, and I poked my head out of the door for a lungful of fresh air. It felt as if days had passed since I'd wandered through the woods to the wild side of town to wait for my mother. I peeked at the time on Jack's phone.

She's late.

How long could it take to bail three people and one dog out of the city jail? *What if something went wrong?* My stomach clenched. It should have been me.

Headlights blinded me as I strained to see down the road in either direction. Several cars pulled up to the pump, but I didn't recognize any of them. I kept looking for the Stepford wife with the silver pixie, but Mom never came.

I let the door fall shut and tucked myself into the corner to wait. What else could I do?

A woman staggered through the door and stopped to gawk at me before locking herself in a stall. Apparently, she didn't notice she looked like an extra on *The Walking Dead.*

Mom couldn't get there fast enough.

Crinkling plastic and coins falling against tile drew my attention away from the door.

"Ivie!"

My head snapped up and tears welled in my eyes. "You're here."

"You look terrible, dear. Red is not a good color on you." She pulled me into a hug. "Did you get one of those

Wonderbras? You're too petite for such a large bosom. I can barely get my arms around you."

"Oh, Mom." I sucked in a deep breath laced with Chanel No. 5 and felt the tension roll out of me. "I'm better now that you're here. Thank you."

"Of course." She released me and shook her head. "I just don't understand how all this happened."

"Not here." I glanced around me, forcing a stiff smile for the woman coming out of the only working stall. "Did you get them?"

"Oh, yes, dear." She smiled and patted my hand. "They're waiting for you outside."

"Good, let's go."

With another cautious scan of the area, I followed my mother out into the dark parking lot. I spotted the group hovering around her ancient Wagoneer, and my heart picked up a new rhythm. Tucking my arm under hers, I pulled her across the pavement.

Jack darted over, meeting me in the middle, and enveloped me in a tight embrace. Tears pricked at my eyes, and I wiped them away.

"Thank God you're safe." Jack kissed the top of my head. "I was so worried."

I melted into his warmth. "I was afraid we wouldn't be able to get you out. I didn't know what to do."

"You did it. You got us out. And I'd do it all over again to keep you safe."

I climbed Jack like a beanstalk, crashing my lips against his without a thought of where we were. I didn't care that we were standing under a streetlight in a public place with God and everyone else watching. I needed his touch.

"*Knock, knock,* Bonnie and Clyde?" Chloe tapped on my shoulder. "Can we get out of here?"

I glanced around. Other than our little group, the street was deserted, but Chloe was right. We shouldn't take any chances.

"Yeah, babe," Jon said. "I already reserved a suite nearby."

I leaned into Jack as we walked to my mother's station wagon then froze—something was missing. "Where's Matt?"

"The police say he's missing," my mother whispered as she climbed behind the wheel. She had no idea.

I stood my ground outside in the cold, staring at the three of them. "Chloe?"

My best friend chewed on the inside of her cheek then stole a peek at Jack.

"Jack? Where's Matt?"

Jack opened his mouth then shut it quickly. They were hiding something.

Jon stepped forward. "He's at the pound."

Twenty

I PACED THE FLOOR OF JON'S hotel suite, certain I'd worn a trail in the vanilla carpet. The room's understated elegance made it the nicest hotel room I had ever been in, bar none. But I couldn't find it in me to care that the sheets had a thread count higher than the national debt. Or that the marble floors in the bathroom were heated. I didn't have the luxury to enjoy the... *luxury.*

I was officially the only suspect in Matt's disappearance, but up until a few hours ago, he wasn't even missing. At some point, they would find me, and I would go to jail—directly to jail, do not pass Go, do not collect two hundred dollars—for his murder. It didn't matter that he wasn't dead.

I imagined rotting away in a prison cell while the man who'd broken my heart and destroyed my life ended up with a new name like Marmaduke or Hamlet and spent his days lounging on embroidered pillows and dining on raw sirloin. At least I could hope they'd neuter him. Either way, I was screwed.

"What are we going to do?" I asked no one in particular.

No one replied.

"Jack?"

He flashed me a weak smile from across the room then glanced at my mother and shrugged.

Chicken. Not that I blamed him. I wanted no part of explaining the situation to my mom. I mean, where would I begin?

Hey Mom, my fiancé dumped me, so I turned him into a skunk, then a rat, then a snake, then a couple of dogs—one at a time. The police think I killed him. He's locked up in the pound where he'll probably be put to sleep, and I'll most likely get the death penalty. Oh, and I've been having smoking hot sex with this delicious magician I just met. You know, the chicken *across the room?*

Yeah, that would go over well. I still hadn't told her I'd lost my virginity. Then again, that experience hadn't been overly memorable. It happened on prom night in the backseat of a banana-yellow 1976 Cutlass Supreme and lasted less than three minutes, most of that time spent hiking my dress up around my waist. Not at all like the last time I had sex in a car.

I wouldn't mind a repeat of that.

"Ivie, sit." My mother pointed to the cherry armchair beside her. "It's hardly your fault Matt went missing. Didn't you say he left you for an aerobics instructor?"

"Yes, but that ho—errr—home-wrecker is saying he's missing, and she thinks I killed him."

"That's crazy. He has to be somewhere."

"Oh, he's somewhere all right. He's in the pound," Chloe mumbled.

My mother's eyes got big, and her hand shot up to cover her mouth. "He's in the *ground*? You *buried* him?"

"She didn't say he was in the ground." I glared at Chloe. "I didn't kill him *or* bury him. He's perfectly fine. He just isn't himself anymore." I bit my lip and tried to find the right words. "Matt's a dog."

"Well, I should say so. Leaving you for another woman? Sleeping around the way he did? To think I've had him to dinner at my home. I even gave him one of your father's watches. I may have to ask for that back."

"No, ugh, you don't understand. He's actually a dog. A Great Dane. He was..." I stopped myself from running through the list of animals. "It really doesn't matter; he's a

Great Dane now. I don't know exactly how this happened, but it seems as if I might be a... a witch." I winced, waiting for my mother's reaction.

But she didn't react. Not the way I expected anyway. Her lack of reaction was a little anticlimactic, but at the same time, I felt something brewing under the surface. Just when I'd thought she'd gone into shock, Mom blinked several times.

"Mom? Are you okay?" I snapped my fingers. "Are you having a heart attack?"

She shook her head and opened her mouth only to close it again. She stood up as if she was leaving the room but turned around and sat down again. "He's actually a dog? You mean eating kibble, barking at strangers, and lifting his leg on trees?" Her voice was hollow, strange. It scared me. It was too much for her sixty-year-old heart to bear.

I swallowed hard. "He squats actually. But even as a man he sat down to pee."

In my peripheral vision, I caught Jack's expression as he fought back a smile.

Mom nodded toward Jack. "And how do you know this young man?"

"Jack? He's a magician, but he doesn't do real magic. His brother is a famous magician." I motioned to Jon, lying across the bed and flipping through a room service menu.

He lifted his head and gave my mom a poster-worthy grin.

"He's on TV. You've probably seen him."

When my mother didn't seem to recognize him, Jon frowned and went back to his menu.

"We thought he could help us, but it turns out he's just a better magician. He still doesn't do actual magic. He's with Chloe. It's a long story." I stumbled over the words, twisting the bottom of my shirt in my hands. My throat constricted when my mother opened her mouth and closed it again. "Are you okay, Mom? I know this is a lot to take in. I wouldn't have told you at all if it wasn't for the predicament I'm in right now."

"I was afraid something like this would happen. You were always such a curious child," she mumbled, playing with the clasp on her bag. "I told your father, God rest his soul, to do something about it, but he wouldn't listen." She looked up at me, beaming. "You were the light of his life. He wouldn't have any of it. I do wish he was here right now."

"Mom, when you say curious, what exactly do you mean? Are we talking 'filled with curiosity' or Wednesday Addams? And what do you mean you told my father—"

"Well, I guess that's that." My mother waved me off as she stood and smoothed the wrinkles in her light blue pantsuit. Her transformation from PTA to CEO was astonishing. She sucked in a deep breath and cleared her throat. "You're going to need the spell book."

"You'll need a gram or two of the nectar of the aconitum plant." Mom looked into my confused face and smiled. "Wolfsbane, dear. It wouldn't hurt to toss in a dash of thornapple just to be doubly sure. It's not really in season, but I'm sure we can make do." She stared off into space and tapped her lips. "It's imperative you add something of Matt's like a lock of hair, maybe a bit of blood. Both would be ideal. You'd be surprised how much is left on a razor or a hairbrush. Men always seem to cut themselves while shaving." She chuckled. "Even stray toenail clippings would do."

I put my hand over my mouth to hold back the gas station burrito I'd eaten for dinner.

"Don't make that face. If they came from him, they'll help. Collect everything as quickly as possible, but you won't be able to do the spell until the day after tomorrow.

You can only work this sort of magic during a dark moon."
Mom spoke as if she was rattling off a grocery list.

Someone had pressed the pause button on my life. No one in the room as much as exhaled. We stood there, mouths hanging open like fish on display in a market.

"Don't just stand there. Let's go." Mom clapped, and the room came to life again.

I stared at my mother with fresh eyes. "You're a-a-a witch?" How did I know so little about the woman who'd given birth to me?

"Oh no, dear, not me. And neither are you." She laughed with a dismissive wave. "Heavens, that's funny. Thank goodness your father never heard you say that."

She was clearly in denial. Had we not just established something wicked this way comes? "Then how do you know all of this stuff? Plants and spells, and did you say something about a book?"

"Well, dear, I was married to a sorcerer for almost thirty years. I was bound to pick up a few things."

"But you just said I'm not—"

"I said you aren't a witch. Witch is such an ugly word. You're a sorceress. You come from a long line of sorcerers on your father's side. My side comes from Denmark."

I'm a sorceress? From a long line of sorcerers? "I think I'm going to be sick." Or faint. Maybe both.

"Take a deep breath, dear."

I fell into the chair Mom had vacated and fanned myself with both hands.

Jack kneeled beside me and smoothed my hair out of my face. "Are you okay?"

"No..." I shook my head then bent down to rest it against my knees. "Definitely not okay. I need a glass of water. With ice. Go ahead and pour some whiskey in it. In fact, forget about the water and just pour the whiskey."

No one moved.

"I'm serious! Raid the mini-bar."

"Oh, no, you don't." My mother bumped Jack out of the way. "You need your wits about you. We need to get straight to work. You said Jack here is a magician? We could use a good magician."

"I'm not a good magician." Jack laughed then cleared his throat. "I just do some fairly simple illusions."

"Hmmm... But you like my daughter. That's not an illusion, is it?" Mom narrowed her eyes and tapped her lips.

"Mom!" I buried my face in my hands, smothering a groan. "Please, don't go there."

"A mother knows these things. I don't need a Magic Eight Ball to see this young man fancies you." She patted Jack's shoulder, and I felt myself flush all the way to my hairline. I had a sudden urge to head to the gallows— or whatever the execution du jour happened to be these days—in Salem.

Jack slid his hand under my chin and lifted my head, forcing me to face him. "I do fancy your daughter." He spoke to my mother, but he looked at me. I expected him to laugh—or run—but he just gazed at me with nervous expectation, as if waiting for me to say something.

"Jack, you don't have to—"

He pressed a finger to my lips. "I have been under your spell, Miss Ivie McKie, very literally, since the first moment I saw you." He touched his forehead to mine and lowered his voice to a whisper. "I will do whatever I can to help you change Matt back. After that, it's up to you."

"Thank you." It was all I could say without opening up the floodgates.

Mom clicked her tongue. "Can you court each other later? We have things to do."

"Okay... You'd better start at the beginning. I'm done freaking out now."

"Um, aren't you forgetting something?" Chloe raised her eyebrows and waited. When no one said anything, she snorted. "Matt? Kind of hard to change him back if he isn't here."

My mouth dropped open. How could I have forgotten? Who knew what would happen to him if we left him in county lockup.

"It's late." Jack squeezed my hand. "There's nothing we can do tonight. We'll go in the morning."

"Jack's right," Jon piped up, crawling to the edge of the bed to grab Chloe around her waist. "There's nothing we can do tonight, so come to bed." He dragged a squealing Chloe into the blankets.

"That would be my cue." My mother excused herself into the adjoining bedroom.

I couldn't argue with that. I wouldn't mind crawling into bed, but I was positive I wouldn't be able to sleep. My mind churned with new information. The desire to see my father's spell book bordered on desperate. I needed to flip through the pages to be close to him, but much like poor Matt, the book was under lock and key for the night. We had to wait until morning to retrieve it from my mother's house. In the meantime, we had to collect all of the other elements required for the spell.

"Jack, can I speak with you for a minute?" I asked, motioning toward the bathroom.

"Sure." He tugged on his shirt collar with one hand and rubbed the back of his neck with the other.

After closing the door behind us, I turned on the water.

"I don't think we should have sex," he blurted.

"I wasn't going to suggest we have sex." For the first time in days, playing "hide the peenstalk" was the last thing on my mind. "Why would you think I wanted to have sex?"

Jack ran both hands through his hair. "Well, uh, we've been having a lot of sex in random bathrooms lately."

"Oh." I bit back a grin. "I guess we have. But that's not what I wanted. I dragged you in here because I don't want anyone else to know what I'm about to do."

Jack crossed his arms and leaned against the sink. "I'm afraid to ask."

I busied myself by picking up a towel and refolding it. "I need to go to my house."

"No." He pushed away from the sink and shook his head. "Absolutely not. You can't go there now. The police have it sealed as a crime scene. Things are already bad enough."

"You heard my mother. I need to get Matt's razor and his hairbrush or anything else I can find. With things as bad as they are, I need to change Matt back as soon as possible."

"No. Jon and I can go in the morning. You need to stay here. Out of sight."

My eyes locked with his, and I clasped his hands. "What if they remove his stuff? I can't take that chance. Besides, it'll be easier to sneak in at night. I can't let another day go by, Jack. I just can't." I gave him a shaky smile. "So are you coming with me, or am I going alone?"

With a crooked grin, he shook his head. "Stubborn witch."

Sorceress.

Twenty-One

JACK CIRCLED THE NEIGHBORHOOD IN my mother's Wagoneer. I stared out the passenger window, watching for lurking police. I didn't see anything out of the ordinary. Mrs. Camp had parked her car across her driveway, but I suspected that had something to do with spying on Matt's house.

We parked at the entrance to the cemetery and walked the short distance back. Jack yanked up the zipper on his navy blue jacket and flipped the collar up to cover his ears. It wasn't much in the way of camouflage, but it would have to do. I'd dressed in the finest in cat burglar fashions—my black Ann Taylor turtleneck and jeans paired with a black windbreaker and a black knit hat I stole from the glove compartment of my mother's car.

Even from the street, the house looked desolate, as if all the life had been squeezed out of it. Bright yellow "crime scene" tape wrapped around the front like some sort of magical force field. I knew better. It was just plastic tape.

"How are we going to get in?" Jack whispered.

I stuck out my index finger and drew a giant O in the air. When he didn't seem to grasp my meaning, I repeated the gesture a few times.

Jack cocked his head and shifted his eyes between my finger and my face. "We're going in through a hole?"

I threw up my hands and shook my head. "Around the back."

His face lit up, and he made a horizontal circle with his hand. "This is 'go around the back,' not this." He mimicked my O.

I poked out my tongue at his grinning face.

"Come on, little witch." He twined his fingers with mine and gave them a squeeze. "Let's go."

Keeping our hands linked, I followed him around the garage, watching for any signs of life at old Mrs. Camp's house. I could have sworn I saw something moving in her overgrown bushes, and my heart almost stopped when I thought her garden hose was a snake. Other than that, nothing. I carefully placed my feet, trying not to make a sound as we crept around the house. Jack stepped on the leaves and mulch, and the crunching sounded much louder in the dark. Mrs. Camp was old, blind, and wore a hearing aid, but I was sure she could hear leaves crunching underfoot at thirty clicks.

"What was that?" Jack barely whispered. His breath came out in a cloud.

With a shrug, I tucked myself further into the shadows.

"We need to hurry." He tightened his hold on my hand and pulled me along in a crouch.

I exhaled once we reached the brick courtyard in the back.

The backyard looked exactly as it had the last time I'd seen it. The iron table and chairs were still hidden beneath waterproof covers, waiting for nice weather to return. More yellow tape stretched across the kitchen door and the French doors to the dining room. I wasn't worried about a little strip of plastic, but I had a better idea.

The window in the laundry room didn't have a lock. It wasn't on the alarm system, and since I'd climbed through that window countless times, I knew I could fit through the opening, even with my new bustline. As often as I'd misplaced my keys, breaking into my—or rather, Matt's house—was my specialty.

Eyes darting between Jack and the patio chairs, I contemplated my choices. Then, pointing to the window just above chest height, I motioned for Jack to give me a boost. He rocked back on his heels and gaped at me as if I'd taken off all my clothes, smothered myself in peanut butter, and invited him to join me in a devil's threesome with Jeremy Irons.

"What? I need a boost."

A light went on in his eyes, and he grinned widely. "You should never, ever give hand signals."

Jack hoisted me up, and I raised the window with a low creak. I was just about to pull myself through when I heard a rustling behind me and froze.

"What are you doing here?" Mrs. Camp's scratchy voice echoed in the night air.

My head banged against the frame as I pulled it back out of the window. "Mrs. Camp. Hi." I rubbed the bump forming on the top of my skull.

"You have a lot of nerve coming back here after what you've done. I expected you to disappear or something."

"It's not what you think. Matt isn't... He's not dead. He's just... missing."

Mrs. Camp scratched the back of her neck. She seemed to be thinking about what I'd said. "Not dead, you say?"

"Oh no, he's not dead at all." I flashed my teeth in a wide smile.

My elderly neighbor licked her cracked lips and returned my smile. "Well, then you'd better follow me. The police are coming." She turned and hurried, in a gait much quicker than I would have expected for a woman her age, across the backyard to her back door. She waved at us to follow.

Jack shook his head. "Something doesn't seem right."

"I don't know what choice we have." Jack helped me down, and we ran to catch up.

"Go now, get inside." She looked over her shoulder toward the road and held the door open. Once we were inside, she closed and locked it. "Follow me." She flipped a switch on the wall, bathing the room in harsh, flickering fluorescent light.

I didn't know what I expected to find in her kitchen, but it wasn't that. My eyes zeroed in on a stack of dingy blue bowls and silver spoons on the wood-grain laminate countertop then a dirty frying pan on the old white gas stove. A shiny brass crucifix hung over the sink and another over the cooktop. The walls were a bright lime green. The yellowed cabinets were probably original to the house, or close to it, and most likely used to be a bright white. Much like their owner's teeth, time hadn't been kind to them. Despite the disarray, the room smelled of lemon cleaner.

Mrs. Camp opened a plain wooden door, exposing a flight of stairs. "The basement. No one will find you down there."

A glance into the gloomy abyss made me shudder. I wasn't fond of basements or the dark, but I heard sirens in the distance.

"They'll be here soon." She banged on the doorframe.

"Come on, I'm right beside you." Jack grabbed my hand and led me down the steps, the wood planks groaning beneath us.

Once we were halfway down, Mrs. Camp shut the door, and I heard a click.

"What was that? Did she just lock us in?" I grabbed Jack's arm and hugged it.

"I don't know, but based on her 'no one will find you down there' comment, I wouldn't be surprised."

Jack used his cell phone to light the stairs, and we made our way to the bottom.

The cellar smelled mildewed, and the dampness coated my skin like a film. A wall of shelves lined the back wall with old boxes stacked on each one. I tried to read the scrawled lettering across their fronts, but most of it was too faded or covered with dust. I could make out "Christmas" on one and "Toys" on another. The rest were anyone's guess.

"Do you think she'll tell the police we're down here?" I asked.

"I hope not."

I nodded even though I was sure he couldn't see me.

After a few minutes of straining to make out my surroundings, I heard heavy footsteps above us. I thought I heard voices too but couldn't be sure. My heart slammed so hard against my ribcage I had trouble hearing anything else. If Jack hadn't been holding my hand, I think I would have had a full-blown meltdown even though *I* was the one with the blue-light-special weapon. All *he* had was the backlight to his cell phone to ward off the forces of evil—and spiders.

Jack shined the light up the bleak staircase, illuminating cobwebs and scratch marks. "What the hell is that crazy old lady doing?"

"I have no clue." I gave his hand a squeeze. "But I'm beginning to regret trusting her."

He clutched my hand tighter.

My body leaned into his like a magnet as I scrutinized the shadows around us. I could deal with "mysterious phantoms," but the thought of creepy crawlies dangling from the dark spaces above made me shiver as if someone had done the Monster Mash across my grave.

"Do you think we should go back up and ask—" A loud popping noise made me jump. "What was that?"

"I don't know, but it sounded like a gunshot." Jack let go of my hand and stepped toward the stairs.

The door creaked open, and a shaft of light spilled over us. "Don't get any ideas," the old woman yelled. "You won't be getting past me tonight."

"Mrs. Camp?" My voice cracked. "Why did you lock us down here?"

"I saw what you did. You aren't right. Something wrong with someone who does what you did."

"What do you mean? What did I do?" I could only imagine the number of things she may have seen me do over the past few days, Jack being one of them. I *told* Matt we needed blinds for the kitchen windows.

"I saw you turn that big snake into a dog. That's just not normal. Not something a good Christian woman does."

Jack pulled me closer to the bottom step, and I saw the barrel of a shotgun pointed at us. When Jack yanked me back, I knew he'd seen it too.

"Get back away from the steps," she yelled.

"Mrs. Camp, you can't leave us down here," I cried.

"I can't let you out to hurt nice people like Dr. Green. I don't know what you did to him, but I'm sure it wasn't right. I told the police about your black magic. They didn't believe me, but I know what I saw." She waved the gun toward the right. "You go sit on the couch until I can figure out what to do with you."

Her words bounced around inside my head.

I let Jack tow me along as he followed the narrow wash of light to an old couch resting against a moist wall. I was reluctant to sit on it. I had no idea what might be living in those cushions.

"Can you call Jon?" I whispered, straining to see him in the low light. I felt him shake his head.

"No signal down here."

A bubble of panic threatened to choke me. "We have to find a way out."

"Are these basements subterranean?"

My mind went blank, and I couldn't formulate an answer. After several seconds, he rephrased his question.

"Ivie, do you know if there is an outside entrance to this basement?"

"I-I don't remember one. I don't know for sure. What if we wait for her to fall asleep and rush the door?"

"No. We can't be sure she'll go to sleep, and we don't know if the gun is loaded. For all we know, she really has called the police. Our best bet is to find an exit down here."

Jack stumbled around in the dark while I held the phone out as a flashlight. A red light blinked on the screen.

"Oh, God... Hurry, your phone is dying."

I shined the light on stacks of boxes looming over me like a madwoman's tower. A few tattered mattresses, spattered with rusty stains, leaned against the wall. An outdated Coldspot refrigerator—the original white coated in the same yellowed layer of age as the kitchen walls—separated the two areas.

"There's a small window over here," Jack whispered. "I might be able to boost you up, and you can get out."

"I'm not leaving you!"

"What about magic? Can you try to work a spell to get us out of here?"

"I don't know. I guess I can try." My eyes fluttered closed, and I concentrated on the barely-there electric current in my fingers. "I feel something, but it's weak. I still don't know how to control this so-called power of mine."

"Come here." Jack tugged me into his arms and rested his chin on the top of my head. "We'll figure something out." He rocked us in silence before chuckling. "We could always have sex. If magic makes you horny, maybe sex would make you magical."

I pushed away from him. "Are you kidding me?"

He wrapped his arms around me again. "I've seen crazier things happen over the past few days."

I added *sex in scary basements* to the list of *crazy* and decided the idea had merit. "You're right." I shifted until I could reach the waistband of his jeans. "On a scale of Luna Lovegood to Hannibal Lecter, it barely makes the grade."

"I was joking," Jack scoffed. "We're not having sex down here."

"It's no worse than an airport restroom." I smirked, but I doubt he saw it in the dark.

"No, it's way worse."

I nudged him. "Come on. If nothing else, it would distract us from our predicament."

"I seriously doubt I could even get it up down here."

"I find that hard"—I swallowed a giggle—"um, difficult to believe."

Jack laughed. "No, it's not hard at all, sweetheart."

"I bet I can fix that." I walked my fingers down his zipper.

"*Ivie.*" His tone was a warning.

"Come on." My knuckles brushed against him. "You know you want to."

He shook his head. "You're going to kill me one of these days, woman."

"Death by orgasm doesn't sound like a bad way to go, Houdini."

Jack wrapped his fingers around my wrist and moved my hand from his groin. "How about death by tetanus?"

"Listen, if you want me to work a spell in this hellhole, you're gonna need to give me a hand."

"Fine." He placed his hands on my shoulders to steer me closer to the wall with the narrow window. "Just remember, you asked for it." His lips brushed my ear. "Close your eyes."

Before I had a chance to comply, Jack began his assault on my senses. The first touch of his tongue to the pulse point in my neck sent a shiver though me. "You're teasing me."

"For starters," Jack murmured. He kissed then suckled the spot.

I leaned into him, swallowing a moan. "Let me guess, you're doing this for the express purpose of revving up my magic?"

His mouth held fast to that point on my neck, biting then soothing the spot with his tongue. Tiny ripples of heat burst through me. With my eyes closed, I felt every thrilling sensation from the top of my head to the bottom of my curled-up toes.

He pulled his lips away with a pronounced pop then slid his hand down my arm and around my waist to crush me against his hardness. "Hey, I'm willing to take one for the team." He caressed my stomach, his fingers dipping beneath my waistband then back again. He reached a little farther each time, yet never far enough.

"Please, don't stop," I begged. "I want you."

"You've had me for longer than you know." He latched onto my earlobe, drawing it between his teeth as he hummed.

The tingles spread like champagne bubbles throughout my body. "Inside me. I need you inside me."

"You want this inside you?" Jack gripped me harder, pressing his jeans-clad erection into me. My legs shook, threatening to give out. "I'm afraid you're going to have to have patience, my little witch."

"No. No patience. Now." My hand fought its way between us, but Jack captured it before I reached the promised land. Somewhere in the back of my brain, I think I knew I'd crossed a line. I'd turned into a regular Amityville whore.

"Not now. But soon. When we're somewhere relatively safe—and clean. Somewhere I can take my time introducing my tongue to every inch of your body. You're always in such a rush. I want a build-up so slow that you shatter into a million pieces beneath me."

"This is torture." I wriggled my hips until I felt him swell against me.

He shuddered, his breath fanning over my neck. "Do you feel it?"

"I want to. Why won't you let me feel it?"

"No, not *that*." Jack groaned. "The magic. Feel it flowing through your fingers. Can you feel it?"

Just as Jack requested, I let the sensations overtake me until I tumbled over the edge in a body-wracking orgasm, the lingering heat licking at my fingertips.

He spun me around to capture my lips. Neither of us would spend any more time in that house of horrors.

"Jack." I pulled away and held up my glowing hands. "I did it."

His face split in a wide smile as he noticed the blue flickers sparking from the tips of my fingers. "Actually, I did it, but whatever gets us out of here."

Shaking my head at his smug expression, I struggled to hold the power steady. I felt as if I was gripping the reins of a wild stallion fighting as hard to pull free as I did to contain it.

Jack's mask of concentration mirrored my own. His jaw flexed, his mouth set in a firm line, and his eyes locked with mine. He smiled briefly as light arced from my body, creating a span that reached a least a foot away.

"See if you can make it bigger," he said, and I cocked an eyebrow in response. "The window, smart ass."

Wiping the grin from my lips, I faced the wall, took a deep, cleansing breath, and imagined the window yawning into a gaping mouth. It shuddered and creaked, slowly stretching. I smothered the urge to squeal as the breach reached the floor and the ground bowed down to greet us.

Jack grabbed my hand and pulled me through the makeshift door before it snapped shut again. We stood outside on the damp grass, staring up at the stars.

"Ivie, I—" Jack rubbed the back of his neck, a range of conflicting emotions flitting across his features. He studied my face then seemed to take note of our surroundings. "I think we need to get out of here."

We kept to the shadows until we hit the blacktop and then set off running. Jack fumbled with the keys, dropping them twice before unlocking the old Wagoneer.

"Go," I said as he cranked the engine.

The tires screeched as we pulled out of the cemetery lot. I watched Mrs. Camp's house, expecting to see her rush out the door after us.

"Oh my God," I said. "I can't believe that just happened."

"Which part?" Jack glanced at me. "The kidnapping or the escape?"

"Both."

He smiled as he weaved through the darkened streets toward the luxury hotel. We pulled into a neighboring parking deck, and he cut the engine. "That was amazing. I still can't believe what you did back there. The window just stretched open for us."

"I know." I struggled to catch my breath.

"You're shaking," he whispered.

I nodded, my heart sprinting.

He stared at my lips. "Are you okay?"

I nodded again, and Jack weaved his fingers into my hair and caressed the back of my neck. I resisted the urge to purr.

"Cat got your tongue?"

He had no idea how close he was. I certainly felt kittenish all of a sudden. "Weren't you scared?"

"Yes." He laughed. "I was terrified."

"I was sure she would shoot us and I would die in my crazy next-door neighbor's basement." That struck me as funny, and I laughed, vibrating the car.

"We didn't get Matt's razor," Jack said.

"I know."

"We can go back tomorrow."

My smile faded as the word *tomorrow* sank in. I didn't want to go back there ever again.

Jack leaned in, and his kiss caught me off guard. I pulled away for a second, dragging him into my seat with me. He slid his hands under me and cupped my bottom. Magic was a waste of the man's talents—though I couldn't help but appreciate his ability to make my panties disappear.

"We should go in." I sighed against his lips.

He shook his head without breaking the kiss. "Not yet."

I slid my hands under his shirt, warming my icy fingers on his hot skin. He froze, and I giggled. But his lips stopped moving, and he jerked away.

A sharp tap on the window made me jump.

"Is everything okay?" A security guard stood outside the fogged glass.

"Yes. We're fine," Jack replied.

"Ma'am? Is that right?"

I escaped Norman Bates's mother to have a random rent-a-cop arrest me in a parking garage? I think not. I let my hair fall across my face and avoided eye contact as I affected a horrible Scottish accent. "Yah. Dinna worry about me, laddie. I'm fine, thank ye kindly."

He flashed a light in my face. "You should really go inside. It's not a good idea to linger in the parking garage in the middle of the night, especially if you've been drinking." The guard double-thumped the roof of the car.

"We will. Thank you," Jack promised with a little salute, and I couldn't help but giggle at his expression. After the security guard walked away, Jack cracked up. "What the hell was that?"

I doubled over in laughter. "I thought for sure I could pull that off. Clan McKie would be so ashamed."

"Yeah, that was... awkward." He got out of the car, walked around to my side, and waited while I got out. "You should get some rest." Jack tucked loose hair behind my ear.

I knew he was right, but sleep was the last thing on my mind. "So where are we sleeping?"

"About that..." He looked down and fiddled with the keys. "I wasn't going to make assumptions. Your mother was on the pull-out when we left, and there's only one other bed in the suite. I don't mind taking the floor if sharing is too strange for you. But I figured since we've already had sex multiple times, sharing a bed wouldn't be a big deal." He flushed. "This isn't coming out the way I'd intended."

"No, I get it. This has been the most unusual week of my life, and I feel like I've known you for longer than the sum of those few bizarre days."

He beamed. "I feel that way too."

"So I would be honored to share a bed with you." My lips tipped up.

"But, sweetheart"—he winked—"I'm not having sex with you."

"The hell you're not. I plan on having my wicked way with you until dawn."

He planted an exaggerated kiss on my forehead before grabbing my hand to tug me toward the elevator. "No."

I let him tow me along. "What's with you being so chivalrous all of a sudden? This is the second time you've resisted my advances. Am I not appealing to you?"

He threw up his arms. "I'm trying to be a gentleman."

Gentleman, schmentleman. I twisted my hand out of his. "Maybe I don't want a gentleman. Did you ever think of that?"

Jack let out an exasperated sigh. "Would you please let me woo you?"

"It's a little late for wooing." Did anyone even say "wooing" anymore, let alone do it? Had I accidentally transported us into the nineteenth century? Next thing I knew, I'd be shopping for a ball gown and scoping out my dowry. "I've already given you my milk for free. You may as well take my cookies too."

"Sorry, babe." Jack caught my wrist, pulling me close until I felt his heartbeat through his shirt. "We're doing this the right way from here on out."

"What about kissing?" I blew out a breath, waving the proverbial white flag. "Will there at least be kissing?"

He leaned in, pressing his forehead to mine. "Just try to stop me."

Twenty-Two

RED STREAKS ETCHED THE MORNING sky. "Red sky at night, a sailor's delight. Red sky in the morning, a sailor's warning," as my father used to say.

Perfect.

My back creaked as I unfolded from the fetal position and stretched. I'd slept with Jack wrapped around me all night. It was both the best and worst sleep of my life.

Despite my best attempts at seduction, Jack refused to have sex with me. I wondered if my ego would ever recover from the crushing humiliation. Forget crazy neighbors, lethal injections, and the gallows. Giving up sex cold turkey, after I'd discovered how much I like it, might be the death of me.

Jack shifted in his sleep and sprawled across the rumpled sheets, monopolizing the bed. He looked magically delicious in nothing but a pair of blue plaid boxers and a day's growth of stubble, his hair even messier than normal.

"At least he let me have the extra pillow." I snorted, pulling it from under his leg. After punching the feather stuffing a few times, I shoved the pillow behind my head and stared at the popcorn ceiling.

What I wouldn't give for a class filled with screaming five-year-olds and a leisurely day on the farm. Instead, I could look forward to the next task on my long list of criminal activities—springing my not-so-great Dane from animal services. I still hadn't decided exactly how that would go down.

I rolled over to look at the clock. It was 8:05, and the shelter didn't open for another hour.

Jack threw his arm over my midsection, and I squirmed at his touch. "So much for not making any moves," I said.

"Who's making a move?" he asked in a sleepy voice.

"Oh, I don't know." I plucked his hand from my stomach and sandwiched it between my thighs. "There's no time like the present."

He popped one eye open to glare at me, taking his hand from between my legs. "*Ivie.*"

"Fine." I crossed my arms over my barely-there tank top.

He snuggled in closer, rubbing his light stubble against my bare shoulder. "Don't be mad."

"Call me crazy, but this feels an awful lot like a move." I wiggled my hips, settling against him.

Jack shook the bed with his laughter. "I'm not making a move. I promise."

"Who's not making a move?" Chloe chimed from the doorway. She wore Jon's black button-down and little else. "Well? Who's not making a move in here?"

I groaned. "Put on some clothes."

Jack rolled away from me to glare at her. "Yeah, Chloe, unless you're planning on joining us, you need to get dressed."

I whirled around on Jack, mouth agape. "Why would you even go there?"

Jack shrugged. "I'm a guy. I will always go there."

Chloe waved. "Please, I'm not here for the entertainment. And for the record, there's nothing wrong with what I'm wearing. I'll have you know this is Armani."

I responded by putting the hijacked pillow over my face.

"But enough about *my* clothes. Why are the both of *you* still dressed?"

"Because," I said, from my hiding spot, "Jack doesn't want me anymore."

Chloe snatched the pillow from my face and threw it at Jack. "Are you kidding me? Look at her? I don't swing that way, but if I did, I'd want her."

"Hey, I never said I didn't want her." Jack turned to me. "That's crazy talk! If we weren't taking a step back to do this the right way, I'd show you exactly how much I still want you." He gave me a quick kiss then went back to addressing Chloe. "Don't mind Ivie. She had a bad night."

"You're both weird." Chloe laughed and sat on the edge of the bed. "Other than a wicked case of cock blocking, what happened last night that was so terrible?"

"For starters, Mrs. Camp tried to kill us," I said.

Chloe gasped. "You mean the feline-o-phobe?"

"That's the one," I said, pointing at Chloe with one hand and my nose with the other. "Jack and I tried to sneak into Matt's house to get supplies for the spell, and she caught us. Then she tricked us into going into her house and locked us in the basement."

"Oh my God, that's insane. I can't believe she locked you in her basement." Chloe threw her head back and cackled. "Did you find any bodies down there? Hansel and Gretel, maybe?"

Visions of spider webs and fingernail scratches in the cracked drywall flooded back to me, and I shuddered. "I'm glad you can laugh about it. I could have been burned at the stake by that crazy old witch." I giggled. "Or bitch maybe? Since apparently I'm the only witch around here." I had no idea why I found it funny that my neighbor kidnapped me and probably planned to kill me. Who knows what she would have done, given the opportunity.

"Don't let your mom hear you using the W-word. She might revoke your subscription to *Good Spellkeeping*." Chloe shook a finger at me with a mock glare before laughing again. "I can't believe you tried to sneak into the house. Did it ever occur to you to tell anyone about your ridiculous idea *before* setting out in the middle of the night? And you..." Chloe glared daggers at Jack. "I thought you'd have more sense than to let her walk into a trap."

Jack shrugged. "It didn't sound like a bad idea at the time. Then again, my brain has been a little deprived of blood lately."

Chloe shook her head. "Don't encourage her. You know damn well it sounded like a foolish idea the moment you heard it. You're a fool for love who can't say no."

"Shut up." I shoved Chloe off the bed. "Trust me, he says no. Far too often for my taste." I gave Jack the evil eye.

"Stop thinking about sex." Chloe ripped the blankets from my grasp. "We need to spring that big jerk from dog jail."

Jack smirked.

"Does anyone have a plan?" I asked.

Chloe winked. "You're the planner. I'm just the window dressing, remember?"

"No plan. We're just gonna wing it," Jack said.

Chloe rolled her eyes. "Cuz that's worked out so well for us."

My mother sat in the driver's seat of her car with a pen, ready to take notes. "Tell me again what I'm supposed to say."

"Mom, you can't read off a napkin in there. You know that, right?" I struggled to keep my voice from climbing up another octave.

"Well, of course. I'm just going to write it down so I can practice."

Chloe snatched the pen from Mom's fingers. "No time for practice, Rose." She tossed it at me in the backseat. "Just remember in here." She tapped my mother's head.

"I see. Well then, what should I say when I get in there?" Mom asked again.

"You want to tell them your dog was picked up yesterday," I said.

"Ask if you can look for him. They should take you back to where the dogs are kept," Jack said before taking a big bite out of his hamburger.

Jon reached over to steal one of my fries and Jack slapped his hand.

"Hey, sorry." Jon held up his hands. "She wasn't eating them."

"It's fine. I'm not really hungry," I said.

Chloe snatched my bag. "Have you ever stuck your fries in a vanilla milkshake?" She pulled an ice cream-coated fry out of her shake and popped it in her mouth. "Delicious."

"Can we concentrate on the task at hand, please?" I asked.

"Sure, sure, sorry," Chloe said with a smile. "Go ahead."

"Mom, do you understand what you need to do?"

"Yes, dear. I think so."

"Okay, good." I faced Chloe. "Are you going to be able to do this? I mean seriously, you're acting like a teenager today." I glanced at the fries she was dipping into her shake.

She rolled her eyes. "I've got this. Have you forgotten who you're talking to?"

Chloe could finesse people better than anyone I knew. She was a healthy dose of magic away from being a witch herself. But then again, what beautiful woman isn't? She taught me everything I knew.

"Fine. Are you ready?" I asked.

"Ready," they said together. Mom and Chloe got out of the Wagoneer.

"Wait." I tossed the red nylon leash to Chloe. "You might need that."

"Just might?" She laughed and slammed the door.

I hated sending them in there to do what I should have been doing.

"It's not safe for you to go," Jack said.

"Reading my mind again?" I gave him a halfhearted smile.

"Just your face." He rubbed the spot between my brows. "They'll be fine."

"I know. I just..."

Jack put a finger over my lips. "Just nothing. They'll be fine."

I gave him a stiff nod and settled back against the seat to wait.

Jon cleared his throat. "Are you going to...?"

"Take them." Jack shoved the fries into his brother's chest.

I fidgeted with a loose thread on my sweater as I stared out the back window. Time seemed to drag, and I couldn't sit still. No one went in or out of the building while I watched for Chloe or Mom to step out with Matt on the red leash. I had no idea what was going on in there. I tried to concentrate on the atmosphere to see if I could sense anything, but I couldn't.

A few more minutes passed, and I saw my mother walking out with Chloe trailing her, carrying the red leash.

I threw the back door open and jumped out of the car. "What happened? Where is he?"

"Ivie, get in the car," Jack pleaded, tugging me into my seat.

"Oh, those people." My mother's face was pinched. She stomped over to the car and got into the driver's seat. "They wouldn't let us have him."

"What? Why not?" I shouted.

"They said something about him being part of an ongoing investigation," Mom said.

Chloe hopped into the front seat and slammed her door. "Oh, you're going to love this. Matt is officially evidence."

"Evidence?" Jack asked.

"Yep. In an ongoing murder investigation." Chloe's face was wild with disbelief.

Jack scratched his head. "What kind of evidence?"

"I've seen *CSI* enough times to guess," Chloe said. "Isn't it always DNA?"

"Well, of course he'd have Ivie's DNA on him," Jack said.

We all stared at each other.

I covered my face with my hands. "This is bad. How am I going to change him back if he's evidence?" I barely noticed Jack pull my hands away from my face. "If he's evidence, they must think they have proof I killed him. Oh, this is very, very bad."

"It's not that bad," Jack said.

Of course it was that bad. If I couldn't change Matt back, not only would they lock me up for killing him, they were going to use *him* to prove I did it!

Chloe waggled her fingers in front of her. "You're going to have to go in there with your crystal-blue persuasion and bring him out."

"I think she can do it," Jack said. "You should have seen her stretch that window open in the crazy lady's basement."

My mother twisted to face me. "What were you doing in a crazy lady's basement, dear?"

I bit my lip. "Don't worry about it, Mom."

"So what's the plan?" Jon asked, stuffing his face with the rest of the fries.

"How many people did you see in there?" Jack asked.

"I think three." Chloe counted on her fingers. "No, four."

"That seems about right," my mother agreed.

"Okay, were you able to get in the back to see Matt?"

Chloe nodded as my mother spoke. "Yes, he was back there. Once we said he was the dog we were picking up, they told us we couldn't have him."

"He's in the back with all the other dogs?" I asked. "They aren't keeping him separate?"

"No. He's in the back," Chloe said. "Probably trying to spell out *help* in his kibble."

"Good." Jack nodded. "We just need to create a diversion." He looked at Jon. "It just so happens we have the perfect person for that."

Jon smiled widely. "Finally, something fun."

Twenty-Three

"WHOSE BRIGHT IDEA WAS THIS?" I wondered.

"Yours," Chloe reminded me, tugging the baseball cap down over my eyes. "I can't get any more of your neon hair under this stupid hat. That is the most ridiculous shade of red I've ever seen."

"I think it's lovely. It reminds me of your father," Mom said.

"Dad didn't have red hair."

"Not usually, no. But when he worked a lot of spells, it would turn. I swear we spent enough money on hair dye to own stock in Clairol."

"Great." I pushed a loose strand of hair under the hat. "That's just what I wanted to hear. I'm doomed to look like a comic book character for the rest of my life."

Jack chuckled and took Chloe's place in front of me to zip up my blue windbreaker. I was glad I couldn't see myself in a mirror. "Are you sure you want to do this?" Jack bent down and looked me in the eyes.

"No, but I have to do it anyway."

"Let's go." Jon grabbed my hand and tugged me toward the concrete block building.

Jack followed close behind.

"Wait, I need a minute." I pulled my hand away from Jon and my eyes flitted between the Blake brothers and the building looming in front of us.

Jack took a cautious step toward me. "Take as long as you need."

"We don't have time for this," Jon said, backing up toward the entrance. "It's show time." In two long strides, Jon reached the door. With a wink, he yanked it open and disappeared inside.

Jack clasped my hands and gave them a squeeze. "Are you ready?"

Taking a deep breath, I gave him a quick nod and let him tow me around the side of the building.

I searched for any clues that would confirm we were in the right place. The cinderblock construction didn't allow for any windows in the back, but the presence of chain-link dog runs told me that was the most likely spot. "Here?"

"It seems as good a place as any." Jack shrugged, his lips tugging up to a half smile. He leaned in to give me a searing kiss before stepping clear of my eye line.

My eyes closed with a flutter, and I extended my fingers as I concentrated on the block wall. "Umm..." Licking my lips, I turned to take one last look at Jack. "I'm going to be super horny when I get done here."

Jack laughed. "I have no doubt."

"Well, just keep that in mind when I jump you later."

"I will." He winked.

Putting on my serious face, I went back to the task at hand, drawing energy from everything around me. My thoughts skipped between the block wall and the memory of Jack's hands caressing every inch of my body. The stretchy band of my power tugged within me, straining against my natural inclination to suppress it. "Let go," I whispered and exhaled slowly.

"I see it, Ivie. The blue light." Jack spoke almost reverently as the current sparked from my fingertips.

"I feel it," I said.

"You can do it. Try to create a door in the wall."

Just as I had in Mrs. Camp's basement, I imagined the wall opening. My mind conjured a heavy door as the heat pushed out from my fingers, curling and wrapping around the imaginary handle.

"I don't know what you're doing, but keep doing it," Jack whispered. "The wall is shimmering in and out of focus."

Jack's voice buoyed me as I worked my magic. "Open." I exhaled a breath and felt the band tighten before going completely limp. I blinked a few times at the new entrance before me. "Holy..."

"You did it." Jack wrapped his arms around me from behind. "Now, let's get in there before someone catches us."

With a quick nod, I grasped Jack's hand and let him lead me into the building. A cacophony of barking greeted us.

"This is an interesting development," Jack said, staring at the locked kennel door in front of us.

We'd somehow managed to enter one of the stalls and were caged just as securely as the dogs around us.

"Hey, buddy. We're not going to hurt you." Jack spoke softly to the frightened dog in the kennel with us before turning his attention to me. "Do you think you can pick the lock with your blue light special?"

With a tight smile, I nodded. "I think I can pull that off without any trouble." *Famous last words.* I pushed the tingling toward the lock, manipulating it until I heard the telltale click. "Got it!" Beaming at Jack, I gave the door a push.

Three things happened at the same time:

The door to the cage we stood in swung wide with a creak.

The doors on every other kennel—including Matt's padlocked cell—opened in sync.

At least twenty-five dogs of various sizes, including my wayward fiancé, rushed out of their enclosures, knocking me over as they made a mad dash for the opening behind me.

"Oh no!" I squealed as Jack spewed a string of obscenities.

"Can you do some hocus pocus to get them back in their pens while I grab the Dane so we can get the hell out of here?" Jack asked.

"Sure," I deadpanned. "I'll just wave my fingers and everything will go back to normal."

Jack blinked at me, his face scrunched up in a pained expression. "Right. Let's just grab Matt and get out of here before we get arrested again."

"Good plan."

The sound of keys rattling in a lock followed by a rush of air at my back froze me in place. My pulse thundered in my ears, almost drowning out the soft squishing of rubber-soled shoes behind me.

"What in the H. E. double hockey sticks is going on in here?"

Slowly, I turned to face a strapping young guy in a county uniform carrying a basket full of kittens. He came to a screeching halt, close enough I could smell the sour litter between their furry little toes. The heat was still sparking in my fingers, but I wasn't about to turn my blue light on helpless kitties.

My eyes shot up to meet his as a slow smile eased across my face. "Hi."

Kitten Guy stared at me with his mouth slightly gaping. His breath didn't smell much better than the litter. "Peggy, get in here!"

I tugged the hat a little farther over my face and took a few measured steps backward toward Jack. My eyes darted to Jack's, and I easily read the panic there.

"Can we help you?" a voice from behind Kitten Guy asked. "What on earth..." I guessed "Peggy" was surveying the situation.

"Oh, I was just looking for a dog." I tilted my head down to hide my face, keeping my eyes glued on the basket of fur in front of me.

"Well, you should have checked in at the desk," she scoffed. "People can't just be comin' back here by themselves. How did you get in here, anyway?"

"She's with me." Jon said from behind Peggy, and I couldn't help but let out a sigh of relief.

"She's with you? How did she get back here? I didn't see her come in with you."

"You were too focused on my stacked deck... of cards, I mean." I looked up and saw Jon beam at Peggy. Her eyes glazed over. The Amazing Jonathan Blake was nothing if not captivating. Jon pushed past her, snaked his arm around my shoulders, and pulled me against him. "My sister."

"Your sister?"

Jon leaned toward Peggy. "Yeah... Poor kid's not right in the head."

"Oh." The woman nodded as if that simple sentence made perfect sense.

"Okay, *sis*, you should go back to the car with Mom while I take care of things." Jon winked at me.

"Umm... okay." My eyes flashed to Jack again, still unnoticed in all the commotion. He had Matt's collar and was dragging him out through the new door in the wall. He gave a quick nod then flashed me a crooked grin.

I turned back toward Jon and the confused animal services employees. I guessed the new plan was for me to go out through the front door. My hand had barely touched the handle when I heard Jon call me back.

"Hey, sis..."

Careful not to look directly at any of them, I spun to face Jon.

"Thank the nice people for letting you play with their dogs."

I had to hold back a laugh. He spoke to me as if I had a screw loose, and he wasn't that far off if my whole plan was any indication. We had gone totally off script, and I had no idea what the new plan was.

"Thank you." I bent my fingers in a pathetic little wave. "Okay, bye."

Without looking back, I made my way to the exit, ignoring the strange looks from the other people in the lobby. I hoped Jon would be close behind. I heard Peggy and Kitten Guy shouting at the loose animals, trying to corral them back into their cages, and I almost felt bad. *Almost.*

The brisk outside air hit me in the face, jolting me out of my trance, and I sprinted toward the car, scanning the area for any sign of Jack or Matt.

"Oh, thank God." Chloe pulled me into the backseat with both hands. "Where's Jon? What happened in there?"

"Where's Jack?"

"Isn't he still inside?" she asked.

"No!" I shrieked. "He went out the back before I left. He should be here." I tried to push past Chloe to extract myself from the vehicle to look for my missing magician. I couldn't bear for anything to happen to him because of me.

"You can't go back there. Be patient. They'll get out," Mom said.

"How?" I asked, crawling to the opposite side of the seat. "How can you be so sure they haven't already been caught?"

My fingers almost curled around the door handle before it was yanked open from the outside. "Miss me?"

"Jack!" Launching myself at him, I wrapped my limbs around him like a vine and crashed my lips into his in a heated kiss. A throat cleared behind me, and I pulled away, hiding my face in his chest. "I thought something happened to you."

"Nope, I'm fine." He kissed the top of my head then popped open the hatch to load Matt in the back. "Your ex just *had* to take a leak at every bush between the building and here."

Chloe poked my arm. "We don't really have time to catch up out here. Jack, do you know what happened to Jon? As far as I can tell, he hasn't come out yet."

Jack didn't respond, but the look on his face told me we were in trouble. "Start the car." Jack pushed me into the back seat.

"What? What's wrong? Is it Jon?" Chloe asked.

Jack slammed the door and hopped into the front. "Go. Drive," he barked, and my mother obeyed.

"Wait!" Chloe cried, pressing her hands to the glass. "We can't leave him."

"We can't stay here. Look." Jack tipped his head toward two police cruisers. "Cops."

"Oh my God. What if they arrest him?" Chloe said.

"He's the Amazing Jonathan Blake; he'll talk himself out of it."

Chloe narrowed her eyes at Jack.

"Don't worry." Jack's expression contradicted his words. "What would they charge him with? He was in plain view of employees the entire time. He had nothing to do with the chaos inside the building. Worst case scenario, he gets arrested and we bail him out again."

"Every single thing that has happened in the past few days has been 'worst case scenario,'" Chloe said, echoing my thoughts.

"Well, I guess we'd better hit the ATM."

Twenty-Four

"REALLY, LITTLE BROTHER? YOU JUST drive off and leave me there? I swear to God, if I see my face on TMZ tonight—" Jon climbed into the Wagoneer, wheezing as he brushed muddy paw prints from his jeans and adjusted his zipper.

We'd picked him up twelve blocks from the animal services building. He was out of breath, slick with sweat, and had been running like a kid who had just knocked over a candy store.

"Collateral damage," Jack said, his face devoid of emotion.

"Collateral damage?" Jon echoed, the same inscrutable look on his face.

Jack nodded. "That's what I said."

Jon blinked at his brother's serious expression. "You left me there to fend off at least two bitches in heat—not to mention several overexcited dogs. I'm lucky I got away with my damn pants. Did you see that crazy old chick, Patsy?"

"Peggy," I said.

"Peggy, Patsy, whatever. The woman was all over me, that's all I know. Christ." He blew out a breath, and we all broke into hysterics. "Don't laugh! I'm not kidding. When she realized my ride had bailed on me, she tried to lure me into her car and practically shoved her mangled, arthritic hand down my pants." Jon grimaced at Jack, holding his hand up like a claw. "Dude, I swear, she's older than Grandma Carol."

"You would have done the same thing if it had been me in there," Jack said.

"No way, not true." Jon shook his head. "I would never violate the bro-code."

"What about the time we *borrowed* Dad's car and went for a joyride down by—"

Jon barked out a loud laugh. "Don't even go there."

"My point exactly." Jack smirked.

Chloe poked Jon's arm. "What are you two going on about?"

"Nothing," they said at the same time.

"Well, good," I said. "We don't have time for a walk down memory lane. We still have to go back to the house to get something of Matt's."

"No." Jack shook his head.

"Jack, I have to." My hand slipped into his. "The spell won't work without it."

"*Ivie...*" Jack looked as if he was in pain. "It's too dangerous. Have you forgotten what happened last time?"

"No, I haven't forgotten. But this time we have Jon, Chloe, and even Mom. We're not going in there on our own. Someone can keep watch."

"Fine. You can keep watch while someone else goes in."

"Jack, no, that's completely ridic—"

"I'll go," Chloe said.

I spun around to stare at my friend. "What?"

"I said I'll go. I mean, I'm the most familiar with your house. I know where Dr. Doggybreath keeps his stuff, and we both know you don't want your mom to accidentally run across your vibrator."

"Chloe!" I choked on my saliva as she giggled.

"Vibrator?" Jon sat forward in his seat. "Now we're talking."

When I groaned, Jack leaned in, whispering against my hair, "We will be revisiting this later."

I changed the subject. "You'll need to find his hairbrush, toothbrush, or his razor."

"Toenail clippings would be ideal," my mother added as if she hadn't heard a word of the previous discussion.

"Forget that. I'm not digging around the trash for someone's nasty toe clippings."

"They just seem to work better in—"

"Forget it, Rose. A hairbrush I'll do. Even a razor. But"— Chloe's face scrunched up in disgust—"I'm not touching his toenail clippings. I love you, Ivie, I really do. But even I have my limits."

"Fine. Get a hairbrush," Mom said. "But make sure it has plenty of hair in it."

"What about this one?" Chloe asked thirty-five minutes later as she shoved a bright pink razor into my hands.

I screwed up my face and stared at her. "Does this look like something Matt would use?"

Chloe shrugged. "What do I know about Dr. Doolittle and his grooming habits?"

After picking through the items in front of me, I turned to Chloe. "None of this stuff belongs to Matt. I told you he was packing his bags just before..." I wiggled my nose. "Did you look for that?"

"I didn't find a bag. Haven't the police been through the whole house? Maybe they took his stuff. Hey, what about these?" Chloe pinched the waistband of a pair of red Betty Boop boxers.

"He never wore them."

Chloe smiled. "Sweet, then I'll keep them."

"I'm going to need to go in myself."

Jack grabbed my upper arm, sending a shiver of need through me. "It's a bad idea."

"Then you tell me what I should do."

"I'll go," Jack said with an air of finality.

"You just want to dig for buried treasures." Chloe waggled her eyebrows, and I felt a blush creeping up my chest.

"He doesn't even know what he's looking for." I stuffed the items Chloe had salvaged back into the black garbage bag before turning to Jack. "If it makes you feel better, you can go with me."

"I don't like it, but I guess we don't have a choice. Someone needs to distract the crazy lady next door before we go anywhere though."

"I'll do it," my mother said. "I'll pretend to be a Jehovah's Witness or something. Who would be suspicious of a sweet old church lady?"

"Wait, so 'Mrs. Kravitz' doesn't know what your mother looks like?" Jon asked.

"Well, if my daughter had ever bothered to invite me over, she might." Mom glared in my direction. "But in this case, that does seem to work to our advantage."

Jack gave half a shrug as my mother climbed out of the front seat and made her way to Mrs. Camp's door, mumbling the entire way.

"Okay, let's go." Jack hopped out of the car, pulling me with him, and we slunk around the house. "This time, let's not get caught, okay?"

"Deal." I stuck my hand out for him to shake, but he grabbed it and pulled me in for a quick kiss, stoking the flame I struggled to suppress. "Hey there, Houdini, I warned you earlier. Don't start something you can't finish."

His lips quirked into a crooked grin, and he gave me another quick peck. "Later."

After I'd climbed in through the laundry room window, I let Jack in the back door. We set out on a quest to find the missing piece of our magical puzzle.

"What about this pair of Converse sneakers?" he asked.

"Oh, gross. Matt's basketball shoes. I can smell them from over here. They're probably teeming with his essence."

"Well?"

My shoulders pushed up. "I'm not sure if sweat counts, but go ahead and throw them by the door. They can be our last resort."

Jack nodded and tossed the Chucks toward the door. "It doesn't look like anyone actually lived in this house." Jack opened the refrigerator. "I mean, look at the stuff in here. Did he seriously organize his food by color?"

I shrugged. "Matt was always a bit anal, I guess."

"An asshole, you mean?"

"Right."

We both laughed.

"What did you ever see in this guy, anyway?"

As I watched Jack glide around the kitchen, tugging drawers and cabinets open, I asked myself the same question. The way Jack's long fingers curved around the door handles, his lean muscles bunching across his back and upper arms as he pushed and pulled made my mouth water. *I could just eat him up.*

Nothing about Matt had ever elicited the same visceral response in me.

"Jack?" I sidled up behind him and stepped out of my jeans, leaving me in nothing but white lace panties and a chunky blue sweater. "What are you looking for?"

"Uh, I'm not sure. Just snooping, I guess." He chuckled but continued to flip through the Rolodex cataloguing Matt's wine collection. "Maybe I'm channeling Chloe."

"I have a better idea." I walked my fingers up his back until both hands rested on his shoulders.

"Hmm?" He shuddered.

I leaned in until my lips brushed his ear. "Let's get naked."

Jack spun around, and his eyes panned down my body to my bare legs. "Ivie, we—"

"Please, don't tell me we can't." My fingers coiled around his forearm. "Just let go."

His Adam's apple bobbed. "You're only saying this because you've been working magic. It's like you're doped up on some sort of magical Viagra."

My hand slid down his side and brushed across his hip to cup the bulge pressing against his zipper. "It feels pretty real to me. I'm almost positive I'd want you even if I hadn't been working spells."

Jack grabbed my wrist, slowing my ministrations but not stopping them. "You don't know that."

"No, I guess I don't. But I know I like you. Even when I'm *not* doped up on magical Viagra."

"We should be looking for something of Matt's." He stepped away, effectively detaching my hand from his body.

"It can wait for just a few minutes. Come on…" I stepped forward, closing the gap between us. "Have meaningful sex with me."

He laughed. "You know, it should really take us a lot longer than a few minutes to have meaningful sex. I mean, it would if you'd ever let me take my time."

"Next time." I brushed my lips against the shell of his ear. "I promise I'll let you take your time next time. This time, for old time's sake, let's go hard and fast."

"I should say no." He nuzzled my shoulder before lifting his face to meet my eyes. "I should run in the other direction, but I don't think I can. You've bewitched me, Ivie McKie."

"I put a spell on you." I slid my hands up his chest.

Jack's voice dropped an octave. "Because I'm yours."

My thighs clenched at his eager tone. *Damn right, he's mine.* "So you're saying yes?" My heartbeat picked up at the prospect of getting some action. All it took was a single look from Jack to put me on the edge of an orgasm.

"I guess I am."

My lips tipped up slowly, and I clutched the front of his shirt with both hands. One hard yank sent his buttons clattering across the floor. "Mmm... much better." A naked Jack was a good Jack.

Jack's breathing picked up, but he stood still, as if in shock. I took advantage of his stunned silence and lifted the hem of my sweater, tugging it over my head and dropping it beside me.

He groaned. "No bra?"

"Nope." I flashed him a cheeky grin. Who would have guessed getting such a positive reaction would become addictive?

Jack growled, grabbed the back of my head, and pulled me in to capture my lips. His warm chest pressed against mine.

"I want you."

"I thought we'd established that." Jack smirked, his long fingers slipping under the waistband of my panties and into my slick heat. "God, you're so wet."

My responding moan spurred him on as two fingers slid into me. I purred, grinding against his hand. "Take me."

My impatience took over and I went to work, forcing the button on his jeans through the eye then skating the zipper down as I walked him backward toward the stairs. When his heels hit the first step, he sat, pulling me down with him. He lay fully prone against the stairs and I was lying on top of him, my hand shoved into his pants, stroking his hardness.

"Does that feel good?" *Like silk over steel.*

"Straddle me," he hissed, gritting his teeth as my fingers curled around his length to free him from the confines of his jeans.

With a leg on either side of his hips, I rocked against his hardness. "Are you grinding your teeth?"

"Maybe." He kissed across my shoulder and pushed my panties aside. He positioned himself at my entrance, then in one smooth movement, he plunged into me. "You're making me crazy, and I'm trying not to lose it."

"Matt used to grind his teeth."

"Christ," Jack grunted, thrusting his hips in a jagged rhythm. "Can we not talk about your ex while I'm inside you?"

"No. Wait." I froze. "Matt used to *grind his teeth* as in grinding his teeth in his sleep. He used a night guard. He kept it in the drawer of his nightstand!"

Jack's hips pivoted as he tried to maintain the friction between us. "Can this discussion wait just a few minutes?"

"No, you don't understand." I threw my leg over and dismounted him, then pulled myself to standing as Jack crumpled.

"No, I guess I don't." He banged his head against a step, over and over again, with a resounding thud.

"His night guard would have his saliva in it." I took the stairs two at a time. "That would work for the spell."

The bedroom was in worse condition than when I left it. Dresser drawers were upended, the contents spilled over the floor. Photos were missing from frames. The clothes Matt had been wearing when I turned him were no longer where I'd left them. In their place were our pillows.

I crawled across the mattress to Matt's side, digging through the nightstand, looking for the clear plastic case holding his night guard.

"Did you find it?" Jack stepped up behind me, fully dressed, and tossed my clothes on the bed beside me.

"Yes!" I squealed, holding up the case. "We've got it. The last piece of the puzzle. Now where were we?" I reached for him.

Jack laughed. "Ah, no. Sorry. Moment lost." He wrapped his arms around my shoulders and kissed my temple. "Let's get out of here so you can change him back."

Twenty-Five

"THROW THE MOUTHPIECE INTO THE pot, dear. We'll boil it down with an ounce or two of Scotch." Mom pulled a bottle of Macallan from an upper shelf and blew off the layer of dust. "Your father was a huge proponent of using a good single malt in all of his spells. I can't say whether it does any good on its own, but if you drink a shot or two beforehand, it does seem to calm the nerves." She elbowed me in the side.

Mom uncorked the bottle and I pulled in a deep breath, savoring the aroma. It brought back memories of my father.

"He used to put a dab behind his ears," Mom echoed my thought. "He often said it was the only cologne he'd ever wear."

"I remember." My fingers skimmed over the cool bottle. "I always think of Dad when I smell Scotch. Even the cheap stuff."

"Oh, your father would have never touched the cheap stuff." She laughed then got quiet for a moment. "Could you grab the herbs, dear?"

I walked across the brightly lit space to collect the filled jars she'd pulled down from the shelves earlier. The faded labels bore the names of different herbs, and I consulted my father's messy script on the recipe card.

It had been years since I'd been down in my mother's basement. As a child, I was terrified of the dark corners and thick cobwebs. That room, the one filled with jars of potions and nectars, always seemed to have the most cobwebs and dust. As I stood there, reading dusty labels, I still found it hard to believe the room had been under a concealment spell my entire life. Instead of dark corners and webs, I discovered only a light coat of dust on the shelves, dozens of ornate bottles and potted herbs, windows that let the light in, and a shiny wood floor. Only after Mom had invited me in could I see the wonder of it all.

"So you think we have what we need to make the potion?" I leaned against the heavy walnut counter and watched Mom stir a heaping cup of Scotch into the pot.

"Oh, I'm sure of it. Saliva, even dried saliva, is better than nail clippings or hair. I would have mentioned it, but you have no idea how difficult it is to come by. The residual spit left on a toothbrush is usually rinsed off every time you use it."

How my mother knew so much about casting a spell to transform an animal back into a human was a mystery I wasn't sure I wanted to solve. But I itched to ask how she managed to keep a garden of poisonous plants a secret from her homeowner's association.

"So where do you get something like this?" I dumped the contents of the jars on the counter and pinched a sprig of wolfsbane, careful to touch the smallest surface area possible. "And this?" I flicked the spiny fruit of the thornapple plant.

"Oh, dear." She fanned herself with her hand. "We've been growing those since you were a baby. Most of the plants are heirloom varieties your father brought over from Scotland. He was the one with the green thumb, but I felt I owed it to him to keep up with it after..."

My head bobbed as my thoughts went back to my father. I wished I'd known that part of him while he was alive. "I'm guessing Dad didn't blow up in his lab during an experiment."

Mom grimaced and shook her head.

"What really happened?"

"Oh, Ivie, it's so complicated."

"Mom, please, I need to know."

"Do you remember the party with the spotted pony—your twelfth birthday?" I nodded, and she went on. "After everyone went home, your father locked himself in his lab to work on a spell. He'd already accomplished the spotted pony and the perfect weather, so I had no idea what else he needed."

I remembered my father tinkering around in his lab for hours on end. He'd get that wild look in his eyes and forget the rest of the world even existed. Too bad his wife and daughter were part of that world.

"Did you do spells with him?"

"Not usually, no. There were the odd few where he needed to borrow some energy, much like you've done with your magician. But for the most part, he did magic alone. He said it was therapeutic. Some men watch porn; your father worked spells. I wasn't complaining... if you know what I mean." She waggled her eyebrows.

"God, Mom, I don't need to know this part."

She flashed a knowing smile. "Don't pretend you haven't enjoyed the benefits of the magic. I may be old, but I'm not dead."

Doing my best to ignore her insinuations, I pushed forward. "So you weren't there when... when it happened?"

"No, unfortunately, I wasn't. I was in the garden, harvesting our newest crop of foxglove. Your father had such a fondness for the pink ones." She patted my hand. "But when I came back inside, I heard him cry out. Oh, Ivie, it was the most horrible sound I'd ever heard. It started out almost human, if not a bit distressed, but soon, it was unrecognizable. Most definitely not a human howl." Her eyes drifted shut and a deep shudder went through her. "Your father's spell had gone very wrong. I'm not sure what was supposed to happen, but I'm certain he wasn't trying to transform himself into a large red Irish wolfhound. The dog even had tips of gray, just like your father."

My eyes went wide. "A dog? Dad turned himself into a dog?"

"He would have laughed at the irony, I'm sure. Angus hated when people assumed he was from Ireland, and he was stuck in the form of an Irish hound. If you ask me, that was what he got for drinking so much Guinness. It would have been funny if I hadn't been so completely terrified."

I knew my mouth was hanging open, but I couldn't seem to close it.

"He tried to help me, bless his little heart, but I just didn't have it in me to work magic. He would bark out answers to my questions, using his paws and his muzzle to point things out. I almost felt like I was playing a strange game of charades. We even pulled out the Scrabble tiles. It worked. For almost eleven years, mind you." She shook her head.

I remembered when Dad died. It had been a difficult time for me. I'd lost him as I was dealing with puberty and trying to find my way in the world. But I always had that dog. He made me feel as if my father was still there, somehow. *Go figure.*

My mother told me we took the dog in to help ease us through our grief. He never left my mother's side. He slept in her bed. She even called the dog Angus. I always found it a bit disturbing. Now I understood.

"You never told me," I muttered.

"What would I have said? 'Ivie, your father didn't really die. He turned into a dog.' They would have locked me up!" She cackled. "No, I couldn't do that. I had to provide for my child. I had to protect my husband. He was almost completely helpless in his new form. The most difficult part of the whole thing was telling everyone he'd died. I had no body. No proof of any sort. We went so far as to stage an explosion in his lab at the university. Goodness, that wasn't the easiest thing to do. Your father had to work an elaborate cloaking spell to pull it off—"

"Wait! Dad could work magic? With paws?"

Mom nodded. "I have no idea how, but thank goodness he did, or I might have been in the same position you are now. I wouldn't have been able to do anything about it though. Your father helped me write this spell." She pointed to the almost illegible words on the card. "It's specifically designed to turn a dog back into a man. He couldn't work the spell himself, and I didn't have the craft in me. I was unable to do anything more than read the words and mix the potion. It takes a powerful sorcerer to work this magic. He never asked, but I knew he wanted me to have you try. He believed you could change him back, but I refused to bring my only child into a world that took her father from me. You understand, don't you? I just couldn't let the craft tear you from me too." She dabbed at the tears forming in her blue eyes. "I know he would be so proud of you. You're easily as powerful as he was."

"What happened to him?" I whispered.

"He vanished one day. Ran off, I guess. I suppose his time had come. The lifespan of a dog is only a fraction of a man's. I never saw him again." Her eyes welled up, and she gripped my hands hard enough to leave bruises. Her face morphed into a fierce expression. "But not to worry. That won't happen again. I won't allow it. You *will* be able to change Matt back. I have no doubt."

"Hello? Anybody home?" Chloe's voice echoed down the stairs.

"Down here," I shouted. "We're prepping the potion."

Chloe's denim-clad legs caught my eye as she descended the stairs. "Ivie, I need to talk to you in private. Hurry, before Jack comes down."

"What?" *Before Jack comes down?* "Why so secretive?" I wondered if we were about to dig up some deep, dark Blake family skeletons or something.

Chloe dragged me into a dark corner of the basement. "You're not going to believe this." She shot a glance over her shoulder. "When was the last time you spoke with Helena?"

"Not since the field trip."

"You haven't checked your messages?"

"No. Why?"

"Listen to this." Chloe pulled out her cell phone and pressed a few buttons then shoved the phone to my ear. "Just listen."

I recognized the voice right away. "Hi, Chloe? This is Helena Ferrell. We met at the Christmas party last year. I work with Ivie. I hope it's okay for me to call you. She had you listed on her emergency contacts. Anyway, I haven't been able to reach her. Is she all right? I've left several messages, but she hasn't returned them. It's really important that I get a hold of her. Just have her call me, okay?"

The message cut off, and I looked at Chloe. "I wonder what she wants."

"I'm way ahead of you." Chloe punched another number into her phone and held it up to my ear with a shrug. "I hacked your voice mail."

I scowled at her until Helena's voice came through the line again. "Goat girl! You didn't come to work today. You all right? You should have dragged your ass in. You got a special phone call. Sexy veterinarian, Dr. Doggy Style, called to see if you were okay. He even left his number for you. He sounded very worried. Well, I didn't talk to him myself, but Mrs. Cooper in the office said he sounded concerned. He wanted to speak with you, but you know her. She wouldn't give out your name or number. I guess he asked for the beautiful teacher accosted by a farm animal on the field trip. Anywho, you need to call him." Helena rattled off the phone number. "You'd better dish the deets to me later. Talk to you soon!"

"The vet left his phone number for me?" My voice came out in a squeak. "Talk about horrible timing."

She grinned. "Two guys head over heels for you? What a terrible dilemma to have."

I turned just in time to see the Blake brothers saunter down the stairs, a big ball of black fur clutched in Jack's arms.

"Karma!" I hurried to Jack's side to pat the scruffy cat's head. "You brought him."

"I told you I would." Jack leaned in to give me a quick kiss then barked out a laugh. "It's a good thing I did, too. He'd shredded my new sheets. Like he was dead set against me ever sleeping in my bed again."

"Bad kitty," I scolded.

The cat jumped out of Jack's arms and rushed toward my mother.

"Well, hello, kitty." Mom bent down to stroke his fur.

"How long before the potion is ready?" Jon asked.

"Once it's mixed up, we need to let it steam until the liquid is all but burned off. It needs to be more of a powder," Mom said. "We'll let it sit until tomorrow night. Ivie can't work the spell until then anyway. She needs to wait for the dark moon."

Jon looked at his watch. "Tomorrow night? That's Halloween. I was hoping to get back to Vegas before then."

"What's the rush, brother?" Jack asked, and we both eyed Chloe. She put on a brave face, but I could tell she was heartbroken at the idea of Jon leaving.

"My job, man. Halloween is a big deal. If I don't get back, they'll get one of those fucking new guys to take my place. Dude, you don't know how it is in showbiz. In the big leagues, you disappear for longer than a few days and they forget your name."

"Maybe we don't have to wait until night." I turned to my mother. "What about sunset?"

"Well, I suppose so." She stroked Karma's fur absently. "There's nothing that says the spell has to take place at midnight."

"Great. It's settled. As soon as the sun goes down, we'll change him back."

"Oh, not here," Mom said.

"What do you mean, not here?" I asked.

"Well, we have to change him back in the same place you changed him originally."

My mouth fell open, and I stared wordlessly at my mother for at least a full minute.

"Didn't I mention that?"

"No, Mom, you did not mention that."

"That would have been good to know, Mrs. McKie," Jack said, pulling my frozen body against his. "Sneaking back in the house with Scooby Doo just might draw attention to us."

"How are we supposed to get inside in broad daylight without getting caught, on Halloween no less?" Chloe asked.

Pushing away from the counter, I pulled myself up to my full height. My lips curved up as an idea struck me.

Twenty-Six

KAY, CHLOE, YOU'RE IN CHARGE of Halloween shopping. We'll all need costumes, but remember, the more discreet the better."

Her eyes lit up. "Oh, I know just the thing."

"No hooker-wear, please. We're not going to a party. We're trying to come in under the radar."

Her face fell, and she blew out a breath. "Fine. Then can I bring Jon with me? With only one shopping day left, the stores may be pretty picked over. I could use his help."

"That's probably a good idea." Jack wrapped his arms around me from behind and rested his chin on top of my head. "It won't look as conspicuous if two of you are buying up all the costumes. Too bad we can't swing by Vlad's Castle and clean out my trunk."

"No." I turned in his arms. "They know who you are now. They may have someone watching your house or even the club."

"You're right." He kissed my temple as I checked costumes off my to-do list. Then he took his warmth with him as he walked over to Chloe and Jon, rattling off suggestions as they headed for the stairs.

"What about me, dear?" Mom perched on the corner of the threadbare red and green plaid sofa that had occupied the family room in what seemed like another lifetime. Karma stretched across her lap as she stroked his fur. "What can I do to help?"

"You've already done so much. The potion is cooling. I've written the spell out using Dad's original as a guide. I stuffed the duffel bags you gave me with everything I could think of to bring. I think I'm good." I blinked against the urge to cry. "Without you, I wouldn't have had a clue what I was doing."

"Oh, that's what mothers are for, dear. But if you're sure you don't need me, maybe I'll just take Kitty here and we'll go pick him up some treats. Would you like that?" She smiled at my cat, and he nuzzled her cheek.

"Rose, we can ride together." Chloe paused with the toe of her black patent-leather Louboutin resting on the bottom step. "The pet store might have something we can toss over Dr. Doggybreath since *he's* a fugitive from justice now, too."

I shot Chloe a scowl. "Thanks."

Her little-girl laugh bounced off the concrete walls as she ascended the stairs, my mom close on her heels. "Hey, what are friends for, right?"

I waited until I heard the front door close. "Are we really alone?"

"We are. Amazing, isn't it?" Jack's arms came around me as he tucked my head under his chin and rocked us from side to side. "This may be the last quiet we get for a while."

"Whatever shall we do?" I giggled.

"I can think of a few things." Jack's lips whispered through my hair.

"Don't tell me: Parcheesi, Monopoly, or chess?"

"Sure. I might even have a few moves I could show you."

"Chess moves?"

"Why not? My, um, *bishop* might enjoy taking your, uh, *queen*."

"Why, Jackson Blake, if I'm not mistaken, it sounds like you're flirting with me."

Jack's mouth found its way to my ear. "You're definitely not mistaken, Miss McKie."

"I don't suppose you'd like to see my old childhood bedroom."

"Hmmm." His fingertips teased the hem of my ivory cashmere sweater as he raised it to expose my stomach. "I would actually love to see your old bedroom."

A slow grin lit my face. "Follow me."

With our fingers linked and butterflies in my stomach, I led Jack to my former room. I stood at the threshold, contemplating what it meant to have him there, and shrugged off my adolescent insecurities. I turned the knob and pushed the door open. The faint scent of Love's Baby Soft lotion and Lemon Pledge wafted out.

"So how many boys have entered the inner sanctum?" he asked, taking in the bubblegum-pink walls—lined with a border of light-purple coneflowers—that hadn't changed since I was six.

I squeezed his hand. "You're the first."

He glanced at me then the bed. "Is it crazy that I'm honored to be the first?"

"No." I beamed. "Not crazy."

Jack may not have been the first guy I'd slept with—heaven knew I'd dated in college—but despite the time I'd spent engaged to Matt, Jack was the first man to truly breach the walls of my heart.

No longer interested in the dated décor, Jack scooped me up, carried me to the double bed, and tossed me onto the fluffy white comforter. He followed me down and stretched out beside me on our own personal cloud.

"You're so beautiful." He leaned in to brush his lips against mine.

Beautiful? My hand flew up to my flaming tangles. *Would he even give the* real *me a second glance?*

"It doesn't matter what color it is." He extricated my fingers from my hair and pressed our joined hands against his chest. "Can you feel what you're doing to me? Not just my body—my heart. You've woven your way under my skin, and it had absolutely nothing to do with magic."

His hand shook, and I felt his pulse racing in time with mine. For the first time since we'd started... whatever it was we were involved in, I felt the weight of the intimacy between us. As I gazed into his eyes, I knew he felt it too. Things had just gotten serious.

I opened my mouth to speak, but he stopped me with his lips, his body pressing me into the soft mattress.

"I want you, Jack. So much." I clutched at him, trying to convey the feelings I couldn't express. I may not have been able to *say* those words, but I could show him how I felt.

"Stop." He grasped my hands in one of his, dragging them over my head to pin me to the bed. "Listen here, little witch, I get to be in charge this time." He pressed a firm kiss to my throat, nibbling the fragile skin as he spoke. "Let me take care of you for a change."

A tremor ran through me, and Jack's free hand snaked under my sweater, caressing the skin low on my stomach before he worked his way up my body, rubbing circles with his thumb as he inched toward my breasts. "Is that a yes?"

I whimpered, and I gave him a shaky nod. I had no idea giving in could be such delicious torture.

He pushed the cashmere until it bunched under my chest and the downy fibers tickled my ribs. I writhed against the fluffy comforter and Jack smirked, never removing his lips from their path across my jaw and down my neck. "Where are those handcuffs when I need them?"

The idle threat in his honeyed voice had me squirming, my thighs clenching and unclenching as I tried in vain to satisfy my aching need. "You're killing me." My breath came out in shallow gasps as he continued his assault on my senses. His kisses turned to nibbles and licks as he worked his way back to my lips.

"I did promise to take my time." He pulled away, releasing my hands, and I lifted my head for him to pull the sweater the rest of the way off and toss it behind him.

"I think these"—his hot breath fanned over my bare chest—"have finally stabilized. And at the perfect size, I might add."

His gaze seared my skin like a caress, and I worried my lip between my teeth. "What if they go back to the way they were?"

Jack kept his eyes on mine as he ran his tongue across my puckered nipple before sucking it and releasing it with a pop. "Then that would be the perfect size. I don't think you get it. It's you I want, not just your random body parts." He licked his lips then kissed me again before switching sides and teasing my other peak until I almost begged him to stop.

"Jack, please." I wriggled as he slunk down my body, my skin pebbling everywhere he touched.

"Patience, my little witch," he said against my stomach. "I told you I'm taking it slow this time."

Slow. If only we could draw it out forever.

Jack kissed down my torso, and my body vibrated with anticipation. Making quick work of my button and zipper, he flashed a lazy grin and curled his fingers around my waistband. He yanked my pants down and away, like a magician pulling a tablecloth from under a full dinner service.

My tongue darted out to moisten my lips, tasting the three little words I'd said at least a thousand times—but never to someone so worthy—as they threatened to tumble out. The connection I felt to the man above me was nothing I'd experienced before, and it terrified and excited me.

"My turn," I whispered, slipping buttons through holes to open his indigo shirt.

My trembling hands slid over his chest, edging closer to his fly, pausing at the brass buttons before working to free his straining erection.

Jack stilled, his mouth curved into a teasing smile as I writhed beneath him, willing him to touch me. His long fingers twitched as they hovered above my hips and the hem of my white lace panties before hooking under the elastic and dragging them down my legs.

"I've wanted to do this since the first time I saw you." Jack drank in my body, causing the ache between my thighs to throb as he kissed from my ankle to my knee.

I let out a shaky laugh. "This isn't the first time we've done this."

His mouth paused halfway to my hip. "Oh, yes..." He resumed his path, lighting little fires as he climbed toward the promised land. "Actually, it is."

My body shuddered when he reached my center, his hot breath fanning across my sensitive skin as his mouth worked its magic. It was official; the guy was trying to kill me. My limbs had turned to Jell-O and my heart hammered out a tune that sounded suspiciously like "Magic Man."

"Going... to make... me faint..." I panted as wave after wave of pleasure crashed over me.

Jack smirked at me from between my legs. "Don't worry, I know CPR."

I gripped his hair in both hands, dragging him up until our noses were practically touching. "Make love to me, Houdini."

He nodded. The man didn't need to be told twice.

Jack rested on his elbows as he cupped my face, and his lips captured mine in a dizzying kiss. Snaking a hand between us, he lined himself up, and with one deep thrust, he buried himself inside me. "Open your eyes."

My eyelids fluttered open, and I locked my gaze with his.

He held perfectly still, giving my body a moment to adjust to his size before rocking into me. Each plunge stretched me further. I loved how he filled me and his weight as he moved above me. With each stroke, the muscles in his back bunched and contracted beneath my palms.

"So beautiful," he murmured, tangling his fingers in my hair and closing the distance between us to press his lips to mine.

I'd never felt so close to another person. Our bodies were entwined, our tongues tangled, our breath shared. But it was more than purely physical. My heart had matched his rhythm, my blood pumping in time with his, and I never wanted to let go of the connection.

I broke free, my lungs screaming for air. "Jack... I-I..." I dove back into the kiss to keep from saying the words.

He groaned into my mouth, a bead of sweat rolling down his forehead as he picked up the pace. "Shhh... just feel me."

What had started as a faint prickle along my skin erupted into a massive chain reaction of fireworks spreading throughout my body. The current spiked, making every nerve ending tingle and my fingers glow. I was close... so close.

"Let go," he whispered, somehow sinking even deeper into me. "I can't hold out much longer."

I wrapped my legs around his waist, trying to keep him captive for as long as I could. "Jack..." I arched my back as pinpricks of light blurred my vision and, exactly as he'd promised, I shattered into a million pieces beneath him.

"That's it. Come for me." He growled deep in his throat, his hips grinding against mine in a furious rhythm, before his body shuddered then stilled. He didn't move for several moments, holding himself above me while his breathing slowed. He rolled over and collapsed into the pillows, hauling me into his arms. "Wow."

I couldn't agree more. I propped myself on my elbow and ran a finger down his chest through the light sheen of sweat coating his skin. My body hummed like a finely tuned engine after winning a race. If I had known that was what he meant by slow, I would have given in sooner. And often.

Jack's thumbs rubbed lazy circles on the back of my neck as he caught his breath. "That was—I can't even. Ivie, I..." He shot up from his prone position to crush his lips against mine, swallowing whatever he was about to say.

A door slammed downstairs. "We're back," Chloe yelled, her voice echoing up the steps.

I fell against the pillow and blew out a breath. "I guess this officially ends our quiet time."

Jack dropped to the mattress beside me with a groan. "Yeah, I suppose it does." He weaved his fingers into mine and brought them up to kiss each of my knuckles. "I wish we could stay like this forever."

I giggled. He'd read my mind. "Be careful what you wish for. You are talking to a witch, you know."

"So does this mean you'll take my wish under advisement?"

"Definitely."

Twenty-Seven

"YOU CAN'T SERIOUSLY EXPECT ME to wear this." Jon's eyes flitted between Chloe and me, and I couldn't help but giggle.

"Yes," Chloe said with a straight face as she watched Jon fumble with his vermillion ascot. "I do expect you to wear that. It's the perfect costume, and you're not going to ruin my theme. Don't forget your groovy hair." A grin spread across her face as she tossed him a blond wig.

"I look like the douche from that Beverly Hills reality show." Jon shook his head. "No one is going to believe I'm some twelve-year-old kid."

"Oh, come on. If anyone could pull off being a twelve-year-old, it would be you." I smirked.

Halloween had arrived, and my nerves were officially shot. Jack had taken it upon himself to massage my shoulders and whisper words of encouragement every chance he got, but nothing really helped. Seeing Jon dressed as a seventies cartoon character did the trick.

Jack bit back a laugh. "Just tell people you're taking your kids out to get candy. I'll bet there'll be so many running around no one will know who belongs to whom."

"Thanks." Jon frowned as he fiddled with the yellow hair helmet.

"Your turn, magic boy." Chloe pointed at the costume in Jack's hands then nodded toward the powder room. "No time for procrastinating. You too, Ivie."

With a shake of my head, I grabbed the bag she'd laid out for me and turned to follow Jack.

"Oh, no you don't." She shooed me in the opposite direction. "You can't be trusted in a bathroom with Jack."

I stalked off to change in the laundry room and turned the bag upside down over the dryer. "This can't be mine." My mouth hung open as I stared at the contents spread out in front of me. "She's got to be kidding."

I adjusted the rusty-brown pleated skirt that flared out from the cinched waist to just above my knee, then battled with the chunky pumpkin-colored turtleneck. The rolled neck scratched at my chin as I pulled on the matching orange knee socks and stepped into the buckled Mary Janes. With a huff, I tugged on the chestnut bobbed wig, tucking strands of my own hair underneath.

I stared at my reflection in the mirror behind the door and blew out a breath. "I'm going to need a new best friend because I'm about to murder mine."

A loud knock startled me out of my thoughts. "Well? How does it look?" Chloe asked.

"How does it look?" I yanked the door open to glare at her. "Why do *I* have to be Velma?"

Chloe was dressed as Daphne, complete with skin-tight purple mini-dress, matching go-go boots, and a long strawberry-blond wig. A bright green scarf capped off the outfit. "Because of course I'd be Daphne. I already owned the boots!" She beamed.

"Shut up." I pushed past her, biting my lip to keep from smiling.

Jack leaned against the kitchen counter wearing an exact replica of Shaggy's costume from the Scooby Doo movies—brown pants, baggy green T-shirt, and a scruffy light-brown wig. "You definitely fill out the sweater better than Velma would."

"Don't encourage her." I righted my wig before it slipped off my head.

"Oh, here. I forgot to give you these." Chloe shoved a pair of thick black-rimmed glasses into my hand. "Perfect! Where's my phone? I need a picture."

"No!" Jack, Jon, and I shouted at the same time.

Chloe poked out her bottom lip. "You're no fun. None of you."

I realized someone was missing. "Scooby Doo, where are you?" I scanned the room.

No sooner had the words passed my lips than my mother stepped around the corner dressed as a run-of-the-mill ghost. She'd draped a white sheet—most likely stolen from her bed—over her head with two holes cut out for the eyes. A resigned Matt followed along behind her.

"Mom?" I asked.

She shook her fist. "I would have gotten away with it, too, if it weren't for you meddling kids!"

Perfect.

"I can't believe I'm doing this." Jon shook his head as he fingered his red ascot and flopped onto Mom's sofa. "When you called me Thursday to say you'd found the girl of your dreams, I had no idea I'd end up trekking across the damn country to go trick-or-treating dressed like Freddie Prinze, Jr."

Jon's words played through my head. *When you called me Thursday to say you'd found the girl of your dreams. Thursday...*

Thursday? "Jack?"

He turned to me slowly, the color draining from his face. "Ivie, it's not—"

"We didn't meet until Friday, after your show. Exactly how many dream girls did you meet this week?"

"Oh, shit, this is awkward." Jon backed away, ducking behind Chloe.

Jack reached for me. "Calm down and listen to me. It's not what you—"

I stepped back. "It's not what I think? Is that what you were going to say?"

He nodded.

"How can you possibly know what I think?" I shuddered as a lick of heat stole through me.

Jack held up his hands as he inched toward me. "Please..."

"You see, what I *think* is I met this sexy magician in a club, and he tricked me into taking my clothes off in the woods. And I *think* we had earth-shattering sex, more than once. Then I *think* he convinced me he wanted something more when maybe what he really wanted was to have his Friday dream girl and eat her too."

"No!" Jack shook his head hard enough to give himself a concussion. "It isn't like that. Please let me explain—"

"Explain?" I barked out a hollow laugh. "That's funny. No, I will not let you explain. I've heard all I need to hear. I'm not listening to any more of your excuses."

Mom placed a hand on my shoulder. "Ivie, dear, you need to calm down. Your fingers are glowing."

Jack moved closer. "You're being unreasonable."

I shrugged Mom off and raised my hands.

"Jack, you'd better get back. Those things are loaded." Chloe yanked on Jack's T-shirt and he relented, mumbling obscenities as he stalked away, Jon trailing close behind. Chloe grimaced as she approached me. "Are you okay?"

"No." I sank to the floor. "I'm not okay. Not. At. All." I blinked to keep back the tears, but they came anyway. So much for meaningful relationships and trusting my instincts. From Magic Man to tragic man in record time. *Life sucks.*

"Sweetie, I think you need to hear him out."

"You can't be serious." I gaped at Chloe. Had she lost her mind? "He's just as bad as Matt."

Chloe rested her hand on my back, rubbing slow circles between my shoulder blades. "I don't think he is. I've seen the way he looks at you. You can't fake that."

I pulled up my knees and rested my cheek against them. "I don't know what to believe."

Chloe smiled. "Just think. Now that you know for certain magic is real, why not true love?"

"I wish I could believe in that. But I'm not a kid anymore. I need to face reality."

My mother bent down, dragging the sheet over her head. "Sometimes you have to take a leap, dear. Faith is a lot like magic. You have no idea how much you have until you let yourself believe in it."

I stepped back as Jack attempted to take my hand. His hot breath washing over my skin ignited a struggle within me against the invisible wall I'd constructed between us. As much as I wanted to have faith, two betrayals in one week made it tough. Especially when I had to deal with re-humanizing my not-even-most-recent ex.

"Are you ready?" Jack's voice held a note of irritation.

As if he had a right to be mad at me. *The nerve.*

With a false air of determination and a twitch of my lips, I nodded. I was far from being ready, but I didn't have time to second-guess myself. The sun would be down in fewer than thirty minutes.

He mirrored my expression. "I don't want to put any more pressure on you, but we're all waiting for you to let us in. Your mom has the potion and the spell. I gave Matt a few Benadryl. Not enough to knock him out, but enough to keep him calm."

"What about—"

"Karma's with your mom."

My head bobbed a few times as I let everything sink in. Matt's fate was up to me. "Okay. I guess we're all set."

"Yep. All set." Jack leaned down but backed off when I flinched away. "Damn it, if you'd just give me a chance to—"

"Let's get this show on the road, okay?" Forcing myself to be indifferent to his pained expression, I tossed my Coke-bottle glasses aside and threw a leg over the windowsill to climb in. I snagged the hem of my sweater on the hardware and fell into the room as I wriggled myself free. "Gah!"

"Are you okay?" Jack whispered through the opening.

"I'm fine." I winced. "But you'd better not have looked up my skirt."

That was the absolute last time I'd break and enter to get into Matt's house. If Mom had told me we'd be coming back, I would have left the damn door unlocked. But no, she'd kept that little bit of info to herself.

"Hurry and open the door," he barked before disappearing from view.

With a groan, I pulled myself up, dusted off my skirt, and went to the kitchen to let them in. We clung to each other as if we were marching to our doom and made our way up the stairs to what was once my bedroom.

The horrid skunk smell lingered, and I held my breath as much as possible, wondering why anyone would have closed the windows I'd left open.

"We have to form a circle," Mom said. She released her pinched nose and reached out to each side. "Link hands. You're going to need the combined energy of your coven to work the spell."

Right.

Everyone spread out, arms outstretched, forming a loose circle with me at the center.

"Now what?" I asked.

"You're the witch," Chloe said with a twitch of her lips.

My mother cleared her throat. "Sorceress."

"Whatever." Chloe rolled her eyes.

I was a whatever. Of course I was. And I was a very powerful whatever, too. I could work that spell with my eyes closed and easily transform a dog to a man. No sweat. It was easy as pie. I kept telling myself that. Over and over again.

But I've never baked a pie in my life.

I gave a slight nod to Chloe and Jon where they stood with their fingers linked together, and they nodded back in unison. I turned to my mother, who hovered close to me. She forced a smile and gave me a quick hug before stepping back into the circle with the others, clasping Chloe's hand.

With a wistful sigh, I turned to Jack. I'd only met him a few days ago, but it felt as if we'd known each other our entire lives. In a sense, I guessed that was true since my life, as I knew it, only started the day before I met him.

But apparently, the day before he met me, he'd found his "dream girl." What did that make me? His nightmare?

I couldn't let myself think that way. We'd had sex, and he agreed to help me. It wasn't as if we'd made any promises or romantic declarations. He owed me nothing.

Jack tipped his lips in a sad smile, and I felt my cheeks burn.

No matter what I'd said, no matter how many lies I told myself, the truth was, he was part of me. I longed to have him stand beside me while I worked the spell, to twine his fingers with mine and no one else's. I wanted—no, needed—direct contact with his skin. Or at least one last kiss before he walked away.

I must have been thinking about it a little too hard because he released my mother's hand and stepped forward.

Just as I was about to apologize for using my magic on him, he whispered, "Can we pause this for just a minute? I need to talk to you in private."

"What the hell, Jack. Now is not the time," Chloe said.

Jack shot her a death glare. "Give me a break. This is important."

He had a lot of nerve, playing on my emotions at a time like that. "Um, I have way more crucial matters to deal at this moment. Either hop back into the circle or see yourself out." I couldn't afford to give in.

Jack gave a somber nod then stepped back and reached for my mother's hand. The four of them formed a circle.

Following my father's instructions, I grabbed the cloth flour sack from the table and tilted it until the mixture poured into my hand. It was more of a dry rub than a potion, but it should do the trick. I dusted my hands with the powder and sprinkled the remainder over the Great Dane, making him sneeze repeatedly.

With a deep breath, I crossed the room to the rumpled bed where the cat lay sleeping and scooped him into my arms. Anxious to move to the next step, I pulled the spell from my pocket and smoothed it out so I could read my chicken scratch. After reciting it in my head a few times, I placed my hand, palm down, on Matt's furry head.

Karma dug his nails into my sweater as I gripped him. I expected him to hiss or arch his back, squirming to escape my arms, but he held fast, a low growl emanating from his chest. Maybe he knew what was coming.

The energy surging through me would flow into him as well. He would serve as the filter, removing the impurities in my magic and sending back only pure power. Understanding that bond between us gave me a sense of comfort. It allowed me to relax, drawing strength from the dark moon.

The heat built more quickly that time, the craft rolling through me like wind charged with electricity. Light, swift, and unfettered, but still hot and thrilling. An angry tornado alive within me. But I wasn't afraid. I didn't have the rage—*or the sex*—to cloud the sensation. For the first time, I controlled the magic. I could discern every molecule, from the prickling of my fingernails growing and the sting of my hair turning a deeper shade of red to the sweet wave of blue heat surging from me. I was intimately aware of it all.

My awareness extended to those encircling me as well. Their thoughts, their fears, their hopes rested like distinct flavors along my tongue, merging into a cohesive whole, intoxicating me.

I even felt Karma's disjointed but human thoughts, as if he had placed them directly into my brain. He seemed to be obsessed with my mother rubbing his belly.

And Matt's unmistakable voice. I didn't know how I'd been unable to hear it before. The image of his face that had been lurking on the edge of the shadows for days appeared as a glistening picture in my mind, as if he were standing before me as a man rather than a dog.

The entire room belonged to me, pulled into my center, yet nothing had moved even a millimeter.

It was time.

After drawing in a slow, deep breath, I let the words roll out.

> *"There, there, my fiancé fair;*
> *This banishment was yours to bear.*
> *From skunk to rat to snake to dog;*
> *You've traveled through a magic fog.*
> *From waning moon the spell was cast,*
> *Your punishment for deeds of past.*
> *Now as the darkened moon is nigh,*
> *Above us in an autumn sky.*
> *I lift your curse and set you free*
> *To be as you were meant to be."*

A long moment passed—a cosmic pause. Then a gust of wind ruffled my hair, and a quick change in light—as if a huge candle had blown out then relit—startled me.

In the blink of an eye, the Great Dane vanished and in its place stood Matt. His dark hair, missing his signature highlights, had gained a streak of white at his temple. He looked a little disheveled, a little confused, and a whole lot naked.

"What the hell... Ivie!"

Twenty-Eight

"**I** THOUGHT YOU WERE WIPING HIS memory?" Jack whispered.

I grabbed the paper where I'd scribbled the spell and groaned, pointing to the last line. *These past three days in sacred haste/Henceforth have all since been erased.* "I forgot to say that part."

"So he remembers everything?"

"I, um, I'm not sure."

"Oh, I remember enough," Matt said. "My kitchen, Ivie? Really? That counter is Carrera marble. Do you know how porous that is? How expensive?"

Jack smirked. "Yeah, he remembers."

Mom shook a finger at Matt. "I suggest you behave yourself, Matthew Green. I won't hesitate to have my daughter change you right back into a woodland creature if you keep up with this nonsense."

Matt flinched, cupping his hands over his... manly bits.

"It's okay, Mom. I deserve it. I had no right to turn him into an animal. Even if he did behave like a dog, I shouldn't have turned him into one." I turned to Matt. "But I didn't deserve the way you treated me, and I'm not someone you want to mess with anymore."

"Can someone toss a blanket over Dr. Doolittle?" Chloe shielded her eyes with her hand. "I could have gone the rest of my life without seeing his... Scooby Snacks."

"No one said you had to look," Matt snapped.

Chloe waved her free hand in his direction. "It's not like I could have missed it. If you were anyone else, I might be impressed."

"It isn't *that* impressive," Jon mumbled in a sour tone.

Jack handed Matt a sheet, and he wrapped it around his waist.

A crash echoed up from the floor below. I spun toward the closed bedroom door, the others mirroring my stance.

"What the hell was that?" Jack asked, pushing me behind him.

Footsteps thundered up the stairs just before the door swung open with a bang. At least a hundred—okay, maybe six—uniformed S.W.A.T. officers pushed into the room, guns pointed directly at us.

"Ivie McKie," one of the men bellowed and I recoiled, my hand going up in response to my name. "You're under arrest for the disappearance of Dr. Matthew Green. You have the right to rem—"

"Hey, whoa, whoa, whoa..." Jack interrupted, blanching as the policeman yanked me out of Jack's grip and whirled me around to handcuff me. "Dr. Green is standing right here, safe and sound."

My mouth fell open as my brain struggled to come up with words. "I-he-it was never missing." My wrists screamed in protest as the cold steel slapped around them.

Not at all like I'd imagined it.

"Officers, please, I think there's been a terrible misunderstanding. Matt's standing right here. Tell them, Matthew." Mom crossed her arms and gave Matt the evil eye.

The S.W.A.T. team continued to detain my little coven, but the lead officer—a tall man who appeared to be in his late forties—paused to look in Matt's direction.

Matt tugged the sheet tighter around himself, shrinking somewhat under my mother's stare. "Uh, that's right. I'm Dr. Green. Is, uh, there a problem, officer?"

"Your fiancée reported you missing." He glanced at me. "Your *other* fiancée. She filed a missing person report a few days ago, adamant that you'd been the victim of foul play. We found your car abandoned in the woods, your house appeared to have been ransacked, and you neither showed up to work nor could be reached for comment. When Miss McKie changed her appearance and fled the state, we had to assume the worst."

"Yes, well, I've been... unavailable, I'll admit. I wasn't feeling like myself. I took a short trip."

"To Vegas, baby," Jon interjected with a wide smile, slapping Matt's back. "He came to see my show."

Another officer—a dead ringer for Robocop—stepped up to Matt. "Do you have any identification?"

Matt glanced down at his sheet. "Do I look like I'm carrying identification?"

"That's definitely him, Stanley." The third officer, a short, stocky guy with a really big gun, holstered his weapon. "A little worse for the wear, if his pictures are any indication. Looks like we may have walked in on something interesting, but I'm not convinced it's anything criminal." He snickered.

Someone snorted and a gale of laughter went around the room.

Jack's eyes flashed with fury. "I'm glad you find this so amusing, but someone needs to uncuff my—Miss McKie."

"Um, I can speak for myself." I nudged the man holding my wrists, giving my hands a little jiggle. "Could you... maybe...?"

"Let her go," the leader said, shaking his head. "Sir, you really should have checked in days ago. It would have cleared up a lot of this confusion before it got out of hand."

As soon as my wrists were free, I rubbed the red marks the cuffs had left.

"I, um, I'm sorry for your trouble, officers," Matt said.

"You should probably check in with your"—he glanced at me again—"fiancée before she calls the National Guard. And for God's sake, can someone please tell me why the crazy lady next door has called nonstop for days, convinced that Miss McKie is a witch who'd turned you into an animal?"

A burst of laughter bubbled past my lips, but I said nothing.

Jon gave the universal sign for *tossin' back the brews* then shrugged. "I'm just sayin'."

"I'll be sure to talk to her," Matt said with a deep scowl directed toward me. "She's probably off her meds again." Then he nodded toward the bedroom door and escorted the officers out.

I glanced around the room. What a disaster. But it wasn't my problem anymore. Aside from Karma, nothing I'd brought to Matt's house would leave with me. Time to leave that badly written chapter of my life behind. I glanced at Jack.

Far behind.

"Chloe." I rested my hand on my best friend's shoulder and leaned in to whisper in her ear. "I'm gonna sneak out. I'll call you tomorrow."

Her eyes locked with mine. "You okay?"

"I will be." I forced a smile at Jon as he wrapped an arm around Chloe's shoulder. "I guess I'll see you on TV."

Jon flashed his cheesy smile. "If you ever get back to Vegas, don't forget to sneak into my show dressed like a hooker."

"You've got it." I laughed. "Take care, you guys." I turned to grab my mom and Karma and get the hell out of Dodge.

"Ivie..." Jack said my name as if it pained him. "This may be the last chance I have, so I need you to listen to me. Please. I put my life on hold for you for the past several days, I think—hope—I've earned a few minutes of your time."

I caught Chloe's face out of the corner of my eye. Her eyes opened wide, her head inclined in Jack's direction, and she mouthed, *Say yes.*

I glanced at Jon then my mother, both of whom nodded. I had no idea what to do. Anxious energy—not to mention a healthy dose of Post Magical Syndrome—pulsed through me, making my instincts unreliable. Taking advantage of my momentary indecision, Mom, Chloe, and Jon left the room and closed the door, leaving me alone with Jack.

I pulled off the scratchy wig and tossed it aside. "If you want me to listen to anything you say, you need to take that off." I pointed to his head.

"Right." Jack removed his Shaggy hair and twisted it in his hands. "You seem to be under the wrong impression about our relationship."

"It's fine, Jack, I get it." I held my ground, pulling myself to my full height.

"No, I don't think you do." He dropped the wig and took my hands. "I just wanted to tell you that over the past several days, I've come to care about you very deeply."

I cleared my throat, prepared to interrupt, but a determined expression settled over his features. I backed down like a coward, putting a little distance between us. What harm could listening do? So what if I'd already said everything I had to say? We were over. So why did my entire being scream at me to change my mind?

He flashed me a shaky smile. "We found ourselves in this completely insane situation, and even before I dragged you out to the woods to have my way with you..." He choked out a laugh. "I felt something in here." Jack pressed my palm against his chest. "I didn't understand it, I didn't know what it was, but I knew I had to do anything I could to hold on to you. It was crazy because it was the second time in a week I'd felt that way about someone."

I wrenched my hands from his. "So your brother was right? There is someone else?"

"Please, let me finish." He frowned, and I nodded. "Jon *was* right, but it's not what you think. The day before I met you, I saw this gorgeous brunette and found myself completely captivated. I was on a routine visit for work, minding my own business, and there she was."

My lips parted, but Jack held up his hand to stop me.

"Unfortunately for me, there was a little accident, and in the commotion, I lost her. I tried to reach out to her but never heard back."

My eyes brimmed over with tears, and I turned my back on him to wipe them away. "I don't understand why you're telling me this. If you were interested in this other woman, why would you start something with me?"

"You really don't get it, do you?" Jack wrapped his arms around me, pulled my back against his chest, and nuzzled my hair. "When I heard Chloe talking about how you were flirting with a veterinarian on your field trip, it took me all of thirty seconds to realize what you meant to me."

"You're not making any sense at all. Are you saying you were jealous of the hot vet?"

"No, Ivie, I was never jealous of the vet. I was jealous of the goat." Jack leaned in to whisper against my ear. "Do you have any idea how badly I wished it was me that day, wrapping my limbs around you in the mud, and not the goat?"

With a gasp, I spun around in his arms. "Jack?"

"I thought I'd lost you. I thought I'd never see you again, and somehow magic brought you right to my doorstep." His fingers curled under my chin, and he tipped my face up to his. "Do you think it was a coincidence? Do you think these things just happen? That a mild-mannered veterinarian and a shy kindergarten teacher would have a magical moment across a field only to meet again as a cocky magician and a feisty witch?"

"That was you?" My voice cracked. I thought back to that day at the farm, to the mysterious man hidden behind a hat and dark glasses. Was that really Jack? "Have you known all along?"

He shook his head. "Not until the plane, when I overheard Chloe talking about the goat."

"But..."

"But nothing. I love you," he blurted. "I'm not exactly sure how or when it happened, but somewhere between that muddy pasture and the bright lights of Las Vegas, I fell in love. I needed to tell you that before you walked out the door and I never saw you again."

I felt the color drain from my face. Every drop of blood in my body had rushed to my heart, setting it off at a pace like furiously beating wings trying to fly out of my chest. "I love you too, Jack. I do. I don't know when or how, but I love you so much."

Jack's mouth crashed against mine. Our noses smashed and our teeth clacked as we struggled to inhale each other.

Our kissing slowed until it was just light pecks.

"I'm going to make love to you until the sun comes up," he said.

"I'd like that." I smiled against his lips. "But maybe not here."

He took my hands and kissed each one reverently before lacing our fingers together. He led me into the hallway.

The whispers stopped when we stepped out of the room, and Jack shared a smile with my mother and his brother.

"Finally!" Jon said. "I thought you'd never work things out. Hey, no offense, I've had a blast, but I'm ready to get the hell out of this place and head back to the sunshine."

Chloe studied the stains in the beige carpet. I wanted to say something but was at a loss for words. I couldn't imagine how she would deal with Jon leaving, as close as they'd gotten over such a short time. I couldn't imagine Jack walking away from me.

Jon tipped Chloe's chin up to look into her eyes. "You coming?"

Her mouth gaped open. "What?"

"There's this little chapel just off the Strip—best damn Elvis impersonators ordained by God and the State of Nevada. You get the choice between skinny Elvis or fat Elvis, though Chubby owes me a favor. I thought maybe we could, you know, get hitched before my next show?" His cheeks pinked.

"Really?" Chloe's eyes widened, and I was sure she would burst out of her skin. "Yes. Yes. Yes." Her arms wrapped around Jon's neck, and he spun her around, dropping her in front of me.

I let out an ear-piercing squeal. "Oh. My. God!" *And the crazy keeps on coming.* Who was I kidding? I was the mayor of Crazytown.

Chloe grabbed my sweater, pulled me into a tight hug, and whispered, "A magical purse would make the perfect wedding gift."

Jon draped his arm over her shoulder. "Well, now that that's settled, I guess it's time we got out of here, wouldn't you say, brother?" When Jack nodded, Jon clapped his back a few times. "Wild couple of days, huh?"

Jack laughed. "Definitely wild."

"Ivie!" Matt's voice barked up the stairs.

I tore myself away from the excitement and tiptoed to the landing. I met Matt's steely gaze and saw the now-tattered sheet wrapped around him. "Yes?"

"Would you please get your miserable, flea-bitten, sheet-destroying cat out of my house and take the rest of your ragged band of miscreants with you? If I never set eyes on any of you again, it'll be too soon."

I cringed. "Sure. No problem. Come here, Karma." I scooped the cat into my arms. "Jack?"

"Yes?" Jack poked his head out with a bright smile. Jon, Chloe, and my mom were right behind him.

"Can we get out of here?"

"You got it, sweetheart."

"Here, let me take the cat," Mom said, reaching for Karma. "You and your magician deserve some time alone, don't you think?"

Jack winked at me. "I think that's a fabulous idea."

"Is everyone riding with me?" Mom asked as we hit the sidewalk.

"Nah, I already called a cab." Jon laid a loud, smacking kiss on Chloe's lips. "Jet's fueled and waiting at the airport."

"Have a safe trip, and take care of my girl," I said.

He smiled. "You know it."

"I'll call you," Chloe shouted as Jon scooped her up, tossed her over his shoulder, and made a run for the cab pulling up to the curb.

"Love you!" I called, waving as they slammed the doors and sped away.

"Well, it's just us," Mom said, crossing to the driver's side of her car.

"Hey, I can finally drive my car!" I remembered, nodding toward the powder-blue Volkswagen Beetle in the open garage.

"You'll need these," Matt yelled, tossing me my keys from the doorway.

For the first time since he'd broken up with me, I flashed Matt a genuine smile. "Thanks." I grabbed Jack's hand. "Oh, hey, I almost forgot." I tugged the antique engagement ring from my right hand and held it out to Matt. "This is yours. I'm sure Candy will be delighted to have it."

He nodded and took the ring. "Well, I guess that's that."

"Yep. It's been"—I was going to say nice but changed my mind—"interesting."

Matt hung his head. "Take care of yourself."

"You too."

Mom pulled me in for a quick hug. "Well, I'll talk to you later. I'm proud of you, dear."

"Thanks, Mom. I couldn't have done this without you."

"Oh, I think you would have done just fine. You're your father's daughter, after all."

Relief washed over me, and I gave the house one more cursory glance before Jack dragged me toward the passenger door of my Bug and held it open. Once he'd situated himself behind the wheel and cranked the engine, he pulled me into a heated kiss.

"Where to, beautiful?"

I thought for a second before a smile split my face. "Surprise me."

Backing out of the driveway, he flashed me an indescribable smirk. "You know, you owe me another opportunity to make love to you slow and gentle. I need more time to learn everything there is to know about your body, mind, and soul."

"Yes, I suppose I do. But you know, I've been doing some seriously powerful magic this evening. I'm pretty keyed up."

"You don't say." He fought back a grin.

My head bobbed a few times. "I do. In fact, if you take the next left, I know of a really secluded spot." I pointed to the turn leading to the back of the cemetery. "I've never had sex in a Love Bug before; have you?"

"No, I can't say I have."

"Whatta ya say, Houdini, wanna have some hot, magical sex with me?"

Jack laced his fingers with mine. "Can't think of anything I'd rather do."

Epilogue

One month later

J ACK AND I PULLED INTO my mother's driveway alongside a shiny black stretch limo. Mom had invited the entire "Scooby" gang to celebrate Jon and Chloe's wedding and apparently, even coming from all the way across the country, they'd beaten us.

"I guess they're already here. Do I look okay?" I ran a hand through my inky-black hair, remembering how much dye it had taken to coax the color back from fire-engine red.

"You look beautiful." Jack raised our entwined hands to kiss my knuckles.

"Especially in that sweater." He licked his lips as his eyes roamed my impressive rack.

I hadn't seen a need to change *everything* back to normal.

"Hey, you two, no having sex in the driveway. Geez, do you ever give it a rest?" Chloe stood on the front steps waving, sunlight glinting off the enormous sparkler on her left hand.

I climbed out of Jack's silver SUV, and we entwined our fingers as we walked toward the house. "We weren't having sex." Not that it wasn't a good idea. Even though I wasn't working magic anymore, I hadn't quite gotten over my taste for sex in unusual places.

"I see you haven't traded in your hot vet for one of his goats just yet." Chloe nudged my shoulder and garnered an eye roll from Jack.

"Don't listen to her, sweetheart. She's just jealous because *you* ended up with the superior Blake brother."

Jack and I had been living together since the day I'd changed Matt back. I hadn't intended for things to move so quickly, but like everything else between us, it just sort of happened.

"Get in here, already. Your mother is driving Jon insane. She keeps asking him about magic tricks. I don't know how you ever lived with her." Chloe grinned, and I knew she was at least half-joking.

My mother moved around Jon to step out of the kitchen just as we reached the dining room. "Ivie, dear, I've missed you." She wrapped me in a crushing hug.

"Mom, I saw you last week."

"That was a week ago. And you're always attached at the hip to your magician."

"Her veterinarian. I don't do magic anymore," Jack corrected, and everyone laughed as he wrenched me out of my mother's grasp.

"Well, I've missed you too, Mom. Dinner smells fantastic." I paused to look around. "Where's my cat?"

"Oh, he's having a nap in the sunshine." She pointed to the spot where a shaft of light filtered through a window, bathing Karma in warmth.

Chloe smiled. "He looks happier than I've ever seen him."

"Are you sure it's been no trouble keeping him? It's not as if we can't take him back. Look how fat he is. I hate to think he's eating you out of house and home—or shredding your sheets."

"No, don't be silly." She waved me off. "He hasn't touched my sheets, and he doesn't eat that much. Although, I dare say he's quite the fan of grilled salmon and raw tuna. But no, he's perfectly content to stay right where he is." She glanced at me, and I saw something in her eyes I couldn't decipher.

"Is everything okay, Mom?"

"Oh yes, dear." She patted my free hand. "Everything's fine. So... still not doing magic?"

Before I could answer, she'd stepped toward the table, straightening the silverware and the pristine white plates.

"No. I'm staying away from magic if I can avoid it. I've finally got my hair back to its normal color." *And my libido tamed to that of a normal twenty-something female.* I winked at Jack, and he blushed, most likely thinking of our romp in the backseat on the ride over.

What? I couldn't help it if the man was unbearably sexy.

"Yes, of course. I'm sure that's wise." She nodded a few times then flashed me a bright smile. "I hope you're hungry. I've made your favorite—grilled liver and onions with roasted Brussels sprouts."

"Yum." I shared a look with Jack as I squeezed his fingers. That was my father's favorite meal, not mine.

Jack took my hint and turned to his brother. "So how was the honeymoon?"

"Dude, fantastic. I swear, it was worth getting married if for nothing else than to take a long vacation in the tropics."

Chloe smacked Jon's head. "That's not even a little bit funny."

"Oh, baby, you know I don't mean it." Jon brushed his lips against hers. "Forgive me?"

"What a pair of saps," I joked, leaning into Jack. "They're making me rethink my decision. Is it too late to change my mind?"

"Definitely too late." Jack turned me until we faced each other. I let my hand slip from his for the first time since we'd stepped out of the car.

"What is that?" Chloe grabbed the hand Jack had released. "Oh my God, is that an engagement ring?"

A bubble of excitement burst out of me, and I erupted in a string of giggles. "It is."

Chloe squeezed the life out of me then went back to staring at my ring. "Holy shit, it's huge!"

Jon pulled Jack into a hug. "Congrats, brother. Welcome to the club, man."

"Thanks."

"So when did you pop the question?" Jon asked.

"Last night. I was going to ask her on New Year's Eve, but I couldn't wait. Sometimes you just know." He laced his fingers with mine again.

Jon laughed, eyeing Chloe. "Boy, do I know it."

"Engaged. Oh, my goodness, that changes everything." My mother rambled, pacing the room and wringing her hands.

"Mom? Are you okay? I thought you'd be happy for me."

She stopped pacing and wrapped me in another hug. "Oh, I am happy. Thrilled even. I adore Jack. I think he'll be a wonderful husband."

"Then what is it?"

"I just wanted your father to be there. He should be able to walk you down the aisle."

"Oh, Mom." I released Jack's hand to pull her in tighter. She hadn't been so upset the last time I got engaged. "You know I would do anything for Dad to be able to walk me down the aisle."

She froze in my arms.

"Mom?"

"Anything?" Her voice got tiny. I could barely hear her.

"Of course! If only it were possible. I'd do anything to have Dad back."

She hugged me again, patting my back before releasing me. "I'm so glad to hear you say that, dear."

Jack shrugged. "So who's ready to eat? I'm starving." He steered me toward the table then stopped dead in his tracks, glancing from the table to me. "Are we waiting for someone?"

Looking around the room, I counted five of us, but the table was set for six. "Mom? Who else is coming to dinner?"

She poked her head out of the kitchen with a cloth flour sack in one hand and a wrinkled sheet of parchment in the other.

"Okay, you're freaking me out here. Isn't that the..." I pointed at the paper with a shaky hand, recognizing the messy words scrawled across it. "What's going on?" I shot a quick glance at Jack, whose puzzled face mirrored my confusion, then peeked over at Chloe's wide-eyed expression.

She mouthed, *"What the hell?"*

"Well, I know you've given up magic, but you did say you'd do anything. If you and Jack are getting married, it's only right he walks you down the aisle. You said so yourself."

My empty stomach twisted and clenched. "Who are you talking about?"

She tilted her head. "Why, your father, dear." She bent down to scoop Karma up and thrust him into my arms.

Jack gaped at the cat. "Karma? I thought your dad turned into a dog. And then he died."

Mom nodded like a bobblehead, pointing to my cat as if he were Odysseus. "I had no idea, of course. Not until the day we were mixing potions. But I always knew if there was a way for my Angus to come back to me, he'd find it." She turned to me and closed my mouth. "I think you should change him back now before we eat."

My eyes darted from Jack to my mother to Karma, the stray I'd picked up from behind a dumpster at school.

Was he my... I looked into his eyes. They were the same emerald green as mine, and then he purred, blinking a few times in the late afternoon sun.

"Daddy?"

Other Books by Erica Lucke Dean

To Katie With Love

Acknowledgments

Writing a book is a lot like giving birth. A lot of blood, sweat, and tears go into the final product. A lot of late nights, chocolate, and Diet Coke, too. I can't imagine making it through the process, alive, without the love and support of countless people along the way.

First of all, to the readers. Without you, there would be no point. Whether one or one million, this book is for you.

To the amazing staff at Red Adept Publishing. What can I say? Lynn McNamee has assembled a kick-ass group of people, and I'm forever grateful to her for that. We may be small, but we are mighty. Thanks to the acquisition team for picking my books out of the slush. Without you, they might have never seen the light of day. Giant hugs, bags of chocolate (the good stuff), and thanks to my editors: Michelle Rever and Cassie Cox. You make me look good. There just aren't enough words to convey how good you make me look.

To the artists at Streetlight Graphics. You guys rock... Seriously! My wildest dreams could not compete with the amazing cover you created for me. Thank you!

To my beta readers, Karen DeLabar, Louise Flynn, Katie Moretti, Lizzie Vance, Amberr Meadows, and Erin Schirer. Thank you for the awesome feedback. You helped shape the final product.

To Kristin Goff for inspiring Chloe. The character may be fictional but the inspiration behind her was real. May you find that perfect purse someday.

To Amber Ivie and her wonderful dog Jackson for lending me your names.

To my fabulous brainstorming-on-Skype team: Michelle Rever, Elizabeth Corrigan, and Laura Kolar. Thank you for twisting my arm until I caved on the "Scooby" scene, for making me laugh through the grueling editing process, and for keeping the crazy "ancient" pop culture references coming.

To my friend and critique/writing partner, Laura Kolar. Where would I be without you? You get my quirks, you understand the way my crazy, messed-up brain works, and you seem to like me anyway. Thank you for letting me bounce ideas off you, for feeding me lines when I had writer's block, and for agreeing to finish my edits if I managed to get eaten by pigs or run over by a train before they were done. Because in my world, those things could totally happen.

To my family, for a lifetime's worth of love and support. Mom and Dad, you gave me the freedom to dance to my own music and never discouraged me from reaching for my dreams, no matter how out of reach they may have seemed. To my sisters, for those nights we listened to "Witchy Woman" with the lights off to scare each other. To my kids, for believing in magic even after you knew the truth. Your imaginations have kept the magic alive in me. And to my great aunt Donna for digging into the family tree to discover we descended from Salem witches. Because that's just too cool for words.

And finally, to my husband, for putting up with my bizarre quirks, my crazy hours, and the countless late nights I spent on Skype with "the girls." Thank you for supporting my dreams even when you don't quite "get" the writer in me. I love you.

About the Author

After walking away from her career as a business banker to pursue writing full-time, Erica Lucke Dean moved from the hustle and bustle of the big city to a small tourist town in the North Georgia Mountains, where she lives in a ninety-year-old haunted farmhouse with her workaholic husband, her 180-pound lap dog, and at least one ghost.

When she's not writing or tending to her collection of crazy chickens and diabolical ducks, she's either reading bad fan fiction or singing karaoke in the local pub. Much like the main character in her first book, *To Katie With Love*, Erica is a magnet for disaster and has been known to trip on air while walking across flat surfaces.

How she's managed to survive this long is one of life's great mysteries.

www.ingramcontent.com/pod-product-compliance
Lightning Source LLC
Chambersburg PA
CBHW051302210726
48287CB00002B/622